Meant to Die

Jennifer Shaw Wolf

Park Press

Cover Design by Sarah Hunter Hyatt

Cover Photograph by Life of Pix

Edited by Lynda Dietz, Easy Reader Editing, LLC

Ebook ISBN: 978-1-7379917-3-1

Paperback ISBN: 978-1-7379917-4-8

Printed in the United States

Chapter One

I'm at the edge of an embankment. Rain pools on the side of the road and runs in small rivulets down the side of the mountain, but I'm not wet. Red and blue beams of light reflect off the twisted metal at the end of the guardrail, but pass through the figure perched on top of it. Rescue workers shout commands to each other, working to free his body from the wreckage.

Damn.

I must have fallen asleep in the middle of my history essay, somewhere between the rise of the Third Reich and Pearl Harbor.

Tanner is sitting on the edge of the guardrail, calmer than he was last time we were here. This time he's just watching the firefighters, not shouting at them that he's not down there. He's not begging me to tell them he isn't dead—yet. Maybe he's finally ready to move on.

"I figured it out, Rand." He says it without looking at me. I almost never get called by my real name during these visions, but Tanner knows me.

I hold my breath, hoping and not hoping that he's going to admit that he's dead. As hard as it is to be dragged here over and over again, I'm not sure I'm ready to let him go.

"There's a storm going on, right? I bet my car was hit by lightning and I was somehow phased out of my body before it went over the cliff. We watched a Star Trek episode about it, remember?"

In another lifetime Tanner and I lived next door to each other. We played football together in the cul-de-sac and binge-watched old Star Trek episodes at his house after school. But that was before my visions became intense, before he became super jock quarterback of the varsity football team, before he called me a freak when I asked him to dance at our ninth-grade graduation ball.

Before he drove too fast on the way back from the homecoming game and missed the corner going home.

I should have guessed a teenager's biggest regret in life would be losing it.

"I was thinking you could Google it or something. I can't be the first person this has happened to. We need to figure this out before they do something stupid like put me in the ground."

I can't tell him that his funeral was months ago. That I broke my "no funerals" rule and went. That I watched his mom and dad most of the student body sobbing over his grave, that they already put him in the ground. For him, it's less than an hour after the accident.

He watches as they lower a stretcher down the side of the hill. "I have to get back before the dance tomorrow. Brie spent a fortune on her dress."

I let him talk without answering. I'm not sure what my role is in this. I can't change his biggest regret. I can't change the fact that he's dead. Am I supposed to convince him he has to move on? My gift or curse or whatever this is didn't come with an owner's manual or some kind of divine guidebook—Dealing with Dead People in Denial, or 101 Ways to Convince Someone That They've Kicked the Bucket. I know there's absolutely no humor in this situation. I must be loopy, or numb, or just cynical. When it comes to Tanner, I'm never sure.

He moves closer to me, sidestepping another firefighter running toward us with a coil of rope. "You'll help me, won't you Rand?" I follow his gaze to the figure slumped over the steering wheel. "Man, I hope I can play the rest of the season. No offense, but Gardner sucks as a backup QB."

Gardner did suck as the backup quarterback. They finished with a 3-8 record even though they wore black armbands and dedicated the rest of the season to Tanner. Not that I follow high school football.

"I'll do whatever it takes. Just don't let them put me in the ground." He pulls his gaze away from the wreck, his eyes pleading. Over his shoulder they finally wrench the car door open. I close my eyes, but I can still see how his body slumps when they pull him out.

He reaches for me, desperate. "It's a mistake. I'm not supposed to be dead! You have to tell them I'm—" As soon as his hands touch my shoulders I'm thrust backward off the guardrail and over the embankment, but instead of landing on the rain-slicked mountainside, I keep falling.

I wake up with a jolt, tangled up in my blankets and covered in sweat. My laptop is open on the bed beside me. The screen is black with a smiling skull and crossbones ricocheting from one side of the screen to the other—my attempt at ironic humor. I close my laptop and move to the unfinished painting beside my bed, trying to capture him the way I've captured my other visitors, but my visits from Tanner aren't like the ones I had before he died.

The penciled-in features and bright blue eyes bear little resemblance to the desperate creature at the edge of the embankment. I study his senior picture clipped to the side of my easel, but I can't reconcile the Tanner I knew with the Tanner from the picture, or the boy from my visions.

I glance out at the hearse parked in our driveway, then down at my phone—four a.m. I stretch my arms and reevaluate the painting, wondering why I can't finish it. Tanner's face is emblazoned in my mind. Every other dead person I see compels me to paint them as soon as their visit ends. Another nearly finished painting stands in the corner—a young woman smiling at a man in a soldier's uniform. He'd waited for her for nearly seventy years. I painted both of their youthful faces perfectly, despite the fact that the woman had passed at ninety-three and I'd never met either of them until she took me walking in a field of bluebells moments after she died.

I give up and stand to work on the other painting. A smudge of red paint in the corner of the canvas stops me. I lean closer.

It's not just red paint, but some kind of doodle—intertwined crosses beneath a red rose, a single drop of blood coming from a thorn on the stem. I don't remember painting it.

I slide my thumb over the image. It comes back red, as if it were streaked with blood.

Chapter Two

"**D**id you sleep at all?"

Mom puts a bowl of oatmeal and strawberries on my nightstand. I set down my paintbrush and lift my arms above my head to stretch my back. I lean to one side, then the other. My shoulders pop and stiffen in protest. "Yeah, I just got up early. I wanted to finish this while her face was still fresh in my mind."

Mom leans over my painting and points to a man standing in the background. "Who is that?"

"The man she was in love with. I think she may have left him at the altar." I take the glass Mom is holding and take a long drink of sweet orange juice, catch a piece of ice between my teeth and crunch on it. "Do you know if she ever got married?" It hits me that it might be awkward if the woman in the painting had a husband, one who didn't know about the man waiting in the meadow.

"No husband, just a sister, Lenae or—"

"—Lynette," I correct her, using the name the woman had called me when we walked through the meadow in my vision.

"Right. Lynette. Eat." Mom points to the oatmeal without asking.

None of this is new to her. I don't have to explain why I know the name of the woman's sister when I've never met either of them. Ghosts have been coming to me as long as I can remember, way before I was old enough to know that sane people don't talk about seeing dead people. Mom has had her own vision, a near-death experience when I was born. My twin sister died and Mom nearly bled to death. Because of that experience, she accepts what I can see as part of who I am. My dad knows about the visions too, but we don't talk about it. He chooses to pretend I'm a normal teenager.

"I want you to go back to bed and try to get some rest. Lynette won't be bringing pictures until later today." She gestures to the painting. "That doesn't need to be finished for a while."

I set the glass on my dresser, stand up and stretch again. My arms and my back ache. My eyes burn from staring at the canvas for almost four hours.

"I'm taking Mark to school. Then I have paperwork to do at the office." Mom screws the cap on one of my paint tubes. "And you need to spend some time on the schoolwork this afternoon. It would be nice if you were able to graduate with the rest of your class next year."

I cross the room and sit on my bed, pick up the bowl, and stir the oatmeal.

"The report on World War II and the Nazis?" Mom waves her hand in front of my face. "The one that should have been sent in a week ago?"

"Right." I set the bowl back down. The report that was so engaging that I fell asleep on top of my laptop.

"You need more sleep." Mom leans over me and tucks a piece of my reddish-brownish, stringy mop of hair behind my ear. "Your training meeting is tonight, right?"

"Right," I say again. My stomach twists in anticipation and dread.

Mark, my younger brother, walks into my room, no regard for my privacy. "Wow, Miranda, you look like hell." I stick my tongue out at him, but I know he's right.

"Mark, watch your language, be nice to your sister, and go brush your teeth. You're going to be late." Mom ticks off her usual list to my brother.

"It's the last day of school. Nobody cares if I'm late. And I could have said Miranda looked like sh—"

"Mark!" Mom says.

"—she needs more sleep," he finishes. His face lights up with a mischievous smile that spreads across his freckles and up to his flaming carrot top.

"Teeth, now!" Mom herds Mark out my door. She stops in my doorway and sighs. "Breakfast, sleep, schoolwork, in that order. I'll be at the mortuary if you need me."

I wave as she heads to the door, still getting after Mark. After she leaves, I stand up and run a brush through my hair in front of the mirror above my dresser. I could be a ghost too, based on the reflection that stares back at me—pale, dark circles under nondescript gray eyes. Thin to the point of being waif-like, not in the model waif-like way, just wasting away, could-be-anorexic thin. That was probably one of the rumors that went around school when my parents pulled me out last year—that I had an eating disorder. If anyone even noticed I was gone.

My official diagnosis is "seizure disorder." Not the kind of seizures that make you fall on the floor and thrash around, but the kind that make you stare off into space, forget everything that's going on around you, and in my case, see and hear people and things that don't exist in the normal world.

I plop back down on the bed, take one bite of the oatmeal, and set it back down. Its already cold, but it's not worth the effort to walk all the way to the kitchen to heat it up. I open my laptop to look at the report. I don't want to go back to sleep, even if I need to be sharp for my meeting tonight. People think spirits only visit in the nighttime. I know that isn't true.

Chapter Three

"You got another thank you note from one of Dad's clients." Mom is sitting at the table, sorting through the mail. She hands me a blue envelope. I rip it open and skim through the card. The curlicue handwriting says: Thank you for the portrait of my mother. Your painting captured the essence of who she was.

"I ran into Tanner's mom in the grocery store yesterday. She looks like she's doing better." Mom flips through the junk mail flyer casually, but I get the question she's afraid to ask.

"The painting isn't finished yet," I say without looking up from the card.

"I know, honey, and she didn't say anything about it." Mom reaches across the table and pats my hand. "I get this one is especially hard for you. But I was thinking that if you finished the painting, maybe it would help you move on."

Move on. Ironic choice of words. Maybe I could do the painting if Tanner would move on and stop dragging me to the accident scene over and over again. I get up from the cabinet and drop the card into the recycling bin. "I have to go."

"Go?" Mark asks. He's playing video games in the clothes he'll probably wear for his entire summer vacation. "You never go anywhere."

"I go." But even as I say it, I realize I can't remember the last time I left the house.

"Oh, that's right. You have training for your new job." Mom says, as if she hasn't enthusiastically reminded me every day for the last week that this was coming up.

"It's not exactly a job, I'm only getting a small stipend. Besides, it's only a couple of days a week. It's not like I'm donning an apron and cheesy ballcap to flip burgers." I'm using the exact words Dad used to convince me to apply for the job. Another attempt to make me into a normal teenager. As if a mortician's daughter would ever be considered normal, even if I didn't see ghosts. I shoulder my backpack casually, even though my stomach churns like a kindergartner leaving home for my first day of school. "See you. It should only be a couple of hours."

Mom waves, actually getting a little misty-eyed. Maybe they're right about me getting out of the house more.

As I walk the familiar path to the rec center, my mind goes back to all the times I walked this way when I was younger. Dad dragged me to Parks and Rec arts classes to get me out of the house the summer after sixth grade. Right when the visions got more frequent and more intense. Madame Vadelorge was my first and only art teacher. She was a little French woman who had taught art at the high school and kept teaching at Parks and Rec even after her hands were too gnarled to hold a paint brush. I'd been drawing and painting almost as long as I'd been seeing dead people, but before her, my talent was raw at best.

She took me under her wing as her protégée. For two years I spent four afternoons a week in the little Parks and Rec studio while she "nurtured my divine gift." She didn't know about my other gift, at least not until she came to me late one night at the end of summer. I was more shocked than she was. A few hours before, I'd left her, alive and well, sipping tea in her tiny apartment. We spent the entire night touring 1960s Paris together—mostly museums—before she disappeared into a little chalet in the French countryside. It was filled with light and from the outside it looked like there was a party going on. It was the trip home she never quite had the time or money for. I'm glad I got to go with her, at least in spirit. I won't be going to the real Paris, ever. Flying is one of my many unreasonable fears.

When I reach the rec center I'm handed a pile of paperwork and a name tag (Miranda Kirk, Beginning Art Instructor). I put the name tag on and clutch the paperwork against my chest as I walk to the last row in the back of the room. It's occupied by a chatty Day Camp Counselor and the Swim Instructor/Lifeguard she's flirting with. He has dark hair, green eyes, and he's built like a swimmer, with broad shoulders and pecs bulging from under a gray T-shirt. The girl is blonde, dark-eyed and has stuffed her oversized chest into a white half T-shirt that could kindly be described as minimalistic. Her name tag is perched on top of her left boob so all I can read is the "Day Camp Counselor" part and not her name. The two of them are sure to be making out in the supply closet by the end of the first day.

I move to the end of the row. Next to the only empty seat is a little girl, nearly hidden behind the dark-haired boy. She's bent over a sketch pad, swinging her too-short legs over the edge of the folding chair as she scribbles furiously with a blue crayon. I glance at her drawing as I sit down, but all I can make out is a sea of choppy crayon waves.

The woman in the front starts the meeting, then drones on for what feels like forever about a youth protection class we all have to take, along with CPR and conflict resolution. I doodle in the margin of my paper, trying to get the eyes right for the man who called me Wendy and showed me every piece of rigging on the boat he never bought before he sailed away into the mist last night.

The lifeguard/swim instructor leans over my drawing. "Are you the art teacher?"

I look up, startled. "That's what it says." I mean to point to my name tag, but it looks like I'm pointing at my nonexistent chest, maybe to further highlight the difference between me and the girl to his right.

"Cool. I'm Adam Holt. We just moved here. And this is my little sister. She's going to be in your class." He pokes the little girl with the sketch pad on the side. She looks up, annoyed. "Remy, this is your art teacher." He squints at my name tag. "Miranda."

The little girl regards me skeptically, a crayon still clutched between her fingers. "Are you any good?"

A strangled laugh forces its way out of my throat. Instead of answering, I hold up the drawing I was working on.

Remy nods. "Not bad." She holds up her own drawing with a challenge in her eyes. In the middle of her sea of crayon waves is a girl's face, her mouth wide open in a silent scream.

"That's so cool." Camp Counselor breaks in. She's using the voice people use when they're talking down to small dogs and toddlers. She leans over and puts her hand on Adam's knee to get a closer look at Remy's picture. "A smiling pink sun in the middle of a blue sky?"

Remy stares back at the girl, unblinking. "No. It's a dead person."

Camp Counselor sits up, her dark eyelashes fluttering with shock. "Well I ... it looks more like ..."

Remy stares at Camp Counselor for a second longer, then levels her gaze at me. As her green eyes meet mine, the air chills and my skin prickles. The crayon drawing comes to life— a girl struggling against blue-green waves flashes into my thoughts. I feel her panic, but I can't see her face clearly.

Remy's voice comes deeper, louder, but far away.

"Actually, she's not dead ... yet."

Chapter Four

"R emy!"

The image evaporates. I'm covered in a cold sweat, gasping as if I was the girl from the picture. Day Camp Counselor and the kids sitting in the row ahead of us are staring at me.

Adam stands, his face flushed. He grabs his sister's hand. "It's time for you to go."

I try to pull myself back to reality, not sure what just happened.

"Not yet," Remy whines.

Adam grits his teeth. "Now. We'll wait for Mom outside."

Remy twists her mouth into a grimace, but she gathers up her crayons and puts them in a little pouch. She tears the drawing out of her notebook and stretches her hand toward me, like she's going to give me her picture. At the last minute she pulls back. "Not yet."

Adam pulls her away and I stare at the picture clenched in Remy's fist. There's something about it, something about this little girl that feels familiar—scary familiar. I've never met anyone who draws dead people like me before and I've never had a vision like this one, one that feels like it was forced into my head.

Adam comes back without his sister. He mumbles an apology as he sits down.

"Don't worry about it," Camp Counselor says, her hand on his arm. "Kids are so weird sometimes. Last summer I—"

I stand. My fingers itch to draw whoever or whatever it was I saw. But I can't do that now, not in front of two complete strangers. "I have to go." I squeeze past Adam and Camp Counselor without meeting their eyes.

"Are you okay?" Adam asks. I ignore the question and move toward the door. When I'm safely on the other side of the room, I glance back just long enough to see the girl point to me and mouth a word I've heard too many times not to recognize: "freak."

I push through the door to the rec center with my fists clenched, my head down—furious at myself for my failed venture into the outside world.

The streets aren't even dark yet, but as soon as the door closes, I feel her behind me. She's so close if I turned around fast enough, I think I could catch a glimpse of a slippery, shadowy, smoke-like figure—at least that's what I imagine she'd look like. Unlike the other ghosts I've known, I've never seen this one. I've never spoken to her, and she's never spoken to me. Everything from her comes as an emotion.

She started coming to me months ago, exactly when I can't pinpoint, because the feelings were weak in the beginning. Probably right after Tanner's accident. Like Tanner, I sense that she doesn't want to move forward. Unlike Tanner, I think she knows exactly what she is.

I've never been scared of any of the ghosts I've walked with. Maybe because they've always been there, maybe because I know they can't touch me. This one gets to me though. Her presence works on my emotions until I can't tell what I'm feeling and what she wants me to feel.

Right now it feels like she's laughing at me. Shame bubbles up red hot into my face. Freak. Freak. Freak.

My first foray into the real world in weeks and I couldn't even make it through one stupid meeting without doing something freakish.

She's beside me now, no footsteps, no breath, just the claustrophobic feeling of someone walking too close, laughing behind my back. I've had enough. I wheel around and face the growing shadows. "Leave me alone!"

"I'm not following you. I mean, I am, but my intentions are good." Adam, lifeguard/swim instructor, is trotting to catch up. "I didn't mean to scare you. You left your paperwork on the chair."

"Oh, um sorry ... um. thanks." My face burns, worse than the shame I felt before, and I fumble as I take the papers from him. "I don't think I'm going to be teaching anyway."

"Why not?" His eyes are really green, he's really close to me, and he's really, really good-looking. I thought I'd forgotten what it felt like to be this close to a hot guy, but it all comes back to me—the sweaty palms, the stammering, the feeling that I'm going to throw up. I'm pretty sure it's all me. She usually makes herself scarce when other people are around.

He keeps looking at me, waiting for an answer. I have to say something. Apparently, he was so focused on his sister that he didn't notice my freaky reaction. "I have a really crazy work schedule. I'm not sure I can—"

"—really, where do you work?"

I rub my palms together, not ready to give him too much information. "I work for my dad, as a painter."

"You paint houses?"

Dang, this guy is persistent. And hot. The voice in my head, the feeling, I can't tell if it's mine or hers. Maybe both. Hot or not, I need to get rid of him. I have a surefire litmus test, one that no guy has passed since Tanner in third grade. All I have to say is "my dad is a mortician" and they run, some of them screaming. It's on the tip of my tongue, but the voice in my head says, Don't screw this up.

"No. Art." I answer. "I paint portraits."

"Very cool. So could you do me sometime?"

"Do ... you? What?" I meet his eyes for the first time, shocked at what he said. Then I laugh. It comes out like someone is strangling a duck.

He blushes, or maybe it's the reddish glow of the streetlight that's coming on. "I mean, could you paint me, uh ... paint my picture sometime?"

"I hope not," I blurt out.

He smiles and leans against the post. "Why? Am I that bad to look at?"

"No. It's just—" Okay, drop the bomb. "I paint dead people, well, pictures of dead people. My dad's a mortician."

"You paint ... dead people." He's preparing to run. I can see it in his eyes. "That's, um, that's really interesting, and maybe just a little bit freaky."

Freaky, freaky, freak, Miranda's a freak.

"I have to go. I'm supposed to be home already." I put my head down and start walking away.

He follows me. "At least let me walk you to your car."

"No car." I pick up the pace. "I'm walking home." I don't have to tell him I always walk. That I don't have a driver's license. That I've escorted too many car accident victims.

"Make you a deal." He catches up fast. "I'll drive you home if you at least try to do the art class. My little sister is really excited about it. And she needs it. We just moved here and she doesn't have any friends yet."

Chivalrous and he cares about his little sister. Her presence is almost a full-blown voice, purring in my head.

"I don't accept rides from strangers." I stare straight ahead.

Nice, play hard to get.

"Good rule. I'll just walk you home, then."

And yet, he's not leaving.

"It's pretty far. Don't you have to get back to the meeting?"

"Seemed like they were wrapping up." He's lying. The woman at the front of the room could have talked all night.

I keep putting one foot in front of the other, not looking at him, but he stays with me. Between her in my head, Adam beside me, and my lack of sleep, I may collapse into a quivering heap right here on the sidewalk. Then he'll know I'm crazy.

He talks the whole way—telling me about his little sister and the school he used to go to. He doesn't seem to mind that the conversation is completely one-sided. When we get to my house he looks long and hard at the hearse in the driveway, but he walks me all the way up to the front door anyway. I turn around to tell him goodbye or whatever I manage to stammer out. He touches my forearm. I'm so used to people not touching me—and ghosts not being able to—that I jerk it away, slamming my elbow into the door.

He steps back and stuffs his hands in his pockets. "Sorry ... hey, I ..." My arm is tingling. I rub my elbow, waiting for him to finish, but instead the silence stretches on. I'm not sure if I should just walk in the door or if I should wait. Finally, he speaks. "... I've been thinking about the dead people."

"What?" I cower against the door. He figured out my secret.

"The ones you paint. They're dead, right? So they aren't going anywhere."

Some of us aren't.

"So they can wait. And then you'll have time to teach the class. It would mean a lot to my sister, and I'd like to see you again." He moves closer. "At least think about it."

Before I can answer, the door opens behind me. I fall backward. Adam grabs my shoulders to keep me from falling. I'm caught up in his arms with my mom standing in the doorway, The shock on Mom's face dissolves into delight almost instantly. "Oh. Hi. Miranda. I thought I heard someone knock. I didn't expect you to be home already." She looks at Adam, like she just noticed he was here. "And who is this?"

"Adam Holt." He releases my shoulders and extends his hand to Mom.

"He walked me home from the meeting." It's all I can do to keep from crawling under the front porch.

"Oh, thank you. That was very nice of you." Mom is shaking his hand and gushing like I've never had a guy at the door before, which I haven't, but she could be a little more subtle about it. "I'm Miranda's mom. Would you like to come in?"

"No thanks. I have to get home." He backs away—hearse and crazy mother equals too much. "I'll see you when class starts next week, okay, Miranda?"

"She'll be there." Mom answers for me.

I walk past her and try to shut the door, but she's still holding it open, calling after him as he walks down the stairs. "It was so nice to meet you, Adam. Thank you again." She hovers, watching him walk all the way down the sidewalk.

I head for my bedroom so I can hide.

"Who was that boy?" Dad asks from the living room.

"A boy who walked Miranda home from the meeting. Isn't that great?"

"I'm not sure—" Dad starts.

Mom cuts him off. "Hush, it's fine." As I close the door to my room she says, "I knew her teaching that class was a good idea."

Chapter Five

Candles flicker on the altar in the front of the room. On either side are white baskets full of red roses that I can't smell. The pews are packed with mourners. They have their heads bowed. Their shoulders shake like they're crying or praying, but I can't hear the words. There's an organ playing somewhere—a solemn tune that drowns out everything else. Red, blue, and golden light streams from a huge stained glass window above the altar. It shows a bandaged man coming from a rock tomb—Lazarus, I think. In the front of the church, draped in more roses is a white casket. The girl inside is beautiful—pale, creamy skin, dark curly hair. She's young—sixteen, seventeen at the most.

I'm not sure why I'm here. I don't know who I'm supposed to be meeting. The girl in the coffin isn't moving. I can't see her standing among the mourners. The whole image is foggy, more surreal than my other visions.

Someone giggles irreverently from the back of the room. I catch a wisp of movement out of the corner of my eye, like a curl of smoke. I spin around, but no one raises their head. No one hears the noise. When I walk toward the front of the room, no one looks up or acknowledges me. The giggle comes again and then changes to harsh laughter.

My body turns cold and electric prickles run up my spine. I can feel her behind me, breathing without breath on my neck. She laughs again. "Find out who I am and I'll help you." She moves closer, breathless lips pressed to my ear. "You will need my help."

My stomach churns as I step to the edge of the big round desk at the center of the Parks and Rec building. "Um, I'm here to teach the art class, I'm Miranda—"

"Great, you're early." The blonde-streaked-with-silver haired woman behind the desk squares her shoulders and stands. "That shows me you're responsible. I hate it when our teen instructors are late. I'm Ms. Perkins." She extends a thin spider-veined hand. According to the clock on the wall above her, I'm almost an hour early for my first class.

I wonder how responsible Ms. Perkins would think I was if I told her I can't teach the art class after all. I must have picked up the phone a million times to call the rec center and tell them I changed my mind. But I keep thinking I'm supposed to do this, that I need to see that little girl again. I need to see what it was about Remy or her drawing that triggered a vision like none I've ever had—a vision at the point of death.

Then there was my crazy dream. I spent hours lying in bed trying to convince myself that it was just a dream. It wasn't vivid like my visions. It was more like I was seeing the whole scene through someone else's eyes, but I'm not sure whose. When I woke up, I sketched what I could remember of the dead girl, but the image burned away like morning fog when it was exposed to the light of my easel.

The laughter and the words still echo in my ears. "Guess who I am" and "You will need my help."

I should be used to no sleep, but I feel more out of it and groggy than usual. I'm loaded down with dollar-store watercolor palettes, a big box of stickers to decorate name tags, and a roll of paper. I've gone over and over what I'm going to do with these kids and tried to remember the lessons that Madame Vadelorge started out with when she taught this class. I wish I had saved some of my early projects, but I don't save anything. None of the ghosts I've walked with have ever carried a suitcase.

The woman consults a clipboard hanging on a hook above the desk. "Beginning Art, room 113. Ron can let you in."

The tall, pimply teenaged boy beside her sets down the comic book he was reading. He gives me a disinterested look, grabs a ring of keys, and waits for me to follow him. He doesn't offer to take any of the stuff I'm juggling. Instead, he perches an updated list of my students on top of the pile in my arms.

We pass a wall of glass that overlooks the pool. I glance at it casually, out of curiosity—not because I'm looking for Adam. I'm distracted so I run into Ron when he stops in front of the door to my classroom, right across from the pool. I lose my grip on my stack, it tips, and everything falls. The covers to the watercolor sets crack as they hit the floor, and some come off completely. The little circles of paint fall out and bounce all over the gray linoleum. Ron doesn't offer to help me now, either. He sorts through the keys and pretends he doesn't notice me crawling around under his feet.

As I reach for a chip of blue paint that's broken in half, Adam walks right up to the window of the pool. A few inches of glass are all that separate us, and I look like a complete idiot. I pretend I don't see him. He taps on the glass. I bend my head lower and ignore the tapping. After a couple more taps, he stops. Ron stands at the door and sighs impatiently while I get what I can carry together and hurry to my feet. I'll have to pick up the rest after I dump this load.

Ron flips on the light, and I'm overwhelmed by memories. The art room is exactly the way I remember it—tables with little cans of pencils and crayons in the middle, easels against the wall by the windows, the smell of paint and clay and dust. The only addition is a gold-framed portrait of Madame Vadelorge—painted by her prize pupil. I haven't seen it since I presented it to the Parks and Rec council almost two years ago.

Ron gestures toward the shelves in the corner, filled with art supplies, including a stack of new watercolors. "You can use any of the supplies on the shelves." He looks at the mess of things I have in my arms smugly. "Let us know if you run out of anything."

I feel like an idiot. I should have asked if Parks and Rec would be providing the supplies for my class. I blew a bunch of my own money for nothing. Frustrated, I drop my armload on the table in the front and turn around to go get everything else. In two steps I stop. Adam is standing at the door, holding the extra supplies I dropped. His hair is wet. He's wearing a swimsuit, sandals, an unzipped Parks and Rec jacket and a huge grin. A red whistle hangs against his bare chest.

"You aren't supposed to leave the pool area without drying off first." Ron says, eyeing the drops of water sliding off Adam's swimsuit. "Or without a shirt."

"Sorry," Adam doesn't sound sorry at all. He sets the roll of paper—covered in his damp fingerprints—and the box of stickers on the table beside the broken watercolors. "I wasn't going to stand by and watch Miranda pick up all this stuff by herself."

"You left a puddle on the floor." Ron points to a few drops of water beside Adam's foot. "That's a safety violation."

"Only if I don't clean it up." Adam flashes a smile in my direction. "Miranda, pass me a paper towel."

I'm so conscious of his eyes on me that I almost can't remember how to work the paper towel dispenser. When I pull the arm down, the click, click, click of the dispenser echoes across the checkered linoleum floor. Ron glares at Adam, Adam smiles back at him and takes the paper towel from me. "Thanks." He kneels down to wipe up the floor. "Good enough?" he says to Ron and throws the paper towel toward the garbage can. He sinks the shot without looking.

Ron grunts something unintelligible and turns back to me. "We expect the room to be left in the same condition you get it in. There's a janitor's closet down the hall with a mop and broom. Lights out and lock the door behind you. Any questions?" I shake my head. He turns and heads back to the desk with a passing glare to Adam.

Adam waits until Ron is a few steps down the hall before he says, "Wow, that guy, anal much?"

I shrug my shoulders, but a voice in my head laughs, hard. The same laughter from last night's dream. It startles me so much that I look around for the source. I was so caught up in my own nerves that I didn't know she was here.

Adam leans against the table behind him, picks up the box of stickers and turns it over in his hand. I wait, watching the clock behind him tick off the seconds. I need to get ready for my class, but I can't move with him around. He finally puts the box down and looks at me. "I need to ask a favor."

I knew it.

"Remember my little sister, Remy? I need you to bring her to me at the pool after class is over."

"The pool? You mean the one that's right there?" I point through the open door to the wall of glass.

"Yeah." He picks up the box of stickers again and shakes it. "Um, I'll be teaching a class and I need someone to get her to me, and, well"—he turns the box over in his hand—"stay with her until I'm finished."

A babysitter? Wow, that's rich.

"You want me to watch your little sister?" My mouth drops open and I lose any composure I might have had.

His tone softens and his voice gets deeper, like he's trying to flirt. "Yeah, you don't mind, do you?" He takes a step closer to me. I'm trapped between his bare chest and the table behind me.

The pieces slide into place: why he was nice to me, why he walked me home, why he's here now. He needs someone to babysit for him. I fold my arms in front of me and do my best to stare him down. "Really?"

He sets the stickers back on the table and starts talking fast. "See, my aunt will be at work, and she has to drop Remy off here. And I really need this job—the lifeguarding and swim lessons thing—I need the money. But there's about a half hour between your class getting done and my shift ending." He looks up at me with a kind of pitiful "please" look that I'm sure would melt a less cynical target. "I'd really appreciate it if you could help me out. And I'd make it up to you. Remy could help you clean up and I could drive you home."

Her voice in my head cackles. That's why he chose you over the blonde chick. She's easy but you're useful.

I avoid his pleading look. I want to say no. I need to say no, but chronic cynic or not, he seems desperate. And I'm not a monster. And he is hot. Oh, so hot. If I left right after class what would I do anyway? Paint? Work on homework? Take a nap and risk a visit from Tanner?

It's only a half hour.

"A half hour isn't very long." I cover my mouth, realizing I spoke out loud.

Adam smiles down at me hopefully. "Only a half hour, except on Tuesdays when I have to lifeguard open swim."

"Tuesdays?" I can feel myself being sucked in.

"You teach two classes on Tuesdays, right? It was on the schedule. Remy could take both classes and then you could bring her to me at the end of open swim."

"Which is?"

"Three." He picks up his whistle and twirls it between his fingers, avoiding my eyes. "So, it's just an extra couple of hours."

"But I'm a complete stranger." I pick up one of the cracked watercolor sets and then set them down again. "How can you just leave your sister with me? How do you know I'm not a serial killer or, or—"

Or a freak who hears voices in her head?

"You teach art to kids. You passed the background check, right? And other than the painting dead people thing." He grins, like he's making a joke. "You seem pretty normal."

He doesn't know you very well, does he?

He leans closer to me. "Besides, no girl as cute as you could be psychotic." He reaches out like he's going to touch my hair —flirting his way to a free babysitter.

I pull away and bump my hip hard against the table. "Ow. Look, I ..."

"Adam, your class is waiting." Another lifeguard wearing the same Parks and Rec jacket pokes his head through the door. "Perkins will have your butt if you don't get out there." He sees me and rolls his eyes. "Stop getting distracted by the girls."

"I'm coming, I'm coming," Adam finishes his closing move and brushes his hand down my shoulder. "See you after class, Miranda. And thanks."

His touch sends an electric current through my shoulder to my face making my cheeks burn red. I can't say no to him. I can't say yes either. I can't say anything.

He walks out the door and then turns back around. "Oh, and Remy is terrified of water, so you'll have to stay out of the pool area until I get done. 'Kay? Thanks again."

Chapter Six

Inside I'm sputtering, but I can't make the words move to my lips. Somehow his touch paralyzed my vocal cords too. I can't tell him that I can't/don't want to watch his little sister. How does someone just assume a complete stranger will babysit for them?

I don't move until he's on the other side of the wall of glass. He waves at me and then sits down on the edge of the pool and with a group of kids. Slowly I regain enough composure to put the stickers and name tags on a table at the front of the room for the early arrivals to work on.

He's using you, using you.

"Shut up," I whisper as I get the watercolor sets from the supply shelf and set one in front of every chair.

One touch and he's got a personal slave for life.

I work on ignoring Her as I fill little cups with water.

You are so pitiful.

The voice in my head, mingled with humiliation, anger, and embarrassment follows me around the room.

Using you, using you.

I rip off big pieces of paper to put at every place.

But he is hot.

I tear at the roll of paper so hard that the cutting edge slices into the side of my thumb. It stings like crazy. I drop the paper on the floor and suck on the cut.

But he doesn't want you. Not really. He just needs you.

I turn around fast. "Dammit! Get out of my head!"

Standing in the doorway, looking shocked, is a woman and her little boy—my first student.

Echoes of laughter ring in my ears. My face burns—again.

"Um, maybe we have the wrong room?" The woman looks like she hopes she has the wrong room. "Beginning Art?"

"No, you're in the right place," I stammer. "I'm sorry I just ..." I scramble for something that won't make me look crazy. "Don't you hate it when you have a song stuck in your head?" I look at the little boy because I can't face his mother.

"Oh, yeah, well." She puts her hand protectively on her son's shoulder. "That is annoying, but I hope your language ..."

Dammit counts as language? Bet he hears worse than that on the playground.

"I'm sorry for that." I bend over to pick up the paper that has unrolled a couple of feet across the floor. When I stand, I keep my eyes on the little boy and try to force her voice out of my head. "Would you like to make a name tag? I have some cool stickers. You can pick some stickers that represent you."

The boy looks at his mom. "What does represent mean?"

"It means ... it means ..." I forgot that there are words little kids don't know and I'm too flustered to think of a good way to explain it to him.

His mom steps in front of me and reaches for the pile. "Just choose some stickers you like. Here. You like dinosaurs."

I walk away from them. How did I get myself into this? More kids filter in—a dark-haired girl in a green and pink shorts outfit, a chubby girl with rosy cheeks and hair so transparent blonde that it looks pink, sandy-haired twin boys who look like double trouble, and a small girl with black braids whose mom peels her hand away and leaves quickly. According to the roster I have seven kids in the group, ranging from age seven to nine.

Remy is the last student through the door. She's standing next to a woman who I guess is her mom. The woman crosses the room to me. She looks harried and she keeps glancing at her watch. "Are you Adam's friend Miranda?"

"Yes," I answer, although "friend" would be a stretch."

"And you'll be able to keep Remy until he's done with his classes?" The woman glances around the room.

"Yes." There's no point in telling her that Adam forgot to mention my babysitting service to me until this morning, although he obviously said something to this woman about it.

"Thank you." The woman squats down in front of the little girl. "You can stay with Adam's friend, okay Remy?" She pronounces the girl's name distinctly. "Adam will take you home. I won't be home from work until late tonight."

"Okay," Remy says. Her eyes follow the woman through the door.

"Would you like to make a name tag?" I ask.

She looks at the pile of supplies on the table. "What do I do with the stickers?"

"Pick some that represent you ... I mean ... oh, just pick things that ..." I fumble again. "That you like."

She stares back at me. "I know what 'represent' means."

"Oh, okay then ..."

"Does it have to be a sticker, or can I draw something?"

One twin shoves the other one into the easels in the corner. Two more easels clatter to the floor. The little girl in the corner flinches, whimpers, and stuffs her hand in her mouth. The boy's mom surveys the scene and shakes her head. I feel like crying too.

"Whatever you want," I say over my shoulder, moving to quell the brewing chaos. "Please don't ... settle down ... stop ..." I reach out and stop the twin running past me. He wriggles out of my grasp.

What was I thinking? I can't teach kids. I've barely been around them, except for my brother, and it takes him about two seconds to make me crazy. These kids—staring at me for some sort of direction—scare me way more than any of the spirits I've ever faced. Dead people I can take, but this crowd ...

In mock-sweet/condescending voice the mother says, "Can I help you get a project started? How old did you say you were?"

"Sixteen." As terrified as I am of the kids, this mother scares me worse. I can't do anything with her staring at me. "You can go if you'd like. Your son will be fine." It's me I'm not so sure about.

"With all these kids?" she says. I'm sure she's thinking that she doesn't want to leave me alone with her darling.

I pick up the easels and try to sound in-charge. "Okay everyone, find a seat. We need to get started." The twins start fighting over a chair. Helicopter Mom sighs again, this time toward heaven.

I glance up and see the painting of Madame V, and breathe a plea to her. Slowly, as if my plea was heard, I remember my own first lesson in this room. I clap my hands and yell, "Freeze!" the way Madame V used to. The kids stop, shocked, and they turn their attention to me. "We need to get to know each other. And then we'll paint, okay?" I pick up a big pad of drawing paper and a wide marker from the supplies and sit at one of the tables. "Everyone get where you can see." They all crowd around me, pushing and jostling for position. I keep my voice low. "I won't start until you settle down." I wait. Eventually the pushing stops and the room quiets. I point to one of the twins, Max or maybe Matt, according to the scrawl on his name tag. "Tell me three things about yourself and then count to one hundred. I'll try to draw you before you get done counting. Okay, go."

He moves in closer. "I'm seven years old. And ..."

I study him for a second and then start drawing as fast as I can.

"I like to play baseball." He screws up his face like he's thinking hard. I have most of his face and the outline of a baseball cap. "And ... I can whistle." He whistles to show me that he can. His brother starts counting. The other kids join in. They lean closer. I'm getting claustrophobic. Little kid sweat is overpowering the marker smell. I'm sweating too, but I draw faster. I finish with a flourish as they say 99, 100.

I hold the picture up for all of them to see: Max or Matt, in a baseball cap, with pursed lips, a bat slung over his shoulder. It's more of a cartoon/caricature then I usually do, but the kids appear impressed.

"Wow. Me next, me next! Can you teach me to do that?" They're all clamoring around me. I'm mobbed with sweaty, sticky little kid hands. The only one not part of the mob is

Remy. She's observing from the corner with wide, but disapproving eyes.

I clap my hands again and yell, "Freeze!" It works better the second time. "I'll do one every time we have class, okay?" I glance at the clock; now the time is going too fast. "But you need to start on your own pictures now. Smocks first and then back to your seats. One, two three, go!"

I hang the picture I drew on the bulletin board while they get smocks. Helicopter Mom says to her son, "I have an errand to run, I'll be back soon," and leaves.

The kids get into their seats, and I tear off a big piece of paper and attach it to one of the easels. I move it to the front and demonstrate a couple of strokes. Everything has taken longer than I thought. By the time I finish there's only about twenty minutes left. "Go ahead and paint whatever you want." To my relief they all start painting.

I walk around the room and look over their shoulders. I'm starting to feel like a real teacher. Then I notice Remy still standing by the front table, staring at a blank name tag.

I walk over to her. "Remy, you haven't started your name tag." I lean into her ear. "Why?"

She shakes her head. "You already know who I am."

"Right," I answer, "but the other kids don't."

She crosses her arms defiantly. "Maybe I don't want them to know my name."

"Why don't you want them to know your name?"

She looks at me like that's a stupid question, something that should be obvious to me. "Because names have power."

I stare back at her. She's positive that I understand what she's talking about. "Names have ... what?"

"Power. You know, like—"

The little girl with the braids knocks over her water. She looks like she's about to start crying again. "Don't worry about the name tag. Just start your painting." I say to Remy, and leave her to help the other girl.

By the time I've finished comforting the girl and mopping up the water, Helicopter Mom is back. It must have been a quick errand. Maybe she was watching from around the corner. I check the time. Class is already over.

"Hang your smocks up and dump out your water. Leave your pictures, I'll let them dry on the racks and you can take them home next time." I let out a huge sigh.

As they put things away, more moms arrive. The twins point out the drawing I made to their mother. "I want to learn to draw like that," Max/Matt says to his mom.

"Did you have fun?" she asks.

"Lots and lots," he answers. His mom beams at me.

Remy is still painting. She's so focused on what she's working on that I don't try to stop her. I work on cleaning up and putting the supplies away. After the other kids clear out, I move to see what Remy's so focused on. She's painting an underwater scene. A girl lies on the bottom of a murky ocean, her hair covers her face in a tangle of blonde mixed with green seaweed. The painting is very good for a nine-year-old.

"Is she a mermaid?" But as soon as the question is out of my mouth, I know I'm wrong.

She looks up from her painting like I've startled her out of a trance. Cold, murky, dread fills my chest as her eyes meet mine. "No. It's the girl from before."

My whole body is cold. I suppress the urge to gasp for breath, feeling like if I did, my lungs would fill with musty water. I force myself to stay calm. "Is she dead now?"

Remy pulls the painting off the easel. "She will be."

Chapter Seven

"**A**ny budding artists like you?"

I look up from cleaning the room to see one of the few adults who seems to get me, my uncle Marshall. He's my dad's foster brother and assistant at the mortuary.

"All young Michelangelos, I'm sure." I hold up a painting that slipped out of the rack; I think it was done by one of the twins.

He steps inside and takes the painting, twisting it upside down. "I'd say more Picasso. I can't decide whether it's supposed to be a truck or a spider."

"Spider truck."

"Actually, that might be kind of useful for the fire department. We could use it to scale buildings and put out the flames." Marshall hands the painting back to me.

I slip it back into the drying rack, trying to decide whether it smeared when it fell on the floor, or if the streaks of red are on purpose. "What are you doing here?"

"Trying to take business away from your dad." He smiles when I raise my eyebrows. "Teaching a basic CPR and first aid class."

"Oh." Marshall has done a bit of everything, from working in a nursing home to being a volunteer firefighter and paramedic to helping at the mortuary. He started medical school, but never finished. At one point I think he was even training to be a cop.

"This one is interesting." He reaches into the rack and taps Remy's picture. "Mermaid?"

"I think so." I'm not in the mood to try to explain Remy's painting to anyone else, especially when I'm not even sure what it means.

"If it's a mermaid, it's the kind that lures sailors to their death." He continues to study the picture. "Kind of dark for a kid. Who painted it?"

"A little girl. They're new to town." I pull the painting away from him, weirdly protective of Remy's painting.

"Short-haired little bird with a big attitude."

"Yeah."

"She was in my class over the weekend. Smarter than you'd think." He leans against the door. "I'm heading back to the mortuary. You want a ride? Not in the hearse this time." He cracks a smile.

"No, I'm actually ... I'm babysitting ... the little bird."

"You?" He smirks. "How did that—"

"Miranda! Where's my sister?" Adam bursts into the room.

"She went to the restroom," I answer, trying not to meet Marshall's eyes or acknowledge the knowing grin I'm sure is plastered on his face.

"By herself?" Adam looks panicked.

"Yeah. She's nine, right? And the bathroom is just across the hall. She can go to the bathroom herself?" Suddenly I'm not sure.

Adam takes a breath. "Yeah, I guess so, sorry. I need to get to my next class. I just wanted to make sure everything was okay."

"We're good." I'm annoyed that even though he dumped his sister on me, he doesn't seem to trust me.

After he leaves, Marshall won't stop smirking at me. "Babysitting, huh? Thought you didn't like kids."

"Shut up," I reply as he walks away.

Ron is alone at the desk when I return the keys. He looks up from his manga long enough to ask if I cleaned up, locked the door, and turned out the light. When I say, "yes," he takes the keys and goes back to his book.

I look at Remy and she stares back at me. I glance at the schedule on the wall and realize that Adam's class won't be over for almost twenty minutes. What am I supposed to do with this kid until then? I look through the glass wall. Adam waves with one hand while he holds a floating kid with the other. "Do you want to go watch Adam at the pool?"

She looks up at me, her eyes wide. "I don't like the water."

Right. Adam said she was afraid of the water. That might explain the two pictures.

I look toward the park on the other side of the street. "Do you want to go to the playground?"

"Nothing better to do," Remy says.

I take that as a yes and start toward the street. We walk in silence, but when I look down at her, I catch her deep green eyes searching my face. Despite her outward defiance, I sense there's something lost and scared inside her. I want to reach out to her, the way I never reach out to anyone. When we reach the far end of the playground, she sits on one of the swings. I sit beside her.

"How long have you been drawing?" I try to make the question innocuous, but her eyes brighten.

She counters with, "How long have you been painting?"

It feels like a veiled reference to what my paintings really are, and maybe that's what my question was as well. I answer both questions honestly. "Pretty much my whole life."

She bobs her head. The movement is so small that I almost miss it. "Me too."

I take another stab in the dark. "The girl in your picture. Do you know her?"

Remy takes a long moment to think. "I don't think so. Her face isn't clear. Not yet."

I consider how to phrase my next question. I don't want to spook her. "Remy how often do you—"

"—Rand, look at that." She points toward the sky, but instead of looking where she's pointing, I can only stare at her.

"What did you call me?" The only person who ever called me Rand was Tanner.

She either doesn't hear or ignores my question. "Look at all those ravens."

I follow her gaze to the huge flock of birds circling the playground. There are so many that they seem to block out the sun. A chill fills the air. The flock appeared out of nowhere, like a bad omen. "I think they're just crows."

Remy shrugs and moves toward the swings. "Either one works, I guess. Some cultures believe crows are psychopomps, some believe ravens are."

"Psycho-whats?" I'm struggling to keep up with her. Part of me is still stuck on her calling me Rand.

She looks at me like I'm an idiot. "Psychopomps. You know, someone or something that guides souls to the other side. Like you." She hops up on the swing.

I step back, suddenly defensive. "Remy, I don't know what ..."

She leans back, eyes closed, stretching her legs out in front of her and pumping higher and higher into the air. "Either way, it means someone is going to die, right?"

Chapter Eight

We swing side by side. Remy sings in what sounds like French. A million questions I don't know how to ask swirl in my head along with the birds that circle above us. Even if I could vocalize what I'm thinking, I'm not sure if I want the answers. I barely know Remy, but I feel like she knows everything about me. I know almost nothing about her, but what I've guessed scares me. And if it scares me, what would a normal person think about her? I want to protect her in a way I've never wanted to protect anyone or anything. That scares me more than anything.

Adam—red faced and breathless—comes running across the road to the playground. "There you are!" He leans against the side of the swing set and breathes in hard. "You scared me to death." Another big breath. "When I couldn't find you after my class, I was starting to worry that you were some sort of psychopath and you'd done something with my sister. Don't do that to me again."

Remy slows her swing with her feet and regards her brother. "Where did you think we'd be? Hanging out in the classroom? Waiting for you to come get us?"

"I just need to know where you are." He ruffles her hair. "'Kay?"

Remy pulls away and rolls her eyes.

I'm standing here—awkward, not sure what I should be doing, when Adam turns on his charm again. "Well, it looks like you two had fun. Glad everything worked out." He smiles. "So I can count on you to be Remy's friend after class?"

I'm not sure how to answer, so I don't say anything. Remy's face lights up with a mischievous grin. "Adam, I think you owe Rand ice cream."

"Rand?" He smiles down at her. I have limited sibling experience outside my own family, but I've never seen a brother treat his little sister like this, like he adores her.

"Yes." Remy grips my hand smugly. "She said I could call her Rand, but no one else." I'm starting to feel like I'm her new prized possession. "And you owe her ice cream."

"Well Rand, I mean Mi-ran-da." He says every syllable slowly and carefully. He leans close to me so I can smell an odd, but not totally unpleasant mix of chlorine and some kind of musky guy sweat barely covered by another scent, cologne or just deodorant, I can't tell. "Would you like to go get ice cream with me? We could go tonight after my mom comes home, so we don't have to take this little twerp with us."

Is he really asking me out? My tongue feels heavy and I struggle to answer. "Um, no, I mean sure, but—"

"She wants me to come, don't you, Rand?" Remy pulls me closer to her side, like I'm the middle of the rope in a tug of war.

"Maybe she's tired of hanging out with you. Did you ever think of that?" Adam says. I get that he's teasing her, that he doesn't really want to go out to ice cream with me, or at least not with just me.

Remy hooks her arms around my arm. "I'm not letting go of Rand. So you have to take us both."

"I guess we're stuck with the cling-on kid." Adam flashes me a smile that takes some of the strength from my legs, even though in another breath, I've convinced myself it's all part of him teasing his sister. "Can I at least have her other arm?"

I stand there like an idiot until Remy nudges me toward her brother with her boney little hip. Adam takes my arm. I stiffen and tingle at his touch all at the same time. He grips my arm tighter and smiles at me, but his face is too close for me to return the smile.

"He needs your phone number too," Remy says.

"Em!" he protests.

She goes for innocent, but her eyes are dancing. "So he can find you if you ever decide to kidnap me, and so he can ask you to hang out without his little sister around."

"For once, kiddo, could you just shut up!" Adam finally sounds like a big brother.

My face is blazing. It makes me feel better that Adam is red too.

We walk to the ice cream shop with Remy clinging to one arm, Adam's arm linked through mine on the other side. It's a slow and self-conscious walk. Remy twitters like a bird to her brother about the art class and about my drawings. She duplicates my brush strokes in the air while she talks. I didn't think she was paying attention.

We get our ice cream—me, plain vanilla; Adam, cookies and cream; and Remy, blue bubble gum with gummy worms on top—and then go back outside to sit at the picnic tables to eat them. I'm smashed, not entirely uncomfortably, between Remy and Adam.

I'm on the brink of enjoying myself when the blonde camp counselor walks by on the sidewalk. She's wearing a pair of short shorts and a mini white tank top. She's with Bianca, a girl who's been one of my chief tormentors since grade school.

"Isn't that the girl who keeps texting you, Adam?" Remy says it loud enough that the girls look over at our table. My recently cooled face flames back up again and I lean back behind Adam.

"Adam!" The camp counselor waves so wildly that her tank top bobs up and down. They cross the street toward us. Bianca looks at me and whispers something to the girl behind her hand.

"Hey, Kari." Adam waves back.

"Hey, Adam." Kari, aka Camp Counselor, slides onto the seat next to Adam. He scoots over to make room, smashing me against Remy. Remy says something under her breath in French. Adam glares at her. I'm guessing he understands what she said. Kari doesn't catch the comment or the look. "We were just talking about hanging out tonight. You wanna come?"

"That sounds great." Adam says. He's completely forgotten that I'm here, even though our short-clad thighs are so close to each other, they're sticking together in the heat.

"There are a bunch of us going." Bianca gives me a sideways glance. "She could probably even come." I catch her meaning, there will be so many people there that even a freak like me won't stick out too much. "Kari was telling me about an old summer camp in Morton. It's super creepy and cool. We could go in the lake, have a bonfire and—"

"No! You can't! You can't go there!" Remy goes from normal to hysterical in half a breath. "Adam, don't ... don't go to the lake, don't take Miranda!"

Adam reaches for her. "Remy, calm down. It's no—"

She's shaking her head; actually, her whole body is shaking. The whole bench is shaking. "No, Adam! You can't go to the lake! Bad things are going to happen!"

Adam goes ashen. "Remy, stop!"

By now all of us are staring at her. Remy's face is flushed, her short hair whipping back and forth as she continues to scream, "No! No! No!"

Adam stands, gasping out an embarrassed apology as he lifts Remy from the bench—literally kicking and screaming. As he pulls her away she grips my shoulder, fingernails digging into my skin through my T-shirt. When I meet her eyes the hysteria is gone. Her expression is deadly calm. My mind is flooded again with blue-green waves, thrashing arms, and a scream that gurgles into nothing.

"Rand. Don't go to the lake. Promise me."

Chapter Nine

She's crying—sobbing, actually. I've never had one cry before. At least not like this.

It took me a few minutes to figure out what was happening. There's always something going on when I'm plunked in the middle of someone's final journey, but it's never been like this. I'm in a bedroom. She's sitting in the corner of the room. Not moving. Just crying.

I have no idea what I'm supposed to do. Who knew death could be this awkward?

She has her head bent, her arms crossed over her knees. Her hair is long and stringy, covering her face. I take a couple of steps toward her, waiting for something, anything to happen. As I get closer I realize she's pleading with someone I can't see. Her voice sounds like a little girl's. "I don't want to go. Let me stay home. Please don't make me go, Mommy. They'll laugh at me. They'll say I'm too fat."

I move closer, feeling like I should answer her. Maybe I'm supposed to play the role of her mother, comfort her or something.

"Don't make me go, Mommy. I don't like my new swimsuit. I don't like the lake."

I bend down, still not sure what to do. The girl's hair is wet. The air around her is heavy and smells swampy, like lake water.

She looks up and our eyes meet.

I recognize her.

I take a step back, tripping over the corner of her bed and stumbling into a puddle of dark liquid. No, not a puddle. The room disappears and I'm in the lake, treading water that I can't feel.

She's kneeling on the dock above me. "Kari?" The name forms on my lips. She laughs and her face rearranges itself into a smirk. "Why did you have to show up? You're such a freak."

The words sting like I was really with her, like I'd gone to the lake and she was telling me I wasn't wanted. But I'm not with her, at least not at the lake. I'm caught in some kind of vision.

Her face changes into a seductive grin. "Go on ahead. I don't want to get my hair wet. I'll be fine, but hurry back. I'll be waiting." She sits at the edge of the dock, leaning back and dangling her feet in the water.

Suddenly she screams, trying to jerk her feet up on the dock, like something bit her. One foot is free, but the other one is being pulled down. She turns onto her stomach, dragging her nails into the dock. She's being pulled into the water. She screams again. "Let me go!"

She's beside me in the lake. Her arms fight the blue-green waves, struggling to keep from going under. She can't keep her head up. Something is pulling her down. She disappears under the dark water.

"Kari!" I scream.

Her face breaks through. She thrusts her head upward, her mouth open wide. Her eyes meet mine as she mouths the words, "Help me!"

Instinctively I reach for her, but as soon as I touch her the colors run, dissolving into a rain-soaked canvas of gray light.

"No!" My voice echoes through my empty bedroom.

I sit up. The lake is gone. I'm drenched, not in lake water, but in sweat. The covers are twisted around my ankles like a hand pulling me under. I kick them off and stumble out of bed.

My mom opens the door to my room. "Baby, what—"

I'm on my feet, staring out the window. My breath slows only when I see the hearse is still parked in the driveway. I slump back on the bed in relief. "Nothing. Nothing, Mom."

She moves to rub my back, wrinkles of concern creasing her forehead. "What did you see?"

"Just ... just a dream. Just a bad dream." I breathe out, but as soon as the words pass my lips another voice fills my head.

No. A nightmare. And this is just the beginning.

***

The hearse is still sitting in the driveway when I lean back from my easel. I breathe in relief, taking it as a sign that my dream really was just a dream. Not all dead people walk with me on their way to the other side, but Pine Grove is a small town. Pretty much everyone here takes my dad's hearse to their final resting place.

I look over the image that haunted my thoughts until I was compelled to paint it. It's not something that I could sell to a grieving family or ever show anyone. Instead of being a painting that captures the essence of a life, this one shows terror at the brink of death. Kari is in the lake beside the dock. Her mouth is open in a silent, frozen scream. Her hands are clawing at the dark water as she's pulled under.

It looks a lot like the drawing Remy did.

I lean forward, examining a shadow behind her and just below the surface of the water. The shape is nearly human, but not quite. In fact, there is something distinctly inhuman about it. I shake my head to clear it. I don't remember seeing anything like the shape in my dream. Like the symbol on my painting of Tanner, I don't remember painting it.

A gentle knock on my door makes me scramble to take the painting off the easel and shove it behind my bed, smearing a few streaks of paint across my sheets. I pull the comforter up to cover them and then sit up in my bed, like I was just pulling myself out of sleep.

"Miranda." Mom opens the door a crack. "Are you up?"

"Getting there." I don't have to try to make my voice sound tired.

She pushes the rest of the way into my room. "How are you feeling?"

"Okay." I bury my paint-stained hands under the covers and glance at the hearse again.

She answers the question in my glance. "No calls yet. What did you—"

"—Is it really that late?" I look at my clock, avoiding her eyes and the question. "I told Ms. Perkins I'd help set up this morning. I need to be there in fifteen minutes."

She looks relieved. "Can I get you something for breakfast?"

I shake my head. "I'll just grab a granola bar and a banana."

"Are you sure you're—"

"—I'm fine, Mom. Really. I need to go."

"Get dressed and I'll drive you so you're not late. But I don't want to make it a habit." Mom smiles, probably enjoying the normalcy of what she just said, but nothing about me will ever be normal.

Ms. Perkins is waiting behind the desk. Her eyes soften when she sees me. "Miranda, right?" Her kindness immediately puts me on edge. "Thank you for showing up today, I appreciate your commitment, but if you're not up to teaching ..."

I glance from her to Ron at the counter. He buries his face in his book, but his eyes flash curiosity before they leave mine.

Ms. Perkins looks uncomfortable, like she said too much. "I heard about what happened at the lake last night with your friends." My blood freezes. "I mean, I assumed you were friends. I saw you together at the ice cream shop yesterday when I was leaving work. It's such a shame, such a terrible accident."

"I'm fine," I mutter, grabbing the keys to my room. I'm anything but fine. I should be thinking about Kari, the girl who I'm now sure drowned in the lake last night, but instead all I can think of is Adam. Did he ignore his sister's warning? Did something terrible happen to him too? Ms. Perkins said what happened to your friends plural, and if she saw me with anyone from here yesterday, it would have been Adam.

I stop in front of the pool, hoping to see him. Instead, the same boy I saw before is standing with a girl who wasn't here yesterday. Was Adam even supposed to be working today? It's Tuesday. He said he was teaching class and then lifeguarding on Tuesday. But he's not here. I only knew him for a day and he's probably gone.

I unlock the door to my classroom and go inside. Madame V's eyes follow me to the drying rack where I left Remy's painting. I'm suddenly afraid to look at it, remembering what she said, what I saw, and what both of us painted. The dark thing that was in my painting is in Remy's as well.

I fold it up, thinking I should throw it away. Before I can decide, the door behind me opens. Remy. She looks more lost than she did yesterday. Her flippant attitude is gone. Her hand is clenched in her mother's.

"Miranda, I'm so glad you're here. I have to get to work. Adam is … well, he wasn't up to coming in today. They still haven't found that girl and he didn't want to leave the lake in case …" She gathers a trembling breath. "I know it's not fair to ask, but I can't miss work. Could you possibly?" She glances down at Remy. "You're the only one we know enough to—"

"—Remy can stay with me." The words, words that sound nothing like me come spilling out of my mouth. I don't want to help. I don't want to watch Remy. I don't want to make any connections. My brain is screaming not to make connections. I can't protect this little girl. People die. Everyone dies.

Remy stares at me with her wide eyes and reaches for my hand. I can't say no. I can't say anything.

"Can you take her back to our house after your class is over? Adam should be back by then." Remy's mom doesn't wait for me to answer. She bends over and hugs Remy, whispering in her ear. "Stay close to Miranda." And quieter. "Don't talk to anyone else." Then she turns and heads back out the door.

Remy is staring at me. I get down on her level and look her in the eye. "Are you okay?"

She just shakes her head. "I can't make it stop, Rand. No one ever listens."

Chapter Ten

R emy spends both of my classes in the corner by herself, drawing. I leave her alone. She's been through enough and really, I'm not sure how to take her. Is she really some kind of kid prophet who can tell who is going to die and how? As hard as my visions are sometimes, what I saw last night was much worse.

She doesn't look up from her drawing until the second class files out. She turns the page over and then quietly helps me put the supplies away. When we're done she finally speaks. "Adam is probably home now. I know you want to talk to him. About what I said to that girl yesterday."

"We don't have to talk about it. Not if you don't want to."

She shrugs and walks over to the drawing she worked on all through class. She folds it up so I can't see it and then pokes it into her pocket.

Remy leads me to an older part of town. It takes us a while to walk there. I didn't think to ask her mom how far away they lived, or if we'd be able to walk it. It wouldn't matter, but it would have been nice to know.

Remy holds my hand for the whole walk to her house. She actually seems cheerful, making little observations about the class. "You did a really good job on the picture of Sophie at the beginning of class today." Or "Matt was the worst of the twins today." Or "Crystal didn't cry at all today." I didn't think she'd paid that much attention, but she knows the names of the kids in class better than I do. Remy is way more observant than I give her credit for. Maybe more observant than anyone gives her credit for.

We finally reach a small house with peeling gray paint and a sagging front porch. Remy takes a key from around her neck and fits it in the lock. She pulls the door open slowly, trying to be quiet, but it still makes a loud screech. In a heartbeat Adam is in the doorway, a plastic water bottle raised above his head like he was expecting to hit someone with it.

"What are you planning to do with that? Drown us with it?" Remy says. She realizes her poor choice of words immediately. Her face goes ashen. "I'm sorry."

Adam lowers the water bottle, looking defeated. His hair is disheveled, like he fell asleep with it wet. He's still wearing a swimsuit and he smells like lake water. "You scared me, Remy. I wasn't sure where you had gone."

"Mom took me to art class. Miranda walked me home." Remy pushes her way inside.

Adam notices me for the first time. "Hey. Miranda. Um, thanks."

"No problem." I'm backing away, but I feel like I should at least ask. "How are you?" The inadequate words come out wooden. I wish I had my dad's gift for sympathy that sounds natural.

He shrugs. "Tired."

"Did they ...?" I'm not sure how to finish that question.

"Find her? No. But they made everyone go home who wasn't part of the official rescue crew."

"Oh. That's not good. I mean. I'm sure it will be ..." But I can't tell him it will be okay. I know it won't. I know what happened to her. "Sorry. I ... I need to get going."

He looks like he wants me to leave, but he shakes his head. "Let me drive you home. Just give me a second to put some pants on and get the keys."

I'm torn. I don't want to walk all the way back to my house in the hot afternoon, but I also don't want to be alone with Adam and Remy again. "You don't need to, I can walk."

"You're a long ways in the wrong direction. I need to get out of the house anyway." He opens the door wider. "Come in. I just need to put shoes on and get my keys."

Awkwardly I walk in and sit on the edge of a threadbare couch. Remy is kneeling down in front of the coffee table. She pulls the paper out of her pocket, smooths it with both hands and pulls a pencil out of a jar on the table. She starts working on the drawing again, the same look of pure concentration on her face that she had for two classes today. She drapes her arm in front of it, so I can't see what she's working on.

We're in a small room with a couple of old chairs besides the couch I'm sitting on. On a stand in the corner is a small TV. It strikes me how dark it is. Instead of blinds or curtains, the windows have heavy blankets stretched across them.

You're the only one who can save her.

I jump and look around. Remy looks up from her drawing, studying my face. Whether the voice is her butting into my personal life, or my own thoughts, I can't tell. It doesn't matter, last night was all the reminder I needed that I can't make connections; too many bad things happen to people. I barely knew Kari and I'm going to be haunted by the expression on her face just before she went under for the rest of my life.

It's the first time my nighttime visions have brought me to someone's actual death. Even Tanner takes me to the accident scene after the crash, after he's already gone. It's the first time I've felt like I could have done something to stop someone from dying. It's the first time I'm haunted by the thought that I should have done something.

Remy is still watching me when the voice comes again. She's the only one who can save you. The voice is close, a whisper in my ear.

Remy giggles, an almost irreverent sound in the quiet room, like the laughter from the funeral in my dream. She looks up, but her smile goes beyond me, like she can see the person whispering beside me.

"Sorry." Adam's voice makes me jump. "I couldn't find the keys. I kinda threw them when I got home." He walks to the front of the house and opens the door for me. "Remy, come on."

She finishes something on her drawing, not in a hurry. Then she folds the paper up, carefully puts it in her pocket, and then puts the pencil back into the jar. Finally she stands up.

It would have been a long walk, but the car ride to my house is short and awkward. Adam and I are silent. Remy is humming something in the back seat, but she doesn't talk either. I feel like I should say something to comfort Adam, but I don't know how close he was to Kari. Against my nature, I'm curious. I want to ask him what happened last night, to see how closely it mirrors what I saw, but I don't feel like I can talk to him about it in front of Remy.

When we get to my house I hurry to unbuckle my seatbelt. Adam reaches over and touches my hand. "Can I walk you to the door?"

I glance around at our empty yard. The hearse is gone. "No. I'm good."

"I want to." Adam says. Remy unbuckles her seatbelt too. Adam turns around and shakes his head at her. "Just me. I'll be right back."

Remy's face breaks into a grin. "If you want to kiss her, go ahead. I've seen you kiss girls before." I turn bright red, mortified.

"Remy!" He hisses, as embarrassed as I am.

I fumble with the door handle, avoiding Adam's eyes. "I can go in by myself."

"I need to ask you something," he mumbles. "Please."

Before I can answer, Remy breaks in. "Don't worry, Adam. Rand won't tell anyone what I said yesterday about the lake. She understands. Don't you, Rand?" I'm trying to exit the car as quickly as possible, but Remy's hand on my shoulder stops me. "I drew this for you. Because I knew you'd understand." I turn around and face her. Her expression looks ready to burst with excitement as she hands me the still-folded paper.

"Thank you." I climb out of the car without looking at the paper. "We can talk later," I call to Adam before he can follow me. I hurry through the front door and shut it behind me.

"Miranda is that you? Why are you so late?" Mom says and then a smile crosses her lips as she peers through the window. "Is that Adam in the driveway?"

I shut my bedroom door on her last words, breathless to see what's on the piece of paper. I unfold it with hands trembling.

It's an old woman. Her hair is long, dark, and stringy. Her back is hunched, her clothes are old and dirty, like she might be homeless. I lean close to the picture, but the woman's face isn't clear.

Chapter Eleven

"Hey Miranda." Against my better judgment, I stop. It seems like most of the things I'm doing these days are against my better judgment, like continuing to teach classes at the rec center.

But I'm here, and even though I did my best to avoid him, Adam is here too, standing in front of the door to my class fifteen minutes before my class is supposed to start. "Do you have a second? I need to talk to you." He looks pointedly at Ron, who came to let me in. "In private."

I take a breath, but then nod. "Sure."

Ron rolls his eyes and takes extra time fumbling with the keys until I think Adam is going to explode. Finally the door creaks open and we step into the classroom. Adam closes the door behind us, almost in Ron's face, and turns to me.

As eager as he seemed to talk to me, he hesitates, raking his fingers through his hair, still wet from the pool. Somehow it manages to stand up in a way that looks both messy and attractive. "What Remy said ... about the lake ... She's just really ... I mean ... she's always been really afraid of the water. Our mom drowned when she was ... well, when Remy was a baby."

"Your mom? I thought that ..."

"The woman we live with is my aunt, my mom's sister. We've lived with her a long time. Remy calls her Mom."

"Oh, I'm sorry. I just ..." There are no words. Being a mortician's daughter has taught me surprisingly little about how to talk to someone about death.

"It was a long time ago. Remy couldn't have remembered, but maybe everything she's heard about that accident has made her scared. That's why she said what she did yesterday. She doesn't want anyone to go to the water, ever, that's all it is."

"It's okay. I understand." I choke on the words, because they're the same words Remy used, and I can't tell him how much I understand. "I'm pretty much afraid of everything." That's something else I can't explain to him, my own slew of irrational fears because I spend my nights with recently dead people.

He nods. "I guess that kind of comes with the territory, right? I mean when you're around death all the time." For a second I stare at him, thinking he knows more than he should. "Because your dad is a mortician, right?"

"Yeah, right." I force a laugh. "Who died and how is pretty much dinner conversation at our house." I want to cut off my tongue. Why would I say something so stupid? Especially when he was just with someone who probably drowned.

"Yeah." He's definitely giving me that freak look. "Anyway. I just wanted to make sure you haven't told anyone what Remy said ... that you won't ... that you won't tell anyone that she said something bad was going to happen at the lake."

I stare at him for a second, but I can understand why he wants me to keep quiet. He doesn't want people thinking Remy is a freak, like me. "I haven't and I won't say anything to anyone."

He sighs. "Thanks." He leans against the door, in relief or exhaustion I can't tell. He looks like he hasn't gotten any sleep since the last time I saw him.

"Are you okay?" I know I shouldn't ask, that I shouldn't care, but despite everything, I do.

"Tired. Stressed, I guess. A lot has happened since we got here. My aunt works a lot and the thing with the lake and ..." He passes his hand across his eyes.

"What happened at the lake? I mean, do you want to talk about it?"

He shrugs. "I shouldn't have gone, I knew I shouldn't have, but Kari and Bianca showed up at my house. I should have convinced them to stay and watch movies or something, but I hadn't really been out like that, not since we moved. It was stupid."

"Did you see her go in?" I'm thinking of what I saw, how it looked like she was dragged into the water and someone or something pulled her under. I shudder with the memory.

"No. I went off by myself. Nobody else was by the water. They were all sitting by the fire, drinking and smoking pot. I'm not into that stuff. Kari and I went by ourselves out on the dock. I was trying to get her to go in the water, but she—"

"Didn't want to get her hair wet." I finish his thought before he can.

"Yeah, actually, how did you ..."

I grasp for an explanation and finally finish with, "She seems like the type."

"Yeah. I guess so.

"I thought it was just an excuse. I think she's afraid of the water. I told her I wouldn't let anything happen to her, that I was a good swimmer and could save her if ..." He bites his lip like he's trying to keep it from shaking. "To prove it, I said I'd swim all the way across the lake, no problem. Dumb, right? She was sitting on the dock when I left. I heard the splash and her scream just before I reached the other side. I tried to get back to her, but I was too far away. By the time I made it back, she was gone. They still haven't found her."

"Do you think she fell in or ..." I want to say, "or did someone pull her in," but I can't get the words out.

"I don't know. I don't think she would have just jumped in. Maybe she slipped or ..." His voice gets quieter. "I shouldn't have left her. Please don't tell anyone what Remy said. We have enough problems without people thinking ..."

"Thinking what?"

He shakes his head. "I don't know. Just—" He puts his arm on the wall, leaning forward, his face earnest, but way, way too close to mine. "Just, thanks for not saying anything."

I step away from him, backing myself farther into the corner. "It's okay, I—"

The door swings open before I can figure out how to finish my thought. Ms. Perkins looks from Adam to me. His face is a couple of inches from mine. His hand is pressed up against the wall behind me. I feel my face burn, knowing how it looks.

She clears her throat. "In light of what happened yesterday I've decided that you shouldn't continue to walk home alone."

"Wait, why?" I ask. "My class ends in the middle of the day."

Ms. Perkins' mouth is firm, but there's a quiver in her words. "Because they haven't found Kari yet, and we can't be sure that she wasn't taken by someone with the intent on doing her harm. I don't care if your classes end in broad daylight. You're the only teen instructor who doesn't drive. I'm not letting you walk home alone."

"Good idea, Ms. Perkins," Adam says. "I can drive you home, Miranda."

Ms. Perkins shakes her head. "No. I already asked Ron to take her home. She's more on his way."

"Ron?" Adam says. "I don't min—"

"—Don't worry about it, Adam," Ms. Perkins says firmly.

Adam looks at her like he doesn't understand. Ms. Perkins crosses her arms, her face set, but I catch the nervous twist at the corners of her mouth.

After a tense pause, Adam shrugs. "Sure, whatever. I'll pick up Remy after class, Miranda." He walks out the door, his hands stuck in the pockets of his jacket, nonchalant, but there's something indignant about his walk and his tone, like Ms. Perkins wounded his pride. He suspects, and so do I, that Ms. Perkins doesn't entirely trust him. He was the last person who saw Kari alive. Who's to say he wasn't the person who pulled her in? Who's to say he didn't kill her?

I think about everything I saw in the vision last night, but I don't know how much of what I see is real and how much of what I see is my own, or even the ghost's perception of what's happening. I've learned my visions come from the dead. Everything I see is clouded by what they see. They share pieces of their lives with me, except this time I don't think it was Kari who was sharing. I don't even know if Kari is really dead or if it was all some bizarre dream.

Ms. Perkins stays after Adam leaves. "In the future please keep this door open at all times, particularly if you're alone with another teen counselor. I don't want rumors to get started." To make her point, she leaves the door wide open as she walks away.

Chapter Twelve

R on is waiting for me when I bring Remy to the front after Adam's lifeguard shift is over. Ron holds his manga book, one finger marking the page while he plays with his keys. He keeps looking between Adam and me as he waits at the desk.

Remy skips over to her brother, oblivious to the tension between the three of us. "We should get ice cream again. Miranda needs to—"

Adam practically growls at her. "Miranda's going home with Ron, and I need to save my money."

Remy looks to me for help, a wounded expression on her face.

"Sorry, but he's right," I say.

"Let's go Mer." Adam grabs his sister's hand. The look that crosses both their faces when he calls her Mer, makes me think he called her that by accident, like maybe he's not used to calling his sister Remy.

I watch them walk out the glass doors. Ron comes up behind me. "Are you coming with me or what?"

"Yeah." But I don't turn around. I just keep watching Remy and Adam as they walk out to the car.

"I'm in the other parking lot." Ron turns and heads out the back way like he doesn't care if I follow. After a minute I do. He's standing by his car when I catch up, flipping his keys between his fingers. Ron's car is pretty much exactly what I thought it would be—too new to be a classic, too beat up and trashy to be considered nice. The back seat is full of comics and manga, the front is full of fast-food wrappers.

I push greasy bags onto the floor and pull the seatbelt around me, steeling myself for the first of what I'm sure will be a series of awkward rides home with Ron. He surprises me by speaking up. "We could go get ice cream if you want."

I shake my head. "I'm good. Thanks anyway."

He stays quiet until we're out of the parking lot. "If you're hungry we could stop for a burger or something."

"No thanks."

"There are a couple of good movies playing at the cheap seats. A superhero flick and some romantic comedy, I think."

I turn to him, suddenly aware—more than that, afraid—that he's trying to ask me out. "I really need to go straight home. I ... I have homework."

His mouth goes hard. "Homework? It's summer."

I'm annoyed by the implication that I'm just giving him a lame excuse, even though that's exactly what I'm doing. "Actually, I do have homework. I do online school, so I have it pretty much all the time."

"Oh. That makes sense."

"Yeah."

Another few hundred yards of silence, then, "I'm kinda smart."

I'm not sure what to say to that, so I let it hang in the air. After a few more miles without any communication he picks up where he left off. "I mean, I could help you with your homework, with math and stuff."

"Oh. Thanks. But right now I'm doing history. That's what I'm mostly behind in."

"Oh." Another long silence. "I don't know a lot about history. Maybe another time, if you need help, I mean."

"Yeah. Maybe."

"Sucks that you have to do online classes over the summer."

"Yeah."

He pulls into my driveway and I'm almost free when he pulls out the bombshell. "He's completely out of your league, you know."

I turn to face him, my face flaming. "What?"

"That lifeguard, Adam or whatever. I mean, even on the off chance he's not a complete psycho serial killer, he's never going to be interested in a girl like you."

I stare at him, anger burning my face as much as embarrassment. There's nothing to say to something like that. I turn away from him, fumbling for the door handle. The door is locked. The switch on my door is broken. "Can you hit the lock? I need to go."

He sets his arm on the back of my seat and leans closer. "You shouldn't be so mean to guys like me."

I turn to him with a death glare. "Let me out."

He's so close I can smell flaming hot Cheetos on his breath. "It's not like a girl like you will get many opportunities to have a boyfriend or get kissed or—"

"LET. ME. OUT." I hope he can't hear the shake of my voice.

He stares at me for a long moment. "Whatever." He smacks the button to release the lock.

I don't bother to tell him thank you for the ride.

Chapter Thirteen

I'm in a church again. Not at a funeral this time. The windows are dark, but flames flicker on a tower of candles burning in front of a little altar. The chapel is empty except for a bent old woman. She's dusting the pews. She doesn't notice me, so I wait. Meticulously she runs her cloth over the benches, straightening the hymnals as she goes. She finally looks at me. "It looks nice, doesn't it? Everything is in order for tomorrow's service." She looks around the room. "I've cleaned this church for long enough. I suppose it is somebody else's turn, don't you?"

"I guess so." This feels normal, comfortable, even if I'm not sure what my role is in her vision.

"Guess so?" She laughs, a young woman's laugh, but she still appears old. "If you don't know, then I'm sure I don't."

"Know what?"

"If it's time for me to go."

Her directness takes me by surprise. "Go?"

"Yes, go. You are the angel who has come to take me home, aren't you?"

In all my passings, I've never been called an angel before, and except for Tanner, I've never been recognized. But this woman seems to know what's going on. "I guess so."

She laughs again. "For an angel, you sure make a lot of guesses. Maybe you're an angel in training, or one trying to earn their wings back after doing something bad. Like in one of those old movies. Am I right?" She sits down on one of the pews and pats the seat next to her for me to sit down.

"I'm really not sure." I walk over and sit beside her. I don't know what else to do. For the first time ever, I wonder if the person who I'm escorting might know more about this process than I do.

"I did some bad things in my life too. Things I regret." She picks a folded piece of paper off the floor and then quickly tucks it into the pocket of the smock she's wearing. Her eyes get far away. "I had a son once, but I chose the needle over being a mom. He didn't have much of a chance. It wasn't his fault, not really. It was mine. If you want to send someone away it should be ..."

I wait for her to finish her confession, for the scene to shift to one where she was the mom she wished she could have been. Instead she goes back to dusting the pew in front of us, humming something that sounds familiar. "I suppose they'll give my room away too, not that I'll be needing it, still it was a cozy room." She adjusts a hymnal that's turned upside down. "I hope they find another lost soul to fill it." She runs her hand over the scarred wood and then the faded red velvet seat. "Well, we'd better get going. Do you suppose they'll allow me to come back and visit sometimes?"

I shrug. "Maybe." I don't know anything about what happens after the moment a soul disappears from my visions.

She laughs again. "You must be a young angel. They haven't taught you too much about your job, have they? Never mind. You'll learn everything you need to know soon enough. Which way do we go?"

For the first time, I'm not sure. "Where do you want to go?"

"Heaven, of course," she says. The old woman in front of me has transformed into a younger woman, maybe early thirties. Her back is straight and her dark hair falls in satiny waves over her shoulders, but her face is still tired and drawn. "Don't tell me you don't know how to get there."

"Actually I ..." I'm looking around the chapel, for some sort of direction, someone waiting or ... there's a stained glass window above the altar, just like in my dream. The picture of Lazarus has been replaced by the image of Christ as a shepherd, but

I'm almost positive it's the same church, the one where the girl's funeral was held. "Have you ever had funerals here?"

The woman laughs. "Dozens. Maybe even hundreds. If you stick around long enough, we could have a front row seat to mine. I wonder who will—"

"A girl's funeral. A teenager. Curly dark hair. Lots of people came."

Her face grows dark. "Why would you ask me about that funeral? I don't know anything about what happened to that girl. It was just an accident. He told me it was just an accident." Her hand moves protectively over her pocket. "There were lots of accidents that summer."

"That summer?"

She looks at me like I should have the answer to that question along with all the others. "The summer all those girls died."

My neck prickles, as if a cold breeze just blew through the church. "What summer? When?"

She looks toward the altar at the front. "So many funerals. So many young people, buried out back." She gestures behind the church. "At first, I thought they were all accidents. Accidents happen, you know, in lakes and on hiking trails, on the road, even at home. Your own bathtub isn't safe. Why there was this old woma—"

"You said at first. What made you think they weren't accidents?"

She turns toward me, her eyes dark with pain, anger, and fear. "I never said I thought they weren't accidents. He told me it wasn't his fault. That it was hers. And I believed him. Until ..." She stares down at the pocket of her smock.

"Until what?" I'm trying to sound patient, the way an angel would, but I feel like there's a reason I'm in this church where the funeral from my dream was held.

"Until I found the note." She keeps her eyes downcast, a single tear sliding down her cheek. "I found this on the back bench, after that girl's funeral."

Careful not to touch her outstretched hand, I take the note and unfold it.

It was my fault. I gave him permission to kill them. I told him what I saw, and he thought that justified what he did. I can't keep him out of my head and I can't make it stop. My death is the only way to save them. If I'm gone he won't know who's meant to die. I'm sorry. For everything.

I look back up at her. "But what does it mean? How do you give someone permission to kill someone? And why not just say who the killer was?"

The woman's eyes go dark and she stares straight ahead. "She was trying to protect him. We all wanted to protect him."

"But why? Who was she? Who was she trying to protect?"

The woman keeps staring straight ahead. "Don't make the mistake I made. Don't love so much you forget what he is."

"Forget what who is?"

"I didn't steal that purse. I don't know where the pills came from." It takes me a minute to realize she's talking to someone else, that she's inside a memory I can't see. "You can't make me leave. This is the only place I have left. I don't care what our agreement was. I won't go." She covers her face with her hands. "Please don't make me go. I have to have a job and a place to stay, or I can't get my son back. He needs me."

"I need your help. Please." I try to bring her back to me. "The girl who wrote the note, do you know who she was? Do you …"

She stands suddenly, her arms outstretched like she's protecting herself. "Stay away from me."

We're not in the church anymore. We're inside an old apartment building. The windows are gray with dust and spider webs. The walls are streaked with dirt and pockmarked with holes. The striped carpet is faded and torn. Her face is dirty and wrinkled, her hair hangs in tangles, her eyes are bloodshot. She backs away from me. "I never told anyone. I never told."

She's backing toward a steep staircase. I take a step closer to her. "Please stop."

She keeps backing away, shaking her head, moving closer to the edge of the stairs. "I kept my promise. I never showed them her note. Not even after she was dead."

She pauses at the edge of the stairs. For a second her eyes clear and I think she sees me as me again. I inch a little closer. "It's okay. I'm not going to hurt you, just tell me who wrote the note."

"Stay away from me!" She shrieks. She takes one final step. I reach for her instinctively. My fingers slip through her outstretched hand as if she were made of dust. She screams and the scene smudges and then disappears like a chalk drawing suddenly wiped clean.

I sit straight up in bed and reach for something to draw with. The woman's face is already fading from the corners of my mind. I startle when I realize what I have in my hand. It's the drawing Remy made.

The woman in her picture is the woman I just watched die.

Chapter Fourteen

"Looking for new clients?" Marshall stands over my shoulder.

It's too late to hide the search on my computer: obituaries. I'm trying to find the woman from my dream. The hearse never went out last night and I haven't heard of any other deaths. I don't know where the church or the old apartment building is. I push my sketch of the old woman under my computer. "More like avoiding my homework."

"By looking through the obituaries? Your homework must be pretty bad." He gets himself a glass of water and sits beside me. "Looking for anyone in particular?"

"Not really."

Marshall doesn't know anything about my gift, but he's always been curious about my paintings. He reaches for the picture I tucked under my laptop of the woman from my dream last night. He stares at the picture. "Is this someone you know?"

"No. I was just practicing faces, trying something different." I take the drawing from him. "Do you remember a summer where there were a bunch of teenage girls who died in accidents? Maybe not here, but somewhere close."

Marshall gets a strange look on his face. "Why would you ask that?"

"No reason. But ... Something feels off about what happened with that girl at the lake."

He puts his hand on my shoulder. "It's because she was so young. Your age, right? It never feels right when someone your own age goes like that."

"Yeah. I guess so."

He takes a breath. "I probably shouldn't tell you yet, but everyone will know soon enough. We found her."

My heart feels sick, even though I already knew she was dead. "You found ... Kari?"

"Yeah. At the bottom of the lake. Her clothes snagged on an old tree limb that had sunk to the bottom. We had to go in with full scuba gear to find her. That lake gets really deep in places, and with the forest right on the edge, things fall in ... kids need to be careful." He breathes out. "A tragic accident, but at least it means there isn't some kind of psycho out there kidnapping teenage girls."

"Accident? Are you sure?"

He studies my face. "Yeah. There were no signs of anything but an accident. Her dad said she wasn't much for the water. She must have slipped or gone in on her own, maybe trying to go after the boy who was with her."

Accident. It's the same thing the woman said last night. They thought they were all accidents. But I remember the look on Kari's face when she went under. She was fighting someone or something that was pulling her down. It hits me then, if someone was holding onto her and there had to be some sort of mark, maybe on her legs or ankles, right? Or maybe her fingernails. I remember how she dragged them across the dock to keep from going in.

"Where is she now?""Where is ... you mean where is her body?" Marshall is looking at me like I'm crazy. "At the mortuary. Your dad did the autopsy last night. I sat in on it."

"Can you take me to the mortuary? Now?"

"You never go to the mortuary." Marshall says.

"I need to see her." I can't believe I'm asking this. Ghosts are one thing, but even though bodies are Dad's business, I've always avoided the mortuary. But I want to see if there are marks on her legs, or wood under her fingernails. Something I missed, something that would show me that my vision was real.

He shakes his head. "I don't think you want to. Her body wasn't in very good shape after being in the water for a few days. I think they're going to cremate it."

"Oh." I sit for a second. Maybe all the evidence is gone, washed away by the lake water. "Dad would have looked for bruises or marks that showed if she was held under the water, right?"

He looks at me with something like suspicion, the way Ms. Perkins was looking at Adam. "Do you know something you aren't saying, Miranda?" He pauses. "If you know anything about what happened to Kari, anything at all, you need to speak up."

"No, it's just ..." I breathe in. Maybe I could tell Marshall everything, or Dad or at least Mom. She's the most likely to believe me. But what do I really know? Echoes of a vision, a dream? I don't have anything like actual proof. Besides, anything I say would pull Remy into this mess. I shake my head. "Just what you said, someone my age shouldn't have died like that."

He nods slowly. "Try not to think about it too much." He stands, reaching for the keys to the hearse.

I hesitate again, but I need to know. "One more thing, if someone had pulled her under the water, would there be any marks?"

He thinks for a minute. "Maybe, but she was a pretty small girl. If she couldn't swim, it wouldn't take much to hold her under."

"And you look under her fingernails for anything that might be there, right?"

"If there was any sign of attack, yes. Miranda, why are you —"

"Just make sure you checked under her fingernails. Okay?"

"I'll make sure, but like I said, her body was in pretty bad shape." He looks at me again like he wants to ask more. He pats my shoulder, like he's trying to comfort me, but he's not sure what to say.

After he leaves I go back to my search. I try different years, accidental death, drowning, suicide, but I can't find anything. I go back to the picture of the old woman. Maybe if I find her, I can find the church. I search for keywords like church and caretaker. Nothing. I think about the apartment building and the woman falling backward down the stairs. I try accident and homeless. The picture on the third hit is the woman from the vision. The article says she fell down the stairs of an abandoned building she was squatting in and broke her neck. They found her yesterday. The article doesn't list a name, just Jane Doe.

But she didn't just fall. She was screaming at someone to stay away from her. Just like Kari, the homeless woman's death wasn't an accident.

Chapter Fifteen

Remy leans over her picture in silent concentration while I clean up after another class. She's drawing a cat this time. Animals and inanimate objects have become my favorite thing to teach, anything to keep her from drawing people. Her face twists in frustration. She looks at the picture of the kitten I demonstrated for the class, scribbles for a minute and then erases again.

I finish putting everything away and perch on the stool next to her. "How's it going?"

She shakes her head. "Yours looks fluffy and alive. Mine looks like a piece of paper."

"I have a secret that will make it easier." I dig into my art bag and pull out my favorite charcoal pencil. Then I fill one of the watercolor cups with clean water. "I didn't show the class this technique because they aren't ready for it yet, but I think you are." I lean over her outline of the cat and add some texture to the fur. "Shade and then get your fingers wet and smudge it, like this. The lines will get softer."

I hand her the pencil so she can copy my movements. I lean over her and guide her hand. After a few attempts, she can almost copy what I've done. She's a natural, but she also has a lot more patience than any kid in the class, even the older ones.

"Does your cat have a name?" I ask.

"He did," she says simply.

I cringe internally. "What was his name?"

"Puffers."

As soon as she says the name, the image of a small gray kitten floods my mind. In a few breaths I've seen the kitten sleep in the sun and play with a piece of knotted yarn. He slips through an open gate toward a busy street. "Stop!" I say out loud.

Remy looks at me, startled. The image is gone. "Mom said she would get us another kitten after we moved, but she hasn't yet."

I shake the vision from my head. I'm not sure where it came from. It takes me a few minutes to recover, but Remy doesn't seem upset by my outburst. She sings a little song while she works on making the kitten look as fluffy as the one I just saw so clearly. After a few seconds I realize the song she's singing has the exact tune the woman from my vision was humming. While she works, I retrieve the picture she gave me before. I wait, smoothing the wrinkles. I've been trying to decide whether I should ask her about Kari or the woman I saw last night. I haven't gotten anywhere with my own research. Remy might be the only one who can help me. "What about this lady?"

"What about her?" Remy asks innocently.

"Does she have a name?"

"She didn't tell me her name." Remy focuses on smudging a patch of fur on the cat's chest.

"Oh."

Remy looks up. "Did she tell you her name?"

I hesitate. Answering that question would be admitting I've seen the things she sees, but I think she already knows that. Finally I say, "No."

"That's too bad. Sometimes if you know their name you can call them back. If they haven't gone too far yet. Names have power."

It's the same thing she said before and more than I've learned in my whole life of walking with dead people. "Did she say anything to you?"

"She told me she was sorry she kept his secret, but she had to."

"Whose secret was she keeping?"

Remy shakes her head. "I don't know." She holds up her drawing. "Now he looks more real." She twists her face in concentration. "If I could draw people better, maybe I could show them what was going to happen. Maybe then they'd listen."

"People aren't great at listening. Especially not to kids." I take the drawing from her and pin it next to mine on the easel.

"I know! That's why I have to show them." She holds my gaze. "Will you help me?"

Her expression, the pleading in her eyes, the trust in her voice, it touches something inside me I've tried to keep closed. I don't think she's just talking about learning how to draw better. "I'm not sure—"

"Remy, time to go home." Adam's voice and his face at the door startles both of us. I wonder how long he's been standing there, watching and listening.

"Look what Rand helped me draw!" Remy says. "It's Puffers!"

A pang of guilt hits me as I look into Adam's pained eyes. In a second I know he left the gate open, the one that Puffers escaped through. I'm not sure how I know that, but I do.

"That's really good, Rem." He turns to me, his voice husky with tenderness or regret. "Thanks for waiting with her again."

"No worries," I say.

He leans against the table. "I know I conned you into this, but I really am glad you said yes." I'm not sure whether a you're welcome is warranted, so I keep quiet.

"There's some kind of street fair in town in a couple of weeks, right?" he says.

"Yeah. The annual Pine Grove street fair. They've been doing it forever." My heart starts beating faster without my permission. I can't tell him that I haven't gone in years. The street fair has too many unknowns: crowds of people, dangerous rides, dark corners.

"I was wondering if—"

"Rand, aren't you ready to go yet?" Ron, who absolutely does not have my permission to call me Rand, breaks into the conversation before I can find out if Adam wants me to go to the street fair with him, or watch Remy so he can go with someone else.

I turn on him, annoyed. "Actually, I don't—"

"Are you all still here?" Mrs. Perkins joins the suddenly crowded art room. "We need to clear out, there's an event this afternoon. I sent Ron to hurry you up."

"We were just leaving." Adam stands up without finishing his thought. "Let's get out of here, Rem."

Remy passes Ron with the glare I'd like to give him, that I think I would give him, if Ms. Perkins wasn't watching us.

Chapter Sixteen

I 'm standing in a little grove of trees. There's a fire in the center of a group of teenagers. I move closer, but none of them sees me.

"Hello?" No one answers. Based on the clothes and hairstyles, what I'm seeing happened years ago. I move closer and try again. "Hello?" No one turns. I can't interact with them. I can only watch. This isn't real, or at least it isn't real anymore. This is more like what I saw before, the girl's funeral, more like an echo of a memory. I look around the circle, trying to figure out whose memory this is. Like before, I feel her presence, but I don't see or hear her.

They're laughing. One dark, curly-haired girl cuddles with a blond guy. She smirks at the lone girl who sits apart from the group. The girl looks different than everyone around her. Her hair is long and straight, dyed black and tipped in blue. Her eyes are rimmed with purple eyeliner and her lips are a deep red. She's wearing a black Megadeath T-shirt and black jeans. Everything about her stands in sharp contrast to the bright T-shirts, cutoff shorts, and laughing kids around her.

The curly-haired girl turns to the loner with an outstretched hand. "Your turn."

The loner glowers at the other girl and the guy she's cuddled up to. He catches her look, but shrugs as if to say, "Can you blame me?"

The curly-haired girl giggles. "We could skip you if you're not into it." She reaches her hand to the couple on the other side of the fire.

The blue-haired girl snatches a silver coin away from her and then flashes a look of defiance at all of them. Her red lips curl into a smile as she slides from her perch on an old stump and slinks like a panther on all fours to the boy who has arm around the curly-haired girl's shoulders. In a surprisingly sexy voice she says. "Ask me anything."

He pretends to think. The look on his face is almost sinister. He cups her chin in a way that makes me think it's not the first time the two of them have been this close. He leans in and whispers in her ear. I can't tell what he says, but a look of triumph spreads over her face as she nods. She sits back on the heels of her black boots and scans the circle as if she's contemplating something. Finally, her glance rests back on the curly-haired girl.

She smiles. Then she moves close to the same guy, sliding her fingers through his hair as she whispers in his ear. Darkness overtakes his features and he nods solemnly. "Definitely Amber."

"What?" The curly-haired girl asks. "What did you ask her?"

Instead of answering, the other girl shakes the coin in her hand and then throws it. It bounces in the firelight and finally lands in the dust next to the Amber's exposed pink-tipped toenails.

"Tails," the boy announces.

The girl with blue hair smirks. "I guess you'll never know." She retrieves the coin and passes it to the next couple. Then she looks back at the boy. He's no longer cuddled up to the other girl. His face is set with a grim determination. The curly-haired girl he was sitting by looks suddenly terrified. She shrinks away from him. "What did you ask her?"

The boy puts his arm back around her, pulling her close to him, but it's not a gesture of comfort. "No worries, Am. Not a big deal."

She leans into him, her head pressed against his chest. She looks up at him through her dark lashes like a 1940s femme fatale. "You have to tell me."

He brushes his fingers across her cheek and then looks back at the girl with the blue-tipped hair, a question in his eyes.

She shakes her head no, but the boy answers anyway. "I asked her which of us would be the first to die."

I'm reaching for my sketchpad before I'm fully awake, trying to draw the faces as they slip from my memory. This vision was foggy, dreamlike, and their faces were distorted by the darkness and dim firelight. The only image that stands out is the fear reflected in the curly-haired girl's eyes. I turn back through my sketchpad to the drawing of the girl in the coffin. Neither face was clear, but I know immediately, Amber is the same girl whose funeral I saw before.

The first to die.

Chapter Seventeen

"It has come to my attention." Ms. Perkins waves a clipboard in the air at the end of our weekly recreation staff meeting. "That there are only three spots filled for our booth at the annual Pine Grove street fair. Now I know you all want to enjoy the fair, but there'll be plenty of time for that after your shift is over." She looks over the crowd. Everyone shuffles in their seats or looks over the papers on their laps, anything to avoid eye contact with her.

I glance down at Remy. She's swinging her legs on a plastic folding chair between Adam and me. This meeting is mandatory, which means Remy got stuck here too. Adam wouldn't let her draw to pass the time. I understand why, but she seems so bored I feel bad for her. She blows a bored/annoyed breath of air heavenward through her bangs.

Ms. Perkins passes the clipboard to a guy on the front row. "The more people who sign up, the shorter the shifts will be, and yes you can sign up in pairs or small groups." She moves onto the next order of business, something about adding educational value to all of our classes. While she talks, the clipboard gets passed around quickly, no one bothering to add their name to the list. It comes to Adam.

Ms. Perkins folds her hands and her tone changes. "On a more somber note, the memorial service for Kari Tomkinson is Thursday afternoon in Morton." We're closing down our program for the day so all of you can attend the service. We'll be taking the field trip vans down for anyone who would like a ride. I know Kari's family would appreciate the support."

I glance over at Adam, thinking I should offer to take Remy that day so he can go to the funeral, but he's staring at the fair sign-up clipboard. His hands are clenched so tightly around the edges that they're digging into his palms. For an odd second I want to reach over and take the clipboard from him, offer one of my hands to squeeze instead, do what I can to make him feel better. I'm not brave enough to make that move.

After a respectful pause, Ms. Perkins goes back to business. "Thank you for all your hard work. I feel like everything notwithstanding, we've had a good start to our year's programming."

Adam stands, still gripping the clipboard. The pain in his face is too much. I reach over, and take the clipboard from him, gently pulling it out of his hands.

He looks at me. "You and Ron?" It wasn't the question I was expecting.

I glance down at the paper in front of me. My name is next to Ron's, filling one of the few shifts. "He must have signed both up. I didn't know about it."

"Oh. Right." He doesn't sound like he believes me.

I'm annoyed at Ron for putting my name on the list and at Adam for thinking I have a thing with Ron. I reach over and cross my name off the list, aware that Ron is watching me. I don't bother looking back at him.

"Are you going?" Adam asks.

I suck in a breath, wondering again if he's going to ask me to go with him. "To the fair?"

"No. I meant the funeral."

"Oh." I try not to let stupid disappointment show in my voice. Adam is upset about Kari, and all I can think about is whether he's going to ask me out. I make up my mind quickly. "I don't really do funerals, but I can take Remy so you can go."

Adam's eyes brush across the crowd before lowering again. "No one wants me there."

I want to tell him that's not true, but as I follow his gaze I notice people staring and then looking away. The suspicion is almost palpable. It didn't occur to me that the empty chairs around us in the meeting might be because of him, not because of me.

"It's no big deal anyway. I barely knew her." Adam keeps his eyes on the floor, even as he starts to take down our row of chairs. Across the room Ron is leaning against the wall, flipping his keys, impatiently waiting for me. I can't take another ride home with him.

I set the clipboard down on one of the chairs and reach for Remy's hand. "You want ice cream?"

"Yes!" She smiles.

I look at Adam, impressed at my own bravery. "What about you? My treat this time."

He glances at Ms. Perkins. "Are you sure?"

"She can't tell me who I can and can't go home with."

Adam's lips turn up into an almost smile. "Okay, but not anywhere in town. I didn't realize how small this place was."

I reach for Remy's hand. "I think I know where we can go."

Chapter Eighteen

A million years ago I used to ride bikes with Tanner to a cliff overlooking the town. On the way we'd stop at a little convenience store and buy a pint of Ben and Jerry's Half-Baked ice cream. He'd eat the brownie and a few bites of my cookie dough and I'd eat the cookie dough and a few bites of his brownie. I'm surprised the store is still in business. I'm even more surprised that I decided to bring Adam and Remy to the spot I haven't been to in so many years, especially since it's less than a mile up the road from the corner where Tanner died.

Adam chooses Cherry Garcia and Remy wants Chunky Monkey. I try a flavor called Americone Dream because I can't handle either the brownie or cookie dough.

"Pull over here," I say as we reach the spot. The cliff is only a few hundred feet off the road, but it's through the woods and mostly hidden from the rest of the world. From it you can see the whole town. Tanner and I used to sit and eat ice cream and plan our adventures. I stop at the top, realizing for the first time that this spot provides a clear view of the corner where Tanner died. I can't keep my eyes off the dented guardrail. Remy reaches over and squeezes my hand like she understands, but there's no way she could know what this spot means to me.

After the squeeze she races ahead of us, scaling up the rocky cliff side. Adam and I set the ice cream and spoons up in the center of the cliff. Remy goes to the edge and dangles her feet over the side. She might be afraid of water, but she doesn't seem to have any trouble with heights. As protective as Adam is of her, I'm surprised he doesn't call her back.

"You can see everything from here!" she squeals back to us. "It looks like a painting."

"Maybe you should bring your art class up here, have everyone try to paint it," Adam says.

"No." Remy's voice goes solemn. "One of the twins would fall off and break his neck for sure."

"She's right." I call back. I'm purposely facing toward Adam and away from the view below us.

Her face sets. "I'm always right."

Adam looks at his sister. She's digging into her ice cream and taking in the view. He lowers his voice. "Thanks for everything. I mean, really thanks. I saw how you were with Remy yesterday. You two have some kind of connection. I don't think she's ever trusted anyone so fast, or maybe ever. She didn't have very many friends where we lived before."

"What about you? Was it hard moving here?" I ignore his thanks. I don't want to talk about any connection Remy and I might have.

"Excruciating. Especially now. Now that everyone thinks ..." He shakes his head.

"It'll get better." But I'm not sure I can make that promise. Small towns can have a long memory. No one here has let me forget I'm a freak. Of course, I'm not a tall, good-looking guy. I'm fairly sure that by the time school starts, at least the girls will have forgotten about him being at the lake when Kari died. "Why did you guys move?"

He sucks in a breath, like he doesn't want to talk about it. After a few minutes he says, "My aunt wanted a new start."

"Oh." I want to know more, but he doesn't sound like he wants to talk about it.

He pulls the lid off his ice cream. "Thanks for this."

"You're welcome." I pick up my own ice cream, and try to dig out a scoop, but the plastic spoon breaks off and the handle bounces out of my hand.

Adam gets a spoonful of his and passes it over to me. "That's why I put mine on the dash, so it would soften up before we got here."

I take a bite, letting it melt on my tongue and then pass the spoon back to him. "Thanks. I've never had Cherry Garcia before. It's good."

"It was my mom's favorite. She used to let me share with her, she said it was my job to keep her from eating the whole thing." He looks far away, beyond Remy, beyond the town. "I was barely seven when she died. I don't remember much about her, but I remember that." He passes me another spoonful.

"What happened to her?" I ask it gently, so if he doesn't want to answer he understands that he doesn't have to.

"We were out on a sailboat with some friends at Lake St. Clair. A storm blew in and the sail came undone and hit her in the back of the head. She fell in. My dad managed to pull her out, but they couldn't revive her. Remy was born a few hours later, after Mom had already been declared brain dead."

"That's really horrible." I know immediately that it's the wrong thing to say, but it's what comes out. Adam stays silent for what seems like a long time. Finally I ask, "What about your dad?"

Adam shrugs. "He couldn't deal, a new baby and a little kid. He passed us off to Aunt Kasey, Mom's sister. I haven't seen him in a couple of years. He sends money sometimes when he's actually working, but mostly he's a deadbeat. Aunt Kasey says my dad lost the part of him that was good when he lost my mom."

"I'm really sorry." I reach to set my hand on his leg, not sure what kind of comfort I can give, but wanting to do something. He intercepts my hand, lacing his fingers through mine and squeezing. An electric spark moves from his hand all through my body. "It was a long time ago," he says, but he doesn't let my hand go, even as he digs another bite of ice cream out of the carton and offers it to me. We sit that way for a few minutes, the sun warming my back, his hand comfortably in mine as we pass the spoon back and forth.

Remy screams.

Adam is on his feet, dropping the carton of ice cream and my hand before I've fully registered what is going on.

"Meri!" He yells, not even noticing his slip as he hurries to the edge of the rock.

Remy is lying on her stomach, leaning over the edge. "My bracelet!" Adam sits next to her, his hand firmly on her back, pulling her away from the edge. "Down there!"

Adam pulls her back and I lean over. The silver charm bracelet she always wears is dangling from the bushes a few hundred feet below us. "I was twisting it and it fell off. It's the one I got from Mom!" Her voice is choked with hysterical tears.

"We can't get it from here," Adam says.

Remy turns to me, tears making trails down her red cheeks. "She bought it for me before I was born. It's the only thing I have from her."

I sit down next to them, evaluating the sheer cliff below us. "We can't climb down to it." I look at the road below us, the switchback where Tanner went off the road. "But maybe if we drive down there we can climb high enough to reach it with a stick or something."

"That's the only way I can think of," Adam agrees. "And even then ..."

"You have to get it for me, Dre," Remy pleads with him. "I have to have my bracelet."

I stare at him. Dre? Maybe Remy's not the only one using a nickname.

He doesn't seem to notice. "I'll try."

We head back to the car. I pick up my untouched ice cream. Remy's and Adam's have bounced down the cliff. Adam drives down to the other switchback, his hands white on the steering wheel.

I reach over and touch his hand. "It's okay. We'll get the bracelet back."

He nods, but looks grim. Remy is crying in the backseat. Adam parks next to the dented guardrail, just a few feet from where Tanner's car went over. He and Remy cross the road to get closer to where the bracelet is, but I'm frozen in place. My gaze travels down the path of torn up rocks and underbrush that after nine months is just barely starting to grow back, to the splintered tree where his car finally came to rest. If I close my eyes I can see the side of his car, shiny in the rain and reflecting the lights from the fire engines and police cars. I can see the rescuers lowering themselves down on ropes. They reach the door and pry it open and—

"Rand!" Remy is yelling for me. "We need you! We can't reach it."

I open my eyes and pull myself from the grim scene, back to the bright sunlight, a tear-streaked little girl, and a silver bracelet caught in a tree.

"I can't get up high enough," Adam says. He's holding a long stick. I can see where he's tried to climb up and slid back on the loose gravel. "I was thinking if you climbed up on my shoulders, maybe you could hook it with this stick and knock it down."

I look from Adam's broad shoulders to the slippery edge, to the pleading look on Remy's face. "Okay. I'll try."

Adam puts his hands on my hips and hoists me onto his shoulders like I weigh nothing. Remy passes the stick up to me. Carefully, Adam climbs on a rock at the base of the cliff. I steady myself with one hand on his head and the other on the stick. He climbs a couple of steps up while I hold my breath, my heart pounding. He stops. "See if you can get it from there."

I stretch up, but the end of the stick just barely brushes the tips of the branch where the bracelet is stuck. "Can you go a little higher?"

"I think so. Hang on." He keeps one arm over my legs and the other he uses to steady himself with tree branches beside him on the trail. He steps up on a narrow rock ledge.

I keep my eyes on the bracelet above us. "A little farther, a little farther." The edge of my stick catches the bracelet. I stretch up as far as I can go. "Can you boost me up?"

Adam cups my feet in his hands and pushes me up until I'm almost standing. I slip the tip of the stick inside the bracelet. "I have it!" I flip the stick backward.

Adam stumbles. I lose my balance, the stick crashing down the cliff behind me. I'm falling down, down ... down the edge of the cliff.

I'm in the seat next to Tanner. He's fighting for control. The car slides sideways—flipping over and over, my stomach lurching and my neck snapping each time it bounces off the ground. We stop suddenly, smashing into the tree in a cacophony of shattering glass, splintering wood, and crunching metal. Tanner slumps forward, a trickle of blood sliding down his cheek.

I think he's gone, but after a few breaths his head moves, slowly rising off his chest. He reaches for the door handle, inches at a time. He grasps it, but the door is crushed against the tree. It won't open. He reaches over and undoes his seatbelt. As he does the words He wasn't wearing a seatbelt come back to me—my dad explaining the details of Tanner's accident the morning after he died.

Slowly his strength returns. He slams his shoulder against the door again, but it doesn't budge. He turns to the passenger side, but it's crushed from rolling down the hill. His fingers move across the seat, searching for something. Finally they curl around his cell phone, wedged in the seat beside him. The screen is shattered. Blood drips into his eyes, but he presses the buttons anyway. The phone is dead.

The phone slips from his fingers—his eyes suddenly meeting mine. "Help me." His voice is weak, but growing stronger. "I wasn't supposed to die here. I wasn't supposed to die like this. I wasn't supposed to die that night! Tell them, Rand!" He reaches for my shoulders "I wasn't supposed to—"

He's gone as soon as he touches me.

Pain radiates through the back of my head. "Miranda! Can you hear me?" My eyes roll open. Adam is bent over me, his hand on his phone. Remy's face is close. I turn my head, my eyes meeting hers. "He wasn't supposed to die that night."

Her fingers grip mine. "None of them were meant to die."

Chapter Nineteen

"You got it back." I say, noticing the flash of silver on her wrist when Remy drops a folded paper on my nightstand.

"No, you got it back." Adam sets a blue vase holding yellow lilies next to Remy's card. "I'm really, really sorry. Putting you on my shoulders was a dumb idea. How's your head?"

"Okay." Throbbing, horrible, and my brain feels muddled. I'm having a hard time deciding what's real. Now for example, it feels like Adam is sitting on my bed with his hand on my leg.

Remy is fluttering around my room. She picks up one of my paintbrushes and runs the soft bristles across her cheeks, holding onto it as she plops on my bed next to Adam. "How long does a concussion last? Because that guy they have teaching our art class is horrible. He has us drawing manga characters and he has no control over the class whatsoever. The twins already broke one of the easels."

"I don't know, Remy. I think he might have to finish out the month." I'm guessing Ron is filling in for my class, based not only on his usual reading choice, but also on the card that Mom brought in for me yesterday from him. I'm afraid it's supposed to be a picture of me—a manga-me with larger-than-life gray eyes, fiery red hair, and a comic representation of a bump on her head. Manga-Me also has a much larger chest than I do and is wearing a much shorter skirt than I'd ever wear.

I reach up and ruffle Remy's hair the way I've seen Adam do. "Besides, I think you could probably use some work on drawing people."

Adam meets my eyes as soon as the words are out of my mouth. I forgot for just a second that Remy drawing people is a bad thing. I drop my hand back to the bed. "Seriously though, I'll try to be back by next week."

"Next week?" Remy whines.

"So I guess you won't be going to Kari's funeral tomorrow," Adam says.

"I can't, sorry. The doctor said I need to stay away from bright lights, loud noises, and any place where there are lots of people." Ironically, all of the things I've been avoiding most of my life. "I thought you didn't want to go."

"I thought if I went with you, then people would stop ... that they'd ..." Adam trails off, digging his fingers into the blankets covering my leg.

"Has it been that bad?" The unfamiliar urge to comfort him wells up inside of me again. Behind it there's this seed of doubt. Could Adam be using me again? Maybe he only wants me to go to the funeral with him so people don't think he had some weird thing for Kari that caused him to drown her. My head hurts too much to try to analyze that thought.

He sets his hand on the bed, inches from mine. My fingers itch to cross the distance and hold his hand the way we did on the cliff. "After you fell, some kids switched out of my swim class, like they were afraid of me. It sucks because I get paid by the kid and I'm down to three."

"After I fell?" I say. He nods. "But it was just an accident." I touch the top of his hand, just lightly, so he knows that I'm here. He turns his hand so his palm is open. My fingers nestle themselves in the hollow of his hand, like they're supposed to be there.

"Yeah, an accident, just like Kari's." He grips my fingers and his face goes dark.

"Adam, I'm sorry I—"

"It wasn't an accident!"

I wince as Remy's voice splits into my throbbing brain.

"Remy, don't!" Adam warns her.

"Rand knows it wasn't an accident, she knows!" Remy insists.

Adam stands up, reaching for her. "That's enough!"

"No!" Remy yells again, her eyes on mine. "Tell him what you saw!" Images of Kari, struggling in the water flash into my mind. I close my eyes and shake my head, the images and sounds reverberating through my skull, nausea churning in my throat, my whole body suddenly hot.

"I'm sorry Miranda," Adam says. "C'mon, Remy. Let's go!" He grabs her leg as she crawls away from him. He's dragging her backward, but she stretches out, reaching behind the bed, almost like she knows it's there.

"No, don't!" It's my turn to yell as Remy hauls out the painting I did of Kari just before she died.

Remy loses her grip on the picture and it falls onto the floor, face up. Adam freezes, one hand still on Remy's foot. I want to throw my body across the picture, but he's already seen Kari's face, her thrashing arms, and her silent scream immortalized by me in oil and canvas.

"I told you she understood." Remy looks smug.

He picks up the painting, studying it. Then he turns to me, his face white with shock and fear. "Why would you ..."

"I couldn't, I needed to ..." But there are no words. Behind the fear, one word is written in his eyes. Freak.

"Remy, we need to go." This time he says it quietly.

Remy digs her hands into the blanket on my bed. "No! Rand understands, we have to find her, we have to—"

"Kari is dead! We can't find her!" Adam explodes. He drops the painting and picks Remy up before she has a chance to cling to me or the bed.

"Not Kari, the other girl. The one who can't leave." Remy is fighting Adam every step of the way, but he's carrying her toward the door.

I stand and move to stop him. My steps are unsteady and my head is pounding. I have to grip the edge of the bed for support. Adam stops and I face Remy. "Why can't she leave?"

"She did something really bad, something she can't fix by herself. She can't let it happen again. We need to—"

"That's enough!" Adam tears Remy away from me, turns toward the door, and runs straight into my dad.

"That is exactly what I was going to say." Dad is filling the door. He's a good couple of inches shorter than Adam, with a smaller frame, but I've never seen him look so imposing.

"We were just leaving," Adam says.

"That's the other thing I was going to suggest." Dad steps aside, holding the door open.

Remy is sobbing now. "We have to help her. Please, Rand."

Her voice fades as Adam carries her away and my dad closes the door behind them.

He walks over and picks up the painting. He studies it for a minute and then sets it on the nightstand, facedown without comment. "How are you feeling?"

I slump back on my bed, fighting tears of pain, frustration, panic, and everything in between. "Not okay."

Dad moves next to me. I've seen him pour out sympathy to complete strangers, hug people who have lost children or spouses, but when he puts his arm around me, it feels as cold and stiff as one of the corpses in the morgue. "I know this is a hard age for you, and boys can be clueless and—"

I push him away, staring at him in disbelief. He sounds like he's reading from some kind of "How to Comfort Your Hormonal Teenage Daughter," website. When I finally speak, I can barely control the angry shake of my voice. "This isn't about a boy. This is about this." I gesture to the painting. "This is about a girl who was murdered. I saw her die, Dad, I saw her drown and there was nothing I could do to stop it."

"You were there, at the lake?" Dad is still trying to find a logical explanation for this.

"No Dad, I was here, in my bed. Asleep. But I saw her drown, just like I was in the water next to her. And then there was the lady on the stairs. I tried to reach for her, I tried to save her, but I couldn't ..." I bury my face in my hands.

Dad places his hand on my back. "Shh, Miranda. You need to calm down. Your head, sometimes delusions are associated with a concussion—"

"No! Not in my head. It's real! It's always been real! Why can't you understand? If I don't find out what happened before, it's going to happen again. I'm the only one who can keep it from happening again!"

Chapter Twenty

I'm in the same church, but this funeral isn't like the other one. There aren't nearly as many people here, and they're almost all adults. The casket is closed—a cheap silver box. There are only a few flowers. A tall minister dressed in black is talking about lost sheep and redemption.

I walk down the center aisle, wishing I could see who is lying in the coffin in front of me. There's no picture beside the alter, no program that I can see, nothing that indicates who this person was.

I look at the mourners instead, trying to judge when this happened based on the clothes they are wearing, but the black suits and dresses don't give much away.

"... she who has an artist's eye lives with her hand in that of the Great Creator." I turn to the minister. For a second I think he's talking to me. I'm standing just below the pulpit, but his eyes stare through me as he continues. "What were once simple figures and crayon drawings became works of beauty. Her gifts were shared with the children she taught. Her love of nature showed in a thousand flowered sketches." He pauses and I hear a hiccupped sob coming from a woman beside me. "But an artist's soul can be a tortured one. We may never know what demons possessed someone so young. What made her believe this was her only choice. We pray for her soul now, that she may have peace ..."

"No peace. No peace. No peace." The voice begins as a whisper of a thought. I stare at the woman beside me, thinking she's the one who's speaking. Her long dark waves seem familiar, but her face is covered, her shoulders still shaking. The voice isn't coming from beside me or behind me. It's coming from all around me. Growing. Not increasing in volume, but in intensity. No one else in the church hears it, but the stained glass window behind the altar vibrates with the words until the depiction of a bandaged Lazarus shudders and breathes as if he were rising from the tomb again.

I fall to the floor, my hands clasped over my ears, but I can't shut the voice out. It echoes in my head until I think my skull will shatter along with the window above me.

"Get out of my head!" I scream.

The stained glass window bursts. A million colorful diamonds rain down on the mourners. I cower, my arms protecting my head.

The world falls silent.

I'm back in bed, shaking, even though I'm holding the covers tight around my head. As I come back to myself, I sit up and reach a trembling hand for my phone to check the time.

Adam's lilies and Remy's card both lie untouched on my nightstand. My painting is on the other side of the room, picture side against the wall. Dad must have moved it. I pick up the folded piece of paper Remy left. At first I think that she's drawn someone else who's going to die. But it's the stained glass window from my dream. Where I expect the words "Get Well Soon," I read, "No peace."

I wad up the paper and throw it across the room. I can't deal with this. No peace for who? For me? For Remy? Or for the girl who can't move on? Despite what I told my dad, I don't have the strength to save anyone.

Chapter Twenty-One

"This is a little different from what you usually draw." Marshall picks up my sketch pad and points at the drawing I started. "Something religious?" It's what I can remember of the stained glass window from my dream. It's unique, a picture of Lazarus coming from the tomb. If I figure out what church has a window like this, maybe I can figure out whose funeral I was seeing.

"Just a stained glass window." I say, tracing the panes around the bandaged figure.

"Pretty good, but aren't you supposed to avoid anything that involves thinking too hard? If I tell your mom you're up for drawing, she might think you can get back to your homework." Marshall's teasing is light this time, gentle. But that's worse than his usual banter. I don't know if I can take any more gentleness.

"Please don't," I answer, but he's right, my head already hurts from a lack of sleep and the after-effects of the concussion.

He hands me back the sketchpad. "What made you decide to draw this?"

"It's something I can't seem to get out of my head."

"Something you've seen before? Maybe in a dream?" Marshall presses.

I lie back on my pillows. I can't make the stained glass window come out quite right. I can't focus and honestly, I didn't pay much attention to it until it shattered. "Something like that."

"Your mom told me ... a little bit about what you see. Not everything, but if you need someone to talk to—" He gestures to my sketchbook. "Someone who believes that there's something to all of this. I'm happy to listen."

I shake my head. How can I explain it to him if I don't even understand it?

"What about the picture? What made you paint this?" He crosses the room and taps the back of the canvas. I'm not sure when he saw it. "It's similar to the one that little girl, Emmy, did, right?"

"Remy, and yeah."

He waits for the rest of the answer. Reluctantly, I give it to him. "I dreamed about Kari. I dreamed someone drowned her."

His eyes get big. I can see him fighting his own doubts. "I don't think that's so unusual. It was a horrible thing that happened. I'm sure you aren't the only one who's had nightmares about it."

"Yeah, except ..." I hold my breath, debating. I don't know if I should tell him about what I saw.

"Except?" He waits long enough that I have to answer.

I let it out in a rush. "Except I dreamed it the night she died. Before I knew anything about what had happened to her."

He lets out a low whistle. I'm waiting for the freak look, but it doesn't come. He reaches for the sketchpad again. "And last night? What did you dream last night?"

"I was in a church, at a funeral. This window was in the church from my dream."

"Kari's funeral?" Marshall says gently.

"No, I don't think so."

"That's interesting." But he says it like it really is interesting, and not like I'm freaking him out. He taps my drawing. "I think I've seen this window before."

I sit up suddenly. "You have?"

"Yeah. I'm pretty sure it used to be in the church in Morton. The one where they're holding Kari's funeral."

"Used to be?"

He nods and then starts searching for something on his phone. He comes up with a picture. "Is this what you saw?"

I take his phone and look at the image. I scroll a little farther down and see another picture of the window this time with a pane missing. "What happened to it?"

"It was destroyed in a freak storm about ten years ago."

I slide my legs over the side of the bed. "How soon are you leaving? I have to go to that church."

Marshall shakes his head. "I can't take you. You're supposed to be in bed, getting better. Your dad would never forgive me."

"But ..." I start.

"But if you hurry you might be able to make the van they have going from the rec center." He stands. "Just be careful, okay?"

Chapter Twenty-Two

I hurry as fast as I can, pulling on a dress, working my hair into a braid. I try texting Adam on my way out the door because riding in the van with a bunch of strangers to a funeral sounds like a special kind of torture.

I start with:

> Hey, if you're still up for going to the funeral. I'll go
> with you.

And then I try:

> My head feels a lot better. I think I will go to the
> funeral after all. Do you want to go together?

And even: Thanks for the flowers and coming by yesterday. Things got a little crazy. Can we talk about it on the drive up to Morton? I'll pay for gas.

He doesn't answer. I take it as a sign that he's joined the Miranda's a Freak club and I'm on my own.

On the counter is a note from Mom saying she took Mark to the swimming pool and then she's going shopping. Dad isn't around either. I breathe a sigh of relief. I don't have to ask or explain why I suddenly need to be at the funeral today. I just leave a quick note:

> Feeling better. I decided to go to
> Kari's funeral.

As much as I hurry, by the time I reach the rec center both vans are gone. I lean against the side of the building and send one more text to Adam:

> I really think we should both go today. Please
> answer.

I hate how desperate it sounds.

"He's not going to show." Ron locks the door to the building behind him. "I mean, it would kind of be like returning to the scene of the crime, wouldn't it?"

"Adam didn't do anything wrong," I yell back at him.

He raises his hands in surrender. "Okay, believe what you want, I'm just saying, don't come crying to me when you end up with worse than a bump on the head."

I let out a frustrated breath, but I don't have the energy to argue with Ron, so I start walking away.

He catches up fast. "Hey, wait, I was just kidding. Well, sort of. I can give you a ride to the funeral." I stop. "That's where you wanted to go, right? Why you were texting Adam? I wasn't planning on going, but if you want to go, I can drive you."

I look at him, imagining the awkward forty-minute ride ahead, but it's not like I have a better option. I have to get to that church, the sooner the better. "Okay, sure."

He smiles. "Great. My car is in the back."

Knowing I'll probably regret it, I follow him to the back parking lot. He gets in and starts the car while I climb in. After a few painful moments of silence he asks, "So how's your head?"

I shrug. "Not terrible."

"You coming back to your class soon?"

"Next week, I think."

"I've been taking your class for you."

"Yeah. I heard."

"Those twins are total brats. I can't get through a lesson without them breaking something. And that one girl with white hair cries a lot."

"Yeah." I breathe in. I can do this, just easy conversation for the next forty miles.

"I don't think your friend Remy likes me very much." Ron reaches under his seat.

"Why do you say that?" My phone buzzes and I reach to check it, but stop when I see what Ron has in his hand. "She gave me this." I take the piece of paper with trembling fingers. It's a manga version of Ron.

"Pretty good, but a little sadistic, don't you think? That reminds me, did you get the drawing I did of you?"

I can't answer. I can only stare at the picture in front of me. Ron's eyes are X's and his head is lolling to one side.

He's dead.

Chapter Twenty-Three

I know immediately that the church is the same one from my dream, even though it's been remodeled. The number of mourners is like the first funeral. There are tons of flowers. No casket, just a gold urn and a huge picture of Kari at the end of the aisle. It's a photograph. I'm grateful that the family didn't ask me to paint her picture.

Ron reaches for my hand as we head move toward the back pew. I pretend not to notice and walk more quickly. I don't want any rumors about Ron and me getting started. The ride was bad enough. Thanks to Remy's picture I was paranoid the whole time that we were going to get into a car accident. Unlike the picture of Kari, there's no indication of how Manga Ron died, nothing to help me figure out how I can stop something from happening to the real Ron.

I'm trying to keep my head down, but I glance up just long enough to see Adam. He's half-standing, looking for someone. As our eyes meet, I realize he's looking for me. Despite the packed church, he's by himself, a margin of space on one side of him. No Remy. When he sees me with Ron he looks surprised and then turns and sits down. I glance at my phone.

I already left. Hoping you made it up in the rec center van. I'll save you a spot.

The text I missed from Adam.

Ron guides me to a nearly full pew and waits while I squeeze into the space, then he squeezes in next to me—way too close for anyone's comfort. He sets his hand on my knee and I push it off twice before he gets the hint and starts playing some game on his phone. The perfume of flowers is overpowering. The music, the benches, everything feels like one of my visions, but I don't sense that anyone is here but the living mourners and gawkers—not Kari, not the woman who cleaned the church, not the girl with curly hair who was in the casket, and not the one who can't move on.

The minister stands. He's too young to have officiated at either of the funerals in my dreams. I raise my eyes to the window behind the rostrum. The stained glass is a picture of Christ holding a lamb, the same as it was in my visit here with the old woman.

The service begins with music, low and solemn and continues with a low and solemn sermon from the man at the front of the church. I sit until the heat and the light, the proximity to Ron, and the smell of flowers gets to me. My head is pounding and I feel like I'm going to faint. I have to have some fresh air. I stand. "I need to go ..."

"I'll come with you," Ron hisses back, less quietly.

"To the bathroom," I finish, thinking quickly of where he can't follow.

"Oh." Ron sits back down.

I walk out as quickly as seems reverent, resisting the urge to break into a run and flee the church. I pass a table full of memories of Kari by the door. A picture of the fat little girl in a pink polka-dot bikini stands in contrast to the model-perfect figure from Kari's latest picture.

A hazy drizzle of rain is falling outside. I welcome the cool mist on my face as I walk away from the church and toward the cemetery behind it. After a few minutes, my head feels better. I look around the cemetery. This might be my only chance to figure out whether either girl is buried here.

I skim the names on the stones as I walk, but there are so many of them. The graves range from mounds of freshly piled earth to markers where the names have mostly been worn off.

I need to find some kind of directory, some place to look up the only name I'm sure of, Amber. There's a figure in a dark coat and a turned down hat. He's bent over one of the older graves, pulling weeds, some kind of caretaker.

I approach him slowly. "Can you help me?"

He looks up, his expression solemn. His face is a pale mask and his eyes are deep and hollow. I can't tell if he's old or young. He wipes the mud from his hands onto the sides of his rain-streaked coat. "I guess that depends on what you need help with." There's something familiar about his face, but I can't decide what it is.

"I'm looking for the grave of a girl named Amber. She died about twenty years ago. I don't have a last name, but I think she died in some sort of accident or ..."

He nods. "Follow me."

I hesitate, but he keeps walking like he doesn't care if I keep up or not, so I finally go after him. I follow him down a winding path, slipping on moss-covered stones and stepping around low trees and overgrown bushes. He's moves faster than I expect him to. I keep almost losing him. The cemetery is much bigger than I imagined. The whole time I'm wondering why he seems to know exactly which grave I'm looking for. Finally he stops at a large reddish headstone. He bends and brushes pine needles and moss away. Between two carved roses I read the name, "Amberlea Dawn Beal, beloved daughter and friend. Taken too soon." Born January 8, 1980, died July 31, 1996.

After a moment of studying the stone I look up at the caretaker. "There was another girl, but I don't have a name for her, not even a first name. I think she died the same summer as Amber. I think maybe she killed herself." I wait, hoping that like before, he'll just know who I'm talking about.

He shakes his head. "Names have power. If you don't have a name, I'm afraid I can't help you."

"She had long dark hair tinted blue at the ends." I study his face, hoping something is familiar. "She died young too. She was an artist and ..."

"... walked as you do, with her hand in that of the Great Creator." He finishes my sentence and I know where I've seen him before.

"You're the minister, the one from her funeral."

"I've presided over many funerals," he says simply.

"You talked about her teaching art to children. You said, 'We'll never know what led someone so young to believe she had no other choice.'"

His misty gray eyes find their way into my soul. "And how would you know that? I spoke those words years before you were born."

"Because I ... because I was there." I set my chin, daring him to correct me.

He studies me for a moment longer, his gaze unwavering. I can't look away either. Finally he says, "Those who are brushed with death and birth at the same instant are forever painted with a connection to the dead that others do not understand."

I pull my sweater closer around me, the rain seeping into my skin, his meaning seeping into my muddled brain. "My twin sister died at birth."

He nods. "You experience memories, memories that aren't your own." It's a statement, not a question. I nod anyway. "Some may call what you have empathy, but it's more than that. You're like an open vessel into which souls pour pieces of their life. You allow them a moment in death to relive what they were in life."

I lean against the red stone, contemplating what he's saying. Stuck on one part of it. "I allow them?"

"As long as you allow it, your mind will always share the secrets of the dead."

"But I can't stop it. I don't have a choice."

His eyes fix mine with a surprising kindness. "There is always a choice."

I consider what he's saying. I think about all the times my life has been disrupted by a soul on its way out of this world. I didn't invite them in, but I guess I didn't ask them to leave either.

His face softens. "The dead share their secrets willingly. The greater difficulty lies in sharing the secrets of the living."

"I don't ..." I begin, but I'm not even sure what I don't understand.

"Holding the past may be a heavy burden, but holding the future"—his eyes meet mine again—"the weight of that gift can prove impossible to bear. The little girl is blessed to have someone to share that weight with."

It takes me a minute to understand who he's talking about. "Remy? Remy shares what is in her head ... with me?"

His eyes move to a far corner of the cemetery. "She needed to share her burden too, but the one she chose to share with ..." He lowers his head. "She didn't choose his actions, but she believed the blame was hers. She couldn't live with that." He stands. He's not talking about Remy anymore, but maybe someone like her.

"That's why she can't find peace."

His nod is slight, almost imperceptible.

"Please, just show me where she's buried. If I have her name ..."

He starts to rise, but another name cuts through the mist.

"Miranda!"

Adam is running toward me, slipping on the wet grass and out of breath. "Why did you leave? When you didn't come back, I thought that ..." He lets the end of the sentence fade into the sound of the rain.

I look back, but I already know the old minister is gone.

Chapter Twenty-Four

"Why are you out here?" Adam leans against a tree. He still hasn't caught his breath and his white shirt is wet and sticking to his chest.

"It was too hot in there. My head hurts and I thought I was going to pass out." I look around, hoping to catch a glimpse of the man again, but there's no trace of him.

Adam looks at the crowd and then back at me. "Coming was a bad idea. Let's just get out of here." He reaches for my hand. I want nothing more than to take it and let him drive me away from this place. Ron appears in the line of mourners coming out of the church. He's looking for me. The picture he showed me in the car brings me back.

"I can't go with you. I have to go home with Ron."

"Why?" Adam asks.

"I can't let him go home alone."

He looks confused, like he can't believe anyone would choose Ron over him. I take a breath, wondering if I could tell him the truth about why I don't dare leave Ron to drive alone. Maybe Adam would understand. Maybe he could even help. He's seen what Remy can do.

Before I figure out how to start, he breaks in. "Look, I'd like to spend some time with just us, so we can talk about things." He takes a breath and for a heartbeat I think he wants to talk about us, about why he held my hand on the rock and in my room and the electricity I feel whenever he's near me. "We need to talk about my sister. I guess you've seen it for yourself.

Remy has ... issues." My heart falls at the same time my stomach churns with anger. He basically just called his little sister a freak. "When she was a little kid my aunt kept saying Remy just had an overactive imagination, that she'd grow out of it, but now that she's older. I mean, I know it's asking a lot for you to not say anything but ..."

"Don't worry about it." I turn away from him, fuming. Adam isn't ready for the truth. I don't know why I thought he could understand.

"Miranda, wait." Adam puts his hand on my shoulder.

"I have to go." It comes out louder than I intend, loud enough that some of the mourners look in our direction.

"Miranda ... I don't ... Are you mad at me?" Adam's confusion deepens. Is he really that clueless?

"Just leave her alone," Ron yells as he walks toward us. "Miranda is with me."

The people stare, their eyes suspicious as they look from Adam to me. He shrinks a little. "Whatever." The stares follow Adam all the way across the cemetery and to the parking lot. He crawls into his car. If I wasn't so mad, I might feel sorry for him.

By the time I get into Ron's car, I'm shaky and exhausted. I just want to go home and curl up into bed, but I'm worried about what I'd see if I did. I don't want to stay with him, but I also can't let Ron go home on his own. I don't know how, but Ron is supposed to die. I can't let it happen again.

We sit in the car for a few minutes, waiting for the windows to defog. "So you want to head home, are you hungry, or what?" Ron says while we wait.

"I could eat." My head is too muddled with all the possibilities. Food might help.

"Great, there's a little hamburger place up the road. We'll grab something there, and then ..." he trails off, like he doesn't quite have the courage to finish. This is a different side of Ron, like behind his clueless, jerk of a façade, he actually wants to impress me.

"And then?"

"I don't know. The weather is starting to clear up, so I thought ..." He trails off again.

"You thought?"

"We don't have to if you aren't feeling up to it, but there's this cool little hike up the mountain. It ends at an old summer camp."

"How do you know about it?"

He shrugs. "My grandma lives out here. I spent a lot of time here in the summer."

"I'm not exactly wearing hiking shoes." I point at my sandals.

"It's not much of a hike, really, just a little trail, a couple of bridges. Kinda cool, but it's okay if you don't want to go." There it is again, like the obnoxious guy from the rec center is gone, and here's someone like me, a little awkward, a little clueless about how to interact with the opposite sex.

My mind races to all the ways Ron could end up dead. Maybe I should suggest that we go home and spend a quiet day sitting on his couch. But then again, second guessing everything might be the thing that gets him killed. My brain hurts from overthinking, so I just say, "Okay."

"Okay?" He seems a little shocked.

"Yeah, okay. Let's get some food and then go for the hike."

"Wow. I mean, okay." He smiles and it almost seems genuine.

We pull into the line of people leaving the church parking lot. I glance back and see the old minister, way over in the corner of the cemetery. For a second I consider telling Ron that I want him to stop, but when I look back, the strange man has faded into the mist.

We get the burgers and then drive up the mountainside. Ron stops by the side of the road next to a worn sign that says "Camp Patawomie."

"There's a picnic area at the end of the trail, where the camp used to be. We can eat there," Ron says.

"Sure." I clutch my bag of greasy burgers and fries close to me and look around for anything that looks dangerous. The trail looks easy enough, not very steep, and mostly green with new grass. It must not be used very much.

We walk in silence down the trail and through the woods. Something feels familiar about this camp, but I can't decide what it is. "There's a couple of picnic tables by the lake." He points through the trees at some falling down structures as we get a little farther down the trail. "A couple of the cabins and other things are still standing." He pauses, reaching back for my hand. I give him a strange look. "I thought you'd like some help." He indicates a bridge across a steep gorge with a little stream at the bottom. Some of the boards are missing. "Your shoes are more slippery than mine."

I let him take my hand and help me onto the bridge. It creaks under our weight. I hold my breath, but the bridge is stable. He doesn't let go of my hand even after we're across the bridge, even though both our hands are slippery with sweat. We walk in silence, glimpsing skeletons of old buildings and what were once brightly colored totem poles. It's not raining anymore, but the air feels heavy, the wind completely still. My feet are starting to hurt.

"How much farther?" I ask, glancing at the dark sky on the other side of the trees.

"We're here." He leads me out of the trees and into a clearing overlooking the lake. He moves to a picnic table. "I'm starving."

"Me too," I realize.

Gallantly he brushes the pine needles off the bench for me to sit down. After I sit, Ron slides in next to me—too close. I scoot a couple of inches away as he fishes through the bag. He hands me a hamburger and then unwraps one for himself. An awkward silence falls over both of us. I look around, trying to think of something to talk about.

"This is a cute little camp. I wonder why it closed," I say.

Ron takes a big bite and then chews loudly. I cringe, but it's mostly internally. "There was an accident." He says it casually, taking another bite.

The hair on the back of my neck prickles. Near the shore of the lake the remnants of a firepit catches my eye. Again, I get the feeling I've been here before. "An accident?"

"One of the counselors fell into the ravine. It's not that far down, but she must have landed just right, or just wrong. She broke her neck."

"Was she ... okay?" I ask, but I already know the answer.

"She died." He swallows loudly. "No one found her until the next morning. She went for a walk alone or something stupid like that."

I stare at the circle of logs below us. My mind repaints the picture—three girls, two boys, a silver coin, the fire coloring their faces with a reddish glow.

Who will be the first to die?

I'm overwhelmed by a sense of foreboding and fear mingled with the strong impression that I've been here before.

Go.

I don't know if the thought is mine or hers. I don't feel her presence, just a tight ball of dread in my stomach. I stand up so fast that I knock my knees on the edge of the table. "We need to leave."

"We just got here." Ron is looking at me strangely.

The voice inside my head is urging me on. Go, go now.

"It's going to rain."

Instead of looking at the clouds, Ron pulls out his phone. "It's not supposed to rain until five or six."

As if to prove him wrong, the wind picks up. A miniature whirlwind of long burned out ashes forms in the center of the fire pit. A crack of thunder splits the air. There is so much electricity that the hair on my arms stands up.

"Yeah, maybe you're right." Ron shoves the last of the hamburger into his mouth. I wrap mine up, barely touched, and put it back into the bag.

"Let's hurry so we don't get caught in the storm." I say. But hurrying might be the thing that kills him. I think of the ravine we crossed, the old rickety bridge. It didn't seem that deep, not really dangerous.

It was an accident.

But I know it wasn't.

Ron reaches for my hand and I take it, holding on tight. I can't watch him die. Why did I let him come here? Why did I come with him?

He looks into my eyes. He has to see the fear there. He doesn't know it's for him. "What's wrong, Miranda?"

"I don't like thunder," I answer.

He puts his arm across my shoulders. "Don't worry. I won't let anything happen to you." He gives my shoulders a squeeze that makes me cringe. "But if you'd rather, we could go into one of the cabins." He tightens his grasp around my shoulders. "And wait out the storm there."

"No." The idea of being stuck in one of those creepy cabins with Ron for any length of time nauseates me. I pull away. "Let's just get back to the car before the storm hits."

"Okay." He takes my hand again and I let him pull me toward the path and the ravine looming ahead.

I stop before we reach the bridge. "Is there another way back, a path that doesn't go over the ravine?"

"Not if you want to beat the storm. The other path out of here loops all the way down the mountain." He tugs my hand as the wind picks up. Another boom of thunder sounds, closer this time. "Come on." He's pulling me and I'm slipping on my shoes behind him. My feet hurt and I'm praying with every heartbeat that Remy's drawing was just a drawing.

We make it to the bridge just as it starts to rain. "It's going to be too slick." I hang back, wondering if going back to the cabins to wait out the storm is the best plan.

"Nah, it's fine." Ron takes a couple of steps onto the bridge. He bounces a little, making it sway. "See no, big deal."

"Ron, don't do that." I'm paralyzed on one side of the bridge. "Just come back. We can wait at the cabins until it stops raining."

Ron hesitates. His face breaks into a sort of grin. "If that's what you—"

It happens all at once, the rush of wind, the clap of thunder, the ropes snapping. I scream. His eyes are locked on mine as he falls.

Chapter Twenty-Five

I run to the edge. "Ron!" He doesn't answer. I get down on my hands and knees and crawl to the edge. "Ron!" I can't see him amid the tangle of ropes and broken boards. I'm desperately looking for a way down when I feel a hand on my shoulder.

I scream, and nearly fall into the ravine myself. He pulls me back. "Miranda, are you okay? What happened?"

It's Adam, his face pale. His hands shake. The rain is pouring down now.

"What are you doing here?" I yell into his face.

"I don't trust Ron. I saw some of the books he reads, pretty hardcore manga stuff and that drawing he did of you, not—"

"He fell!" I crawl back to the edge. "The bridge broke. I saw him go down. I don't know if he's okay."

Adam stands, scared but determined. He reaches for the rope on the side of the bridge that's still attached. He jerks on it, testing its strength, then he moves toward the edge, using the rope to keep himself steady. "I might be able to get down to him, to see if he's all right. It's not that far." He inches down the slope, slowly, slowly. I sit on the edge, praying that he doesn't fall, praying that Ron is okay.

"Stay where you are!" A deep voice commands from the other side of the ravine. I look up to see Marshall. "Both of you, STAY WHERE YOU ARE!"

"Ron fell!" I yell back. "We need to help him."

Marshall moves to the edge and peers over, a grim look on his face. "Stay there!" he commands again. "I'll radio for help, and I have some gear in my truck. I'll see what I can do."

Adam climbs back up and sits next to me. He takes off his jacket and holds it over the top of both of us. The rain comes down in sheets while we wait for Marshall to come back. It seems to take hours. He comes back in full climbing gear. He anchors himself to the far end of the bridge. He tightens his helmet. "You two, get away from here, out of the rain. Find some shelter."

"No!" I yell back, my whole body is trembling. "What if you fall too?"

"I'll be fine. I've done this kind of rescue before. Besides, help is on its way." He turns around backward and starts to climb down the ravine.

Adam puts his arm around me, directing me toward the cabins. I turn around once. There is something horrible and familiar about the sight of Marshall climbing down the side of the ravine. It takes me a second to sort out whose memory it reminds me of. Then it hits me: Marshall looks just like one of the firemen, scaling down the cliff to retrieve Tanner's body.

Adam directs me back to the cabins. We go to the closest one, but it looks like the roof has caved in. "That one, over there!" Adam yells over the wind. The second one looks more intact, but when Adam tries the door, it's stuck shut. He leans closer, examining it. He pulls a knife from his pocket and slips the knife in the edge of the door. He twists and something snaps. The door springs open.

The cabin is dark and dirty. The windows are covered in grime, spider webs and tattered blue curtains, but the roof looks solid. Bare wooden bunk beds line two walls and there's a little table in front of the window. Adam sits on one of the bunks.

I sink onto one opposite him and cover my face with my hands. "No, no, no, no." It's the only words I can get out. A thousand things I did wrong run through my head. I shouldn't have agreed to go on the hike. I should have made Ron go home the minute I saw the picture. I should have let him take me back to the cabins to wait out the storm.

Adam switches sides so he's sitting next to me. He puts his hand on my back. "Hey, it's going to be all right. It wasn't that far of a fall. He's going to be okay. I heard him groan as I was starting down the cliff. He probably just broke an ankle or something."

"No, no, no, no." I shake my head. Ron is dead. I know he's dead and it's all my fault. Why did I think I could save him? Why did I think I could stop this?

After a few minutes of patting my back Adam gives up trying to console me. He gets up and walks toward the window. "Still raining," he says, like the weather is the most important thing in the world.

"What if Marshall slips too? We should have stayed with him."

"He seems to know what he's doing." Adam picks up a little piece of wood and starts scraping at it with his knife.

After a few minutes, the scrape of his knife starts to get on my nerves. "Why are you doing that?"

"It calms me down. My dad taught me to whittle when I was a little kid. I mean I know it's not like the stuff you draw, not real art, but it's something to do with my hands."

I nod. I'm wishing I had a pen and paper, anything to keep my mind occupied, although I'm afraid of what I'd draw now.

"What were you guys doing out here?" Adam finally asks.

"Taking a hike. Ron bought me lunch and we came out here to eat it."

"But why did you go with him? No offense, but he doesn't seem to be your type."

"How would you have any idea what my type is?" I snap back at him.

"I mean, I guess I don't. But I didn't think Ron was really anyone's type."

I shoot him a dark look and he goes back to carving his stupid piece of wood. It's not even taking any kind of shape. I lean back on the bunk, my head pounding again. The mattress is long gone and all that's left is a hard plank of wood. I stare at the planks above me, wishing I could have a redo on the last three hours. Maybe if I hadn't decided to go to Kari's funeral none of this would have happened. The weight of guilt settles like a lead blanket on my chest.

I study the swirls of graffiti on the bunk above me. I trace over a pattern that looks familiar—intertwined crosses, surrounded by lines and swirls, an anatomically correct heart with a crack in it, and a rose dripping blood from a single thorn. I turn away. The dark drawings make everything worse.

The part of me that was determined to figure out what happened, to prevent it from happening again, has shriveled up and hidden away. The girl from the camp could have been one of the girls who died by accident that summer. I should look around and see what I can find out about the girl who died here, but there's too much death already.

I close my eyes, but I can't shut the pattern out. There's something familiar about it. I open my eyes and trace it with my finger, wiping away some of the dust in the process. It reminds me of wiping away a mark in the corner of my painting of Tanner. The symbol is the same.

I study it more closely. The crosses aren't actually crosses. I think they're supposed to be Ts. The swirls could be letters too, T-I-F. Tif. I trace the other letters: T-I-M. Tif and Tim, two figures intertwined with a heart and a rose with a single drop of blood. What does it mean and how did it end up on my painting? I rub my hand across the board, trying to see the other patterns more clearly.

"What are you doing?" Adam sits on the bunk.

"Someone drew all over the bunk above this one." I say.

"Let me see." Adam crawls onto the bunk next to me. "A little dark." For a few minutes he lies beside me, studying the pictures on the bunk above. He flips his body around so he's looking at the corner by our feet. "There are more over here." I maneuver myself in the small space, trying not to touch him, but it's impossible.

"Look at this one." He brushes spiderwebs from another picture. "I wonder what this girl did to deserve so much hate."

The picture is like the others, a simple drawing done with a permanent marker. The only difference is this one has been partially scratched out, probably with a knife like the one Adam was using. I run my fingers over the deep cuts in the wood. Most of the picture is rubbed out, but I can still see dark curly hair, full lips and one staring eye. The face, like so many things in this cabin, looks familiar. I pull out my phone and take a picture of both of the drawings.

Adam props himself up on one arm. He's so close I can feel heat radiating from his body. "Are you feeling better?"

I shiver. "Not really."

"You're shaking. From the cold or because of what happened?"

"Both." My hair and my T-shirt are wet from the rain. My head is pounding and I can't focus.

He slides his arms around me. I tighten into a little ball inside myself, but I don't move away. He rests his head on the top of mine. "It's been a hell of a day, for both of us."

I nod.

He leans down so our eyes meet. His breath is warm against my skin. He's probably been in this position lots of times, lying next to a girl with his arms around her. For me this is a first. He pushes a piece of my wet hair out of my eyes, then runs his finger down my cheek. "I'm sorry, for all of this."

"It's not your fault." But I'm not even sure of that anymore.

"I really wish we could just start over." He moves his other hand, the one behind my back, grasping something.

I grab his arm to stop him. "What are you doing?"

He holds up his knife. "Folding the blade in. I didn't want to accidentally stab you." He drops the knife and it clunks on the floor below us.

I'm not sure that's really what he was doing or what he wants to start over. He leans closer, his face inches from mine. A nervous bubble forms inside my stomach. I suppress a giggle that wants to escape. There's nothing funny, but I think he's going to kiss me. I'm going to get my first kiss right after I watched someone die. I'm paralyzed, not sure whether I should stop him.

The door flies open.

Chapter Twenty-Six

My dad is standing in the doorway of the cabin. It takes me a few terrified heartbeats to register that it's him and about thirty humiliating seconds to extricate myself from Adam's arms and climb out of the bunk. From where Dad stands, it looks like me and Adam have been in here making out while everyone else was trying to save Ron.

Before he can say anything about Adam or ask what's been going on, I ask, "Is he okay?"

I've seen my dad deliver bad news before, so I recognize the shadow that crosses his face immediately.

"How?" I ask before he even answers the question.

Dad uses the tone he reserves for grieving mortuary clients. "The rope from the bridge got wrapped around his neck when he fell. He broke his neck. He probably died instantly."

"No." Adam says from behind me. "I heard him when I was at the edge of the ravine. He was groaning or ... or something. He was alive."

Dad's expression hardens when he looks at Adam. "And what brought you out here?"

Adam shrinks into his jacket. "I followed Miranda. I don't trust Ron, didn't trust him. I just, I don't know, had a bad feeling about the situation."

Dad nods, almost as if he's agreeing with Adam. "A lot of that going around. You two need to head back to the scene of the accident. The sheriff has some questions for you."

I glance sideways at Adam. He looks as gray and downtrodden as the soggy, falling down camp. As we follow my dad back to the ravine, Adam reaches for my hand. I'm so surprised that I let him take it. He gives a quick squeeze and then lets go. I'm not sure what he means by the gesture, but I don't have enough strength to analyze it.

I brace myself for a stretcher covered by a white sheet or worse, but there's only a closed ambulance, flashing lights, fluttering yellow tape and sheriff's deputies huddling around the ravine like it was an open grave. Marshall walks over and gives me a long hug. "Are you okay?" I nod my lie. If I could, I would run as fast as I could away from this place.

"Marsh, could you follow the body back to the station? I'm sure the coroner could use your help. Not many cases like this in Morton, at least not recently." Dad shudders at the word recently. "I'll make sure the kids get back okay."

"My car is here." Adam speaks up. "I parked it down at the trailhead. I can get home by myself. I could even take Miranda if you need to stay."

I feel the weight of suspicion as all eyes rest on Adam, my dad included. The sheriff breaks the silence. "We'll see how things go after we talk to both of you, separately."

Adam goes pale, but he nods. He follows one officer into an SUV while I'm directed to another. Adam gets a straight-backed dark-haired guy with a mustache, while I get a blonde woman who has a sympathetic smile.

Dad follows me, but he's waved away. "You know you can't be with her for this part, Doug," the blonde officer says.

He hesitates, but then nods. He gives me a stiff hug. "It'll be okay. I'll be right out here."

"Would you like a blanket?" the officer asks as I slide into the SUV.

I start to say, "No," but my teeth are chattering so much that she gets the blanket anyway.

"How are you doing?" she begins.

A horrible wave of guilt and frustration and helplessness washes over me. Stupid tears start flowing. Not just slip-down-your-cheeks tears, but full-on body-wracking sobs. I can't control my mouth any more than I can control the sobs.

Between them the truth slips out. "I thought I could keep him safe. I thought if I were with him, nothing bad would happen."

She puts her hand on my back, alternating between patting and rubbing, like Adam did. "Why did you think Ron wasn't going to be safe today? Do you know someone who wanted to hurt him?"

"No, I just …" There's no way to explain any of this.

"Just what?" She prompts. Her voice is gentle and coaxing, but there's an underlayment of suspicion that wasn't there before.

"I just felt like something bad was going to happen. This camp is such a creepy place, and that bridge didn't feel safe and the rain came up all of a sudden and I … I couldn't save him." I break down again.

She waits until the body-wracking sobs calm down to shoulder-shaking sobs. "Let's go back a bit. Why did you come out here in the first place?"

"For a funeral. For Kari's funeral. Ron and I both worked with her. I missed the van, so Ron offered me a ride." She types something into a computer she has on the dash.

"But why didn't you go home after the funeral? Why did you come here?"

Why, why, why? The question drums inside my brain with the rain on the vehicle's roof. "It was Ron's idea. He bought me lunch and he wanted to go for a hike.'"

"Have you ever been here before?"

For some reason the question rattles me. Everything about this place feels familiar, familiar and sinister, but I shake my head. "No. Ron knew about it. He wanted to show it to me."

"What kind of relationship did you have with Ron?" she probes.

"None, really. We saw each other at work. We've talked a couple of times. He drove me home a few times. I … I … hardly knew him."

"But you rode with him to the funeral?"

"I missed the van." I remember the texts I sent to Adam. "I asked Adam to take me, but he'd already left."

She nods, typing again. "And what is your relationship with Adam?" Her voice changes when she says his name. They all think he did something to Ron. The police officer who escorted him to his car looked ready to slap handcuffs on him. Maybe I should be more suspicious. But despite him ending up at the wrong place every time, I don't believe he's a murderer.

I look for the right word. "Friends? Maybe? His little sister is in my art class and I babysit her after class is over. We hung out together a couple of times. Honestly, I hardly know Adam either. He hasn't lived here very long." Not that that detail really matters, since outside of my family I can't really say I know anyone.

"Any idea why Adam decided to follow you and Ron out here today?"

"He said he didn't trust Ron. He didn't like the kind of books he reads or something."

"Books?" Her forehead wrinkles.

"I don't know. The only kind of books I've seen Ron read are manga. I don't know anything about them."

"I see." But she types for longer than her I see warrants. Finally she stops. "Tell me everything that happened today from the time you left for the funeral with Ron until the bridge broke."

I tell her everything I remember. I don't say anything about the drawing in the car. I can't let her think I'm crazy and I can't drag Remy into this. I wish Marshall had stayed. He may not be fully on board with the "Miranda sees dead people" thing, but at least he's willing to listen.

She types for a long time before she finally asks. "Was Ron on the bridge alone when it broke?"

"Yes." My voice is almost a whisper.

"Why is that?"

I moisten my lips. "I was afraid. The bridge didn't look stable." I kick my foot out from under the blanket to show her my sandals. "I have slippery shoes on and it was raining. I told him we should go back to the cabins and wait out the rain."

"And what did he say to that?"

"At first he told me it was fine, he bounced the bridge a little bit, to show me it was okay, but I think he was getting ready to come back to my side when the ropes broke."

"So he was facing you?"

I nod and close my eyes, but it just makes the image of Ron's face when he fell sharpen in my mind.

"And when did Adam get there?"

"Right after Ron fell. He must have heard me scream."

"Which side of the bridge was Adam on?"

"The side where I was."

"But you didn't see him until Ron fell?" There are a hundred questions behind that one.

"No."

"Did either of you go down into the ravine after him?" she asks.

"I wanted to, but Adam stopped me. Then he started to climb down, but that's when Marshall got there. He told us he'd go down. He told us to get away from the edge and out of the rain."

She hmms and I think the questions are over, but she keeps going. "What did you and Adam do until your dad got to the cabin?"

I'm not sure what that has to do with the investigation. "Sat there in shock. He ... he tried to make me feel better. He told me Ron would be fine, that he heard him groaning or something like that."

"I see." She writes again. "And how are you feeling now?" It's kind of an afterthought.

I stare at her. What a stupid question. Finally I say, "Not ... not okay."

She nods sympathetically. "You can go back with your dad." I unwrap from the blanket and try to hand it to her. She shakes her head. "Keep it, for now." She's looking over her report, not really paying attention to me, so I wrap the blanket back around my shoulder and open the door to the SUV.

I'm almost out when she puts her hand on my shoulder. She's looking down at her computer. "Did you or Ron have anything sharp on you?"

"Sharp?" I ask.

"Like a knife."

My mind fills with the sound of Adam's knife scraping against the piece of wood, but she didn't ask about Adam. "No."

"Hmm."

"Why?" As soon as I ask the question, I know I should have kept my mouth shut.

She looks up, her eyes meeting mine. "According to the report I just got, there's a possibility that the ropes on one side of the bridge were intentionally weakened, maybe even cut with a knife."

Chapter Twenty-Seven

The ride home with Dad is another kind of interrogation. He asks almost the same questions that the officer asked. My answers to him are more honest, but more biting. I'm angry and confused and my head hurts and I'm done pretending I'm normal and everything is okay.

He starts with, "Why did you go to the funeral today when you were supposed to stay in bed?"

"I had to go to that church today."

"Why?"

"I saw it in a dream last night. I needed to find one of the girls who was buried there."

His face goes pale. "Why did you want to find her?"

I stare back at him, forcing him to see my resolve. "Because I think she might have been his first victim."

He stares at the road. "Whose first victim?"

"Whoever killed Kari, and the woman on the stairs, and now Ron."

Dad is quiet for a long time. "What if those were all accidents?"

"What if they weren't?"

He waits for a few miles, like he's trying to figure out how to handle me. "I think they're going to hold your friend Adam for questioning."

I turn back to face him. "Adam? Why?"

He sighs. "You're right. It's possible this wasn't an accident. It's possible that Kari's drowning wasn't an accident either. I don't know anything about a woman on the stairs, but some things have come up, things from Adam's past."

"What things?" I ask.

"There was some trouble in Canada. A police officer was shot and Adam seemed to know more about it than he should have."

"He didn't kill any of them."

"Did the ghosts tell you that?" I can tell Dad's trying hard not to sound ironic, but he's failing. He still doesn't believe me.

"No. All of this has happened before, way before Adam came here." I face him, full-on, daring him to call me a liar. "The ghost did tell me, or rather she showed me that. She did something while she was alive that she won't forgive herself for. She can't move on. Maybe if we find out who the killer is—both then and now, maybe then she can leave."

Dad's voice goes soft, his frustration exchanged for the gentle pandering I hate. "There are lots of ways to be sick, not just in your body, but in your mind. Sometimes people see things that seem very real, but it's just the chemicals in their brain, making them think they—"

"You still think I'm crazy?" I laugh, but there's nothing funny about it. "Do you know why I went with Ron today? It was because I knew he was going to die. I saw—" I shake my head, still not willing to drag Remy into this. "I saw something that made me sure he was going to die, and like an idiot I thought I could prevent it, but I actually caused what killed him. Do you have any idea what that feels like? Do you know what it is to know someone is going to die and not be able to stop it?"

He stares at me, shocked, then asks. "Miranda, did Adam tell you he was going to hurt Ron?"

"No."

"Then who?" Frustration and fear creep into his voice.

"No one. I just ..." But there's nothing I can say that would make him understand. "You wouldn't believe me if I told you the truth."

He doesn't say anything for a while. I can almost see his mind working, building his argument, searching for the right words. Finally he says. "I'm not saying what you see isn't real ... to you. I'm just saying that maybe this whole thing is too much for you. Wherever the visions are coming from, it isn't your responsibility. We can find someone to help you ... manage things."

I close my eyes. There's nothing I can say that will make him believe me. Maybe he's right. If I am crazy, or even if I'm not, maybe I can shut everything out. Maybe if I took antipsychotic drugs, everything would go away.

There is always a choice.

The old minister's words come back to me like a thunderbolt. What if he's right? What if I can choose not to listen? If I can choose to keep the visions out of my head, maybe I can choose to be normal. I look over at my dad. He looks older, more haggard, more worried than I've ever seen him. Maybe he's right. Maybe this isn't my responsibility. Maybe it never was.

***

I'm at the edge of the cliff again, rain clouding my vision. The firefighters scale down to the smashed car. The car door opens. I close my eyes, willing the vision to go away.

"Miranda! Help me!" Tanner's voice is far away and right next to me. It's a whisper and a cry that echoes in my head. I open my eyes and he's standing in front of me, pleading with me. "Don't let them bury me. I wasn't supposed to die."

"No. No. No!" I say the words out loud. "I can't help you. You're already gone. You died in the car crash."

His image wavers and his voice trembles as he reaches his hand toward me. "No, Miranda. I didn't die in the crash."

"Leave me alone!" I strike out at him, slicing my hand through his body.

His form dissolves into mist. I step backward. Water sloshes against wood. The ground beneath me has transformed to the docks beside the lake. Kari's face breaks through the water.

"Help me!"

I back away, covering my face and cowering on the dock. "No! There's nothing I can do. Go away!"

"Help me. Help me." I cover my ears and back away. Her plea echoes around me, turning from desperate into a mocking chant.

I open my eyes, forcing myself to face her. "I can't help you!" A look of desperate pain crosses her face before her body melts into the ripples of the lake, like she was only the girl from my painting and her colors had washed away. The dock and the lake dissolve with her.

A hummed tune fills my ears. Next to me, the woman is humming as she dusts the pews. She looks up and meets my eyes. "She can't do this alone. She needs you."

"No!" I scream it louder. The wind picks up behind me, blowing my hair into my face. The woman's face trembles with fear and sadness. "I wasn't brave enough. You have to be."

"No!" I scream back at her.

My voice blends into a wind that tears through the church. Before I even touch her, the entire image—the woman, the church, and the pews vibrate and shatter like the stained glass window above me.

I'm at the camp again, standing at the edge of the ravine, watching Ron. He reaches his hand to me, but he stays where he is. To touch him, I'd have to go out on the bridge. I can't. His eyes lock on mine, full of condemnation. "You knew. You knew and you didn't stop it."

His words pierce me to the soul, but I shake my head, tears streaming down my checks. "I couldn't save you. I couldn't save you. I can't help anyone."

"You're wrong. You can still—"

"No!" The bridge collapses under him. He disappears into a dark nothingness. It grows until everything around me is sucked in with him. The void reaches to claim me too. I'm clawing at rocks and mud at the edge of a yawning pit, an open grave. They stand ready to bury me. Their faces are no longer real. They're cartoons and paintings and graffiti swirling in a muddying mix of colors and screams and pleas.

"Leave me alone!" I scream at all of them.

The silence yawns around me like the open pit. I'm back in bed, tears streaming down my face, my throat raw from screaming. I think it's over, that I banished them all to a place they can't reach me. I open my eyes and take in the familiar room that isn't mine. It's tiny and dirty and smells like cigarette smoke. There's a Black Sabbath poster on the wall and black curtains block out two long windows. I stand, moving in spite of myself toward a carved gold mirror that sits above a shabby dresser. The image that stares back at me isn't my own.

It's her.

I reach up to touch the blue-tipped black hair. Her eyes are red and there are smudges of black eyeliner and black mascara on her cheeks. The top of the dresser is marred with drawings and graffiti—images I recognize. Lying in the center is Adam's knife. I pick it up.

Using you. Using you.

The room swells with laughter. The voices are back, surrounding me, mocking me. Shame and guilt seep into the depths of my soul until I can't face the image in the mirror.

Using you. You let him use you.

I draw the blade across my wrist. I don't feel it, but the cut fills with blood that drips down my arm.

You only have one choice.

Choice. There is always a choice.

I drop the knife and it clatters to the floor.

"No!" I yell at the girl in the mirror.

There's only one way to get away from him.

"Stop it! Get out of my head!" I yell as loud as I can.

Your fault.

"No."

"Miranda!" Mom's voice is outside the door even though this isn't our house. The doorknob rattles. "Miranda! Let me in."

Let me in. Let us all in.

"No! No, no, no! I won't let you in! I won't let you!"

Using you. Using you. The room pulses with the words. You let him in. You let him use you. Your fault.

"Miranda open this door!" Mom sounds frantic, but if I cross the room, she'll see me. She'll see who I've become. She'll know that this is all my fault.

"Marshall, help me!" she yells.

It's your fault they're dead. It's all your fault.

"No!" I scream. "Not my fault. It's your fault. Leave. Me. Alone! My choice! My life! I choose to be left alone!"

Someone has to stop him.

"How?" I scream.

The door bursts open with a crack of splintering wood. Marshall must have kicked it in. He's standing with my mom, in the hall of my own house. I'm in front of my own mirror, in my own bedroom. The face staring back at me is terrified and haunted, but it's me.

My arm drips red, but there's no knife in my hand, only a paintbrush. Mom pulls me into her arms. "Baby, baby, baby." She says it over and over again as she strokes my hair.

Marshall wraps his arms around me and Mom, bundling us both into one big hug, like he wants to protect both of us. The shame and guilt drain away like the closed door was a floodgate that kept the emotions inside me.

"Are you hurt?" Marshall grabs my wrist, smudging the swirls of letters that cover my right arm.

"No." I pull my arm away, staring at what I painted there. All that's left is a smear of red paint and the letter T.

"What did you see?" Mom says.

I can only blink in response to her question. It was too much, too many images to try to explain it.

Mom puts her hands on either side of my face and holds me at arm's length. Tears are streaming down her face. "We'll get help. We'll find a way to make everything go away."

"I'm okay." As soon as I say the words, I know they're true. The only voice inside my head is mine. The only emotions I feel belong to me. "They're all gone. I sent them away and they're not coming back. I made my choice."

Chapter Twenty-Eight

"**M**iranda, wait up."

The sound of Adam's voice makes my heart flip like a caught fish and then sink like a dead one. I knew I was taking a risk venturing out of the house, but Mom told me I had to pick up my last paycheck at the rec center myself. Classes there have been indefinitely postponed due to tragic events. I could care less about the money, but I knew Mom won't stop her anxious hovering until I made some attempt at normalcy.

For the past two weeks I've practiced shutting everyone out, living and dead. It's worked so far. No nightly visions, no feelings radiating from someone is in my room I can't see. I fully expected Ron to come back again. Because of the way he died, I assumed he'd be stuck here, like Tanner, but I haven't seen either of them. Dad took the hearse out in the middle of the night last night, and I slept right through it. I never had to meet the man who's lying in the morgue now. I don't know what his biggest regret was.

I stop and turn to face Adam. "Hey."

"Hey." He smiles like he's genuinely happy to see me. "You look a lot better. I mean you look good, really good."

"I feel better, no more concussion." I tap my head. Then I really look at him. If I look better, he looks worse. There are dark circles under his eyes and he looks tired, the way I looked before, like he's the one walking with the dead. "What about you?"

"Oh, you know, being questioned by the police every couple of days, losing my job, suspicious looks from strangers, and avoiding the world. It's been a fun-filled summer."

"I'm really sorry," I say, although except for the parts about the job and the police, he's describing almost every summer I've lived through.

He huffs out a breath. "Not your fault." He looks up at me, almost shyly. "Remy misses you. You should come see her."

"Yeah." But as I say it I know I have no intention of seeing Remy. I miss her too, but she's so interconnected with the visions I'm trying to escape that I can't risk going back there.

"Miranda." Ms. Perkins steps out of the building. "I know it's a lot to ask, but we're still planning on our street fair next week and we're low on volunteers. I know you had signed up with Ron, but it would mean a lot if you could run the art booth for a couple of hours."

I look at her, doubtful, but I don't have the heart to tell her no. "I'll think about it," I say instead.

"Thank you." She pats my arm. She's effectively ignored Adam this whole time, but manages a dark look for him as she walks away.

"I guess looks can't kill." Adam leans against a light pole. "It doesn't matter to any of them that the police couldn't find enough evidence to hold me."

"What about your knife?" It comes out before I can stop it.

He pulls out his pocketknife. "You mean this? Ironically, it's too sharp. They said the ropes were most likely cut with a dull, serrated knife. Actually, the going theory is that the ropes weren't cut at all, just rubbed against the supports for too long. The wind from the storm just finished the job."

"Just another accident," I say.

"You sound like you don't believe that." Adam says.

"I don't know. All I know is that it's not my job to figure out what happened." I press against the wave of guilt that threatens to swallow me with that statement.

"I don't know why you thought it was," Adam says.

"Yeah."

We both stand awkwardly for a few minutes, not sure what to say to each other. Finally he says. "So tell me about this street fair."

"It's the biggest event in town, or so I've heard. I haven't been since I was a little kid. They shut down all of Main Street from the city building to the park. It's mostly vendors and a few kids' things like bounce houses and stuff. A few big rides, if you're into that kind of thing."

"I am, actually. You?"

I go for honesty, because, at this point, why not? "Let's see, I'm afraid of heights, high speeds, loud noises, bright lights, and crowds, so no, rides are not my thing."

"What is your thing, then?" He sounds like he's sincerely interested in what I like.

"Art, mostly." It makes me sound so one-dimensional that I think about it for a minute. "Teaching, maybe. I actually really liked my class, even if I'm deathly afraid of kids."

"Art and kids, that sounds like you might actually like the street fair. I know I would. We should go together. Maybe I could help you with whatever you do in the art booth," Adam says.

I look at him strangely. "Why?"

He leans against a lamppost and something of his old cockiness comes back. "I didn't think I was being that subtle. Usually when I give a girl flowers, or hold her hand, or come after her when I don't trust the guy she's with, she gets the hint. And if that doesn't do it, I'd think trying to kiss her would seal the deal."

"All of those things happened under extenuating circumstances," I point out. "So why do you keep coming back? Why do you want to spend time with me? Are you still looking for a free babysitter?"

He cringes and I know it was a low blow. "I'm sorry for that, I was just—"

"Desperate?" I finish for him.

"Yeah, something like that."

"No worries, we all do stupid things when we're desperate. See you around." I start to walk away.

"Miranda wait."

I stop.

"That's not it, at least, not anymore."

"Anymore?" I turn back to face him.

He hesitates for a few minutes, staring at the ground like he's trying to collect his thoughts. "There's something about you. The way you don't have to prove yourself to anyone. The way you look at someone like me or Remy and don't judge us the way other people do. The way you are so sure I'm innocent when the rest of the town is convinced I'm some kind of serial killer." He moves closer. "The way you can look into my eyes and it seems like you know everything about me, but you like me anyway." He blushes. "At least I think you like me."

"I do," I say. "I mean, I do like you."

"That's good." He steps a little closer. "Because I like you too."

He's right in front of me. I look up and meet his eyes. His lips twist in an nervous smile. Then he leans down. It happens right there in front of the city building with cars passing by and people on the sidewalk. My first real kiss. I'm embarrassed and elated and excited and scared and all of those emotions belong to me. It feels right and normal, even if everyone watching thinks the two kids kissing on the sidewalk are a couple of freaks.

Chapter Twenty-Nine

"Hold still."

"That tickles. When are you going to let me see?" His hand covers mine.

I pull away. "Stop. You're going to mess it up."

I'm in a strangely familiar cabin, sitting on a strangely familiar bunk, except this time it's covered with a foam pad, a rumpled sleeping bag, a blanket, and some kind of tattered stuffed animal. There's a boy sitting beside me on the bunk, wearing a white T-shirt with the sleeve rolled up. I'm drawing something on his shoulder. Everything is blurry and soft around the edges, like staring at the scene through the fog of memory.

Dammit.

Maybe it was Adam's kiss or the fizzy, floaty feeling in my stomach when I went to bed after texting him for an hour. Whatever it was, I let my guard down and she got into my head. I know it's her, the one who can't move on. She feels like me or I feel like her. I pull back, ready to stop the vision and push her out of my head. The nearly finished image on his shoulder stops me.

"Are you finished? Can I look?" He twists around.

"Not yet. Hold still." The voice isn't mine. Despite the haziness of the vision, the emotions are crystal clear. This boy is more than a friend, and I know what I'm drawing.

I watch her hand—my hand—move back to his arm, finishing the last swirls around the rose. Instinctively I pick up

a red pen and color in the rose and the drop of blood. "Okay."
A wave of insecurity washes over me. What if he hates it? What
if he laughs?

"Okay?" he says.

"Okay, you can look now."

He squirms and turns his head. "I can't quite see it."

I go to the next bunk over and dig through a perfumed
backpack. Contempt and jealousy mingle in my stomach as I
dig past a hoard of cosmetics until I find the mirror she uses
every morning to do her makeup. I hold it up to his shoulder,
angling it until he can see what I've drawn.

He lets out a low whistle. "That is incredible."

"You like it?" I ask. A lock of hair, mousy brown, falls over my
eye. I brush it back. I hate my hair.

"I love it. As soon as I can, I'm getting it made into a real
tattoo."

My chest swells with pride. "For reals?"

"Absolutely for reals. We could do matching tattoos." He
puts his hand on my arm and runs his thumb over my bare
shoulder. A shiver of pleasure runs the length of my body. I try
to push past the emotions to see him. His features are soft
around the edges and he's not facing me full-on. It's almost like
she can't quite remember what he looks like, or maybe it's too
hard for her to look at him. "Better yet, I could have this one
done and I could draw one for you." He takes the red pen from
me and draws a sloppy heart on my thigh, just where my
cutoff jeans meet bare skin. I laugh.

"See, I told you it tickles," he says.

"Too bad I'm not ticklish," I answer.

"Oh really." He takes both of my wrists in one hand. With
the other he inches toward my knee.

"Don't. You. Dare."

"Oh, I think I dare." He pushes me onto the bunk, trapping
me with his thighs straddling my waist. My heart pounds
against his palm holding my wrists. He smells of musky boy
sweat, sandalwood and lake water. Elation, infatuation, desire,
and something that could be the beginning of love pulses
through my body. This is the first time a boy has paid

attention to me. This is the first time anyone has looked beyond my freakishness.

No. Adam paid attention to me. He kissed me. Just today. I shake my head. I feel like I'm losing myself, like she's taken over all of me. I should push her away, push him away. But I don't want to leave. He releases my wrists, but I don't move. He leans closer, moving his mouth toward mine.

The cabin door bangs open.

A girl stands in the doorway. She has curly black hair and beautiful eyes. Her body is curvy and slender in all the right places. She looks from him to me in disbelief. My blood boils with embarrassment and jealousy. He stands quickly, rolling his sleeve down to cover my drawing.

"Amber," he says as he crosses the room. "Is it time to walk the kids to dinner already?"

"No." She moves closer to him, purring like a kitten. "We're talking about having a bonfire tonight after lights out. We'll play some games. Everyone's invited." But when she says everyone, she strokes his arm possessively.

A wave of anger and jealousy roils through my stomach and threatens to swallow me. The rage directed to the girl in front of me is murderous. I hate her. She's everything I'm not, everything I can't be. She has every boy here wrapped around her finger. She can't have him.

My fingers dig into the sides of the bunk.

First to die.

That thought brings me back to myself. I force myself to back away from him, from her, from the body and mind that aren't mine. Slowly, I extricate myself from her completely. I push the vision away until I'm back in my own room. My heart pounds in my ears. It takes a long time for the anger and jealousy to fade.

When I'm finally free of her emotions I reach for my phone, scrolling until I pull up the picture I took of the drawing in the cabin. The drawing on the boy's shoulder is the same as the one that was above the bunk. The same as the one that appeared on my painting. If the boy she was talking to was Tim, then maybe the girl's name is Tiff.

The old minister said names having power. I moisten my lips, but can't bring myself to call her name out loud. Not when I just got free of her. Instead I try to draw his face. I can't remember the shape of his nose, or what color his eyes were. Nothing about the boy was clear beyond the way she felt about him.

My phone dings a message from Adam.

> You still awake? I can't sleep. I want to see you. Tomorrow?

I take a breath and remind myself that I'm done with this. I can keep them out of my head. I can have all the normal things I never thought possible. I can have a real boyfriend. I don't have to let myself be dragged into someone else's mistake. I don't have to relive the past or see a future I can't change.

I type back:

> Absolutely.

> Remember how we talked about going to the street fair?

> Yes. That sounds awesome.

Well, I got a new job. A new temporary job. I'm running some of the rides at the fair. I have a crash course in being a carnie and then I have to work both nights of the fair. But if you can stay after, they said I could have one guest to ride the rides with me for free.

I text back.

> Okay.

He seems to have forgotten that I don't like rides. It doesn't matter. I just want to spend time with him.

One more slight catch. I need someone to watch
my sister. My aunt has to work and I can't do the
job unless someone stays with Remy.

Using you, using you.
I ignore her. I don't need a disembodied voice telling me what to do or how to feel anymore.
I type back:

Of course. It will be fun to hang out with Remy.

Thank you, thank you, thank you! My aunt will
pick her up when she gets off work. Then we'll
have the rest of the night together.

Sounds perfect.

I curl up onto my bed. I'm not sure about how I'm going to convince my parents to let me go out tomorrow. For parents who have been trying to get me out of the house for the last thirteen years, they're suddenly very particular about where I go and who I'm with. Somehow I'll make it work. I close my eyes and drift away into a dreamless and deathless sleep.

Chapter Thirty

I should have guessed what Mrs. Perkins had in mind for me for the street fair. Someone must have told her about the drawings I did for the kids in my class. I'm stuck drawing caricatures as fast as my fingers can create them. Next to me is a donation jar for the rec center. Another couple of teen teachers at the other end of the table are painting kids' faces, another donation jar beside them. Between us there's some space to color. I'm grateful for Remy. She keeps the supplies organized and restocked. She's also pretty good at telling the kids to wait their turn and that they only get two stickers.

I haven't had a chance to sneak away to see Adam yet. His job keeps him across the carnival from us. Every once in a while I catch a glimpse of him taking tickets or running one of the rides. I don't have time to really watch him, but every time I see him there's this odd feeling of ownership, or at least the feeling that he's in some way mine.

I've just finished my umpteenth cheesy couple drawing when I notice Remy drawing furiously on a piece of paper. Before I can see what she's working on, Kari's friend Bianca comes to the booth. She's wearing a pair of cutoff jeans so short that her pockets are hanging below the frayed hem and a half-cropped pink T-shirt with the word "sweet" splashed across her chest. I don't recognize the guy with her, but I'm already working on their couple caricature in my head. At least the one I'd like to do of them. I'd draw him with a tiny head and overdone ape-like chest. For her, I'd narrow the waist and accentuate her hips, just enough to make her question if the shorts she's wearing make her butt look big.

"Miranda." I immediately don't like the tone in her voice. "What are you doing here?"

Apparently me sitting under a sign that says "caricatures" with an easel and a large piece of paper in the middle of the street fair didn't clue her in. "Working the rec center booth." I answer as simply as I can. "Would you like me to draw you?"

She walks around slowly, taking long exaggerated looks at some of the samples I've hung up next to my easel "These aren't too bad." She sniffs. "But I like your work with dead people better." She laughs at her own joke. "What about it Miranda, could you draw me dead? I heard you painted one of Kari just before she died." Her voice is needle sharp and thinly coated with venom.

My heart freezes. How could she possibly know that? The only people who have seen that picture were my parents, Marshall, Adam, and Remy. The picture was gone from my room when I came back after Ron died. I'm sure my dad destroyed it.

"And what about poor Ron? Did you do a picture of him, hanging from the rope bridge?" She shakes her head. "Seems kind of odd to me, you used to paint dead people and now the people you paint seem to end up dead."

Something inside of me starts to boil, a rage that I'm not sure is completely my own. "Do you want a picture or not, Bianca?"

She laughs. "I'm curious. What will I look like dead? Something like this?" She lolls her head back on her neck, rolls her eyes back and lets her mouth fall open. She looks absolutely hideous and the boy with her looks extremely uncomfortable.

"No. Like this." Remy holds up the picture she was working on. The drawing is something like my caricatures, but in Remy's childish style and a more detailed background. It's clearly Bianca. She's lying on the ground, in front of the Ferris wheel. Her legs are at odd angles and her eyes are staring at nothing.

"What the hell! You little monster." Bianca rips the paper out of Remy's hand, crumbles it up and throws it back at her. "Let's get away from this freak show."

My heart is racing. I can't let this happen again. I put my hand on her shoulder to stop her. "Bianca, stay. I'll draw your picture. No charge."

She pushes my hand away. "Don't touch me, freak."

I try again, desperate to stop events that are already set in motion. "Okay, but please, stay away from the Ferris wheel."

Bianca turns on me, her face is a sheet of white fury. "You are a complete psychopath and a freak. I know Adam had something to do with Kari's death and I know you helped him. I'll figure it out Miranda, and then you'll be the one at the bottom of the lake."

She stalks away, her boyfriend plodding after her. When they're gone, I pull Remy into a corner of the booth. "Why did you do that?"

Remy's expression is matter-of-fact. "She asked. She wanted to know what she would look like dead, so I showed her."

"You can't just ... people are going to—" I start, but finally I give in. "What did you see?"

Her eyes get big. "I tried to show you what was going to happen. I tried to get in, but it was locked."

"You tried to get into my house?" I'm suddenly freaked out by the image of Remy prowling around, trying to find a way into my house.

"No." She taps her forehead. "I couldn't get inside there. It was bad when your head was hurt, but it's worse now."

It takes me a second to comprehend what she means by that. "You tried to show me what happened to Ron?"

She nods. "I couldn't get through. I couldn't warn you. You were the only one who could see what I can see, the only one who would listen, but you aren't listening anymore."

I squat down so I'm at her level. "Do the things you see scare you?"

She nods. "Sometimes."

"What if I told you that you don't have to see them anymore? What if there was a way you could keep the visions out?"

She looks confused. "But if I did that, how could I help her? How could I help the girl who can't leave? She wants us to find out who he is."

"Who ... the bad guy is?"

"Who the murderer is," Remy says in a firm voice. "He'll keep killing until we find out who he is. They'll keep coming to me, but it will always be too late."

I want to ask her more, but I'm interrupted by a voice from the other side of the booth.

"Excuse me Miss Artist, could you draw a picture of me?"

It's Marshall, decked out in a tight blue T-shirt with the words "Pine Grove Fire Department" stretched over his left pec. He turns to the side and strikes an impressive bodybuilder-worthy pose. "But maybe that's not my best side." He turns again, puffing out his chest and flexing his biceps. "No." He shifts his stance again, looking over his shoulder. When he turns again, he kicks the wadded-up paper that was Remy's artwork. He quits posing, leans down, and unfolds it. He studies it for a minute, his face wrinkling with concern and fear. "What is this?"

"Bianca," Remy says before I can think of a good response.

"Hmm, and what did Miss Bianca do to deserve a picture like this?" Marshall smooths out the wrinkles out the paper and studies the drawing.

"She wasn't very nice to me or Remy when she came by the booth," I say quickly.

Remy shakes her head. "That's not why she looks that way. It was because she fell."

Marshall looks at me for an explanation, but I can't give him one here, not with so many people around, even if I was sure he was ready to hear the truth. He's looking at Remy with an intensity I've only ever seen once before, when he was heading down the cliff to rescue Ron. "How did she fall?"

Before Remy can answer, her Aunt Kasey walks up. "Hey Miranda, I got off early, so I can get Remy out of your hair."

"Not yet!" Remy complains. "Can't I stay and ride the rides with Miranda and Adam?"

Marshall raises his eyebrows at me. He was there to hear the half-truth I told my parents about helping out at the street fair. I neglected to mention spending time with Adam.

"It's late," Remy's aunt says.

"At least can we get some food? I'm starving." It's funny how quickly Remy can change from the deadly serious girl who is wise in a way most people never will never be, to a typical I want it now nine-year-old.

"I don't think so, baby. Food here is expensive. We'll get something when we get home." Kasey's words droop in exhaustion.

"You can't come to the street fair without at least trying a mountain burger, or one of Twisties' waffle donuts." Marshall's interest moves from Remy to her aunt. She's about his age and despite the stress she carries, she's very pretty. Her hair is long and dark and her eyes are a deep brown.

"I don't think we've met," Kasey says.

"I'm Miranda's uncle, Marshall." Marshall extends his hand.

"And I'm Remy's aunt and guardian, Kasey."

"Very nice to meet you," Marshall says. "If you'd like to stay a bit longer, I'd love to show you the fair and buy Remy something unhealthy to eat."

Remy's eyes get big. "Can we?"

I can see the indecision in Kasey's eyes. She still looks tired, but there's a new spark in her eyes. Marshall was goofing around with the poses, but he is built like a bodybuilder. He has curly dark hair and striking blue eyes. Although I don't remember him ever having a serious girlfriend, he's never had a problem getting a date.

"I have a few things to do in an official capacity until I get a break." Marshall points to the seal on his T-shirt. "Then I'm free for about an hour. Just enough time to take you and Remy around, let you taste some of the local cuisine and maybe even get in a couple of rides." He winks at Remy.

"But not the hammerhead," Remy says.

"Okay, not the hammerhead," Marshall agrees. "I don't like going upside down anyway."

Kasey looks from Marshall to Remy. "I'm not sure how I can say no."

"Then don't," Marshall says. "I'll be back in less than twenty minutes."

As soon as he's gone Kasey leans closer to me. "Tell me about your uncle." I don't get a chance to answer before two more couples line up to get their pictures drawn. While I work, Remy says something about needing to use the bathroom and they leave. They must meet up with Marshall somewhere along the way because they don't come back.

Ms. Perkins arrives just as my shift is supposed to be over. She looks at my money jar. "Oh Miranda, this is wonderful! If you could stay just a little longer—"

"I can't." I cut her off before she can guilt me into staying. Adam is walking toward us. The corner of my mouth turns up its own as he gets closer. He's wearing a dark green carnie polo shirt that's a little too small. It brings out the color in his eyes and emphasizes the definition in his chest. Watching him walk toward me takes my breath away. I can barely believe he's coming to get me.

"Rand, you ready to go?" he says.

"Yep." My mouth turns up again and a flutter of pride moves from my stomach to my chest.

Ms. Perkins frowns her disapproval, but I've completed my shift, so there isn't much she can do.

"Yeah." I slip my hand into Adam's and ignore the way she looks at us.

Chapter Thirty-One

"So any idea who the guy is with Kasey and Remy?" Adam asks as we walk toward the lights of the carnival.

"My uncle, Marshall. Well, sort of my uncle. He was my dad's foster brother for a few years. His mom was a drug addict and he doesn't have any other family, so we claim him."

"They looked like they were having fun," Adam says. "It would be cool if Kasey met someone. She kind of put her whole life on hold to take care of me and Remy."

"It'd be cool if Marshall met someone too." I bump him with my hip. "Maybe we could be cousins."

"Kissing cousins?"

"Absolutely." I lean over and kiss him quickly, impressed with my own bravery.

He pulls away and takes my hand. "So what first? The guys I work with said they'd let us have cuts, so no waiting in line."

Across the concourse I see Bianca and the guy standing in line for the Ferris wheel. My stomach churns with dread and frustration at her stupidity. They're the next ones to get on.

"Ferris wheel," I say quickly, pulling Adam behind me.

We get to the ride just before Bianca and her date are about to get on. I step to the front of the line, Adam trailing after me. The ride operator, hairy everywhere but his head, nods at Adam and then opens the chain to let us through. When Bianca and her date step forward he holds up his hand. "You'll have to wait for the next round."

"But, but, we were here first!" Bianca sputters.

"Sorry." The man doesn't sound sorry at all as he turns to help Adam and me into our seatbelts.

"This is a lame ride anyway," Bianca says. The dread I felt as soon as I saw Remy's drawing eases as Bianca stalks away from the Ferris wheel. I don't know if it's enough to save her, but it's the best I can do right now

For my whole life, well at least the part of my life that I actually left the house, I've watched couples go up to the top of the Ferris wheel and wondered what it would be like to go on it with someone special. I didn't believe it would ever happen for me, and not just because I was terrified of going up that high in a little metal chair. Now that the moment is here, I wish I could enjoy it.

Adam slides his arm across my shoulders as soon as we're strapped in. "I thought you said you don't like heights?"

I laugh. Now that I've stared down my demons, or at least the ghosts that came to disrupt my peace, sitting in a little metal chair hundreds of feet above the world doesn't seem so scary. "Tonight, I'm not afraid of anything."

"Good." He slides closer. "I like that you feel safe with me."

I turn to look at him. The lights from the wheel are reflected in his eyes. "I do feel safe with you." That wouldn't be such a big statement except that almost every other girl in town thinks Adam is a serial killer—a super-hot, charming serial killer, but still a serial killer.

"Would it be cliché if I told you that you look beautiful tonight?"

"Completely cliché," I throw back. I know I'm blushing, but maybe the glow from the lights around us hides it. Two weeks of mostly undisturbed sleep, a little highlighter and lip gloss, some curl to my hair, and I'm looking a little less like a zombie. Still, it's the first time a guy has ever told me I looked beautiful. "Thanks."

I glance over the side and see Bianca in the line for the hammerhead ride. Not my responsibility, I remind myself as Adam leans toward me. Just as we reach the top of the wheel, right where I'd always imagined getting kissed, he presses his lips to mine. I wrap my arms around his neck and kiss him back. I open my eyes and the lights and sounds swirl around me. I'm dizzy with the height and his kiss.

He pulls away and twists a piece of my hair around his finger. "Miranda I—"

My phone vibrates, completely spoiling the mood. I pull back, panicked that maybe my parents have figured out where I am, who I'm with, or that I lied to them. I check the caller ID and then answer. "Marshall?"

"Hey, Miranda, where are you guys?" He's shouting, but I can barely hear him because someone is throwing a fit in the background.

"Currently at the top of the Ferris wheel." Kissing a hot guy. I add in my mind.

"Any way you can get down here, like now?"

I envision my parents standing at the base of the Ferris wheel, ready to take me home and lock me back in the tower that until now I created for myself. I glance at Adam, still sitting forward, his hand on my knee. "Um, top of the Ferris wheel," I say again.

"Miranda!" The shrill and panicked voice is familiar.

"Remy?" Adam asks.

I nod and hold the phone away from my ear. "Remy, what's wrong?"

"You need to come. You need to come now!" She's on the edge of hysterical. I look over and spot the bright pink of Bianca's shirt, still in line for the hammerhead. "Please, please, Rand!"

"Okay, we'll be there as soon as we can. Just try to stay calm." I hang up the phone.

Adam, who heard every word, looks at me. "Which one of us is going to play sick so they'll let us off?"

I agree to take the fall. Adam starts yelling to the operator as soon as we're about halfway to the loading station. "Can you let us off? My girlfriend doesn't feel very good."

I don't miss the word girlfriend. It's almost enough to make me queasy enough to actually throw up. The ride operator must have a serious aversion to someone getting sick on the ride. He lets us off as soon as we reach the bottom.

"This better be important," Adam says when we get to the bottom. "And you owe me a do-over on the Ferris wheel, or at least the other part."

I blush again, but he's already holding my hand and pulling me toward a sobbing Remy on a bench beside the ice cream stand.

"Rand!" Remy reaches for me. Between gulping sobs she gets out two words. "I lied."

"What are you talking about?" I'm trying to pull her away from the crowds and Adam and Marshall and everyone else, but there isn't anywhere to go.

"The girl, the one who was mean to you." She hiccups a sob. "I told her she was going to get hurt, but I lied."

"You lied?" Relief floods through me. Remy lied. Bianca is safe. "Why did you lie?"

"I wanted her to be afraid." Remy says.

"It's okay then. If it was a lie, nothing—"

"But now, it's all changed. I saw ..." Remy stares at me, pushing a kaleidoscope of images into my head. It hits me like a sped-up movie that's missing most of the frames—Bianca, dangling from a broken seat belt, sobbing, just about to fall, but she's not falling from the ferris wheel, she's falling from the —

The screech of metal vibrates the air around us. Marshall is gone, running before I even register where the sound is coming from. A boom of metallic thunder punctuated by screams comes next. I turn in horror. The egg-shaped cage is suspended upside down at the top of the hammerhead's arc. The metal door flaps open and a bright pink T-shirt catches on the edge of it. Bianca kicks to gain her balance and one sandal breaks loose. It falls to the ground and bounces once, like an omen of what's to come.

Chapter Thirty-Two

"Hold on!" Marshall's voice rises above Bianca's screams and those of the crowd. He scales the side of the ride, finding handholds and footholds where there should be none. I can barely watch. I didn't see the end of Remy's vision. I don't know how this ends for either of them.

Marshall gets closer. The ride shifts. Bianca is almost thrown free. Her date has his hands and feet wedged against the sides of the ride, struggling to hold himself in. He can't help her. Marshall reaches the top of the cage. Slowly he reaches his arms out to Bianca. "You need to try to come to me." His voice is calm, but loud enough that I can hear him far below. "If I get any closer, the ride will roll."

She shakes her head. Her fingers have welded themselves to the bars of the cage. Her body trembles with the effort of holding on.

Marshall inches closer. "You can do this. You're going to be okay."

He stretches his hand to her leg, the one closest to him and wraps his hand around her ankle. If the ride shifts again he'll fall. They'll both die. "I'm going to hold on until we get a better way to get you down. Don't let go. You weren't meant to die today."

The wail of a fire engine sounds in the distance. The police clear a path for it to come through. They park just to the side of the hammerhead. The ladder begins to extend slowly, too slowly. The ride creaks. Bianca slips. Marshall tightens his grip on her ankle. There's no way he can hold her in place.

She's going to die.

"No," I whisper.

Whatever fates or demons were unleashed when Remy drew that picture have no mercy. There's no way to recall what's been done. I can't watch, but I can't turn away. The ride creaks forward like a death clock, counting down the seconds until they fall. Marshall's footing slips. As he regains his balance the ride shifts. Bianca falls backward, screaming. Somehow he holds her as she dangles from one caught leg, the seat belt flapping beside her. It's the last image I saw of Remy's vision.

I bury my face in Adam's chest. I can't watch someone else die. He wraps his arms around me. I feel him exhale with the crowd around us. I pull away and look. A firefighter at the top of the ladder reaches out, grabbing Bianca under the arms and dragging her to safety. She's lowered down to another firefighter on the ladder. Then they reach and take Marshall's hand. He's safely on the ladder. Then they're helping Bianca's date down.

A cheer goes through the crowd. I sink to my knees, joining Remy in a sobbing heap. "She's safe. She's safe." I say it over and over again.

I lied. I lied. I lied. Another voice echoes in my head. I turn, thinking that it's Remy, but the voice is in my head. She's part of me now. I don't know if I'll ever be able to break free of her again.

Chapter Thirty-Three

H ow's Marshall?" I ask as Mom sits on my bed the next morning.

"Shook up, sore, but other than a few cuts and bruises, he's fine. Same with the girl he rescued," Mom says.

"It's crazy what he did to save her," I say.

"Yeah, I guess he broke about a million safety rules, but he saved the girl. I guess they might let it slide." Mom reaches over and tucks a piece of my hair behind my ear. "You looked really nice tonight. I meant to tell you that when you left to go volunteer at the fair and"—she hesitates and I hear the question in her voice—"babysit Remy."

"I did volunteer at the fair, and I did hang out with Remy, but ..." I try to formulate exactly what to say to her.

"But you really went to spend time with Adam," Mom finishes for me. She sounds more sad than angry.

"Yeah," I answer.

"You really like him?" she asks.

"I think so."

Mom lets out a long breath. "Adam seems nice. He's definitely charming and good-looking, but ..." She seems to be trying to collect her thoughts.

"But?" I prompt even though I'm pretty sure I don't want to hear the rest of her sentence.

"Did you know he was one of the last ones to operate the hammerhead?" Mom asks. I shake my head. "Or that the ride had a safety inspection about a half hour before he went on his break, and everything seemed to be working fine then?"

"What are you trying to say, Mom?"

"Just that he's been in close proximity to a lot of bad things that have happened this summer."

"I have too," I point out.

"I guess that's true. But what do you really know about him?"

"I know he's not a killer," I say.

"Did they tell you that?" Mom looks around the room, like they—the spirits I've walked with—might be with us right now.

I hesitate, trying to figure out how to formulate my answer. Mom has never had any doubts about what I see, until now. I think the other night when I sent all the spirits away freaked her out more than it did me. I looked over her shoulder a couple of days ago on the computer and saw a search on the word "schizophrenia." I think she might be moving toward Dad's side of the "Miranda is losing it" debate.

"No," I finally say. "It's just a feeling I have. I trust him. He makes me feel ..." I search for the right words, but they don't come. It would be so much easier if you could sketch a feeling.

"He makes you feel like you're worth paying attention to," Mom completes for me. I feel my cheeks get red. "I can see where that would mean a lot to a girl who's been ignored and bullied her whole life."

I bristle at her brutally honest assessment. It doesn't sound like Mom. More like she's parroting something she read in a book, or something someone told her to say. "So you think he's only interested in me because he's what, grooming me to be his next victim? Honestly Mom, if Adam wanted to kill me, he's had plenty of opportunities already."

She knows she hit the wrong nerve. "Baby, I just want you to be okay. I just want you to be happy. I feel like you might be a little too close to Adam to make an accurate judgment."

"If I told you they think he's all right would that be better? Does their opinion matter more than mine?"

"Miranda, that's not what I mean and you know it." She raises a sigh to the ceiling. "This is so hard. I never had to parent you like I've had to parent your brother. You've always just done the right thing. I mean, you provide a lot of other things to worry about, but lying and then going out to be with a guy? A guy who might or might not be dangerous. That's kind of out of the realm of what I'd have to discuss with a normal teenage daughter, much less what I'd have to talk about with you."

"So what, then, I'm not normal?"

"That's not what I meant," she says quickly.

"But it's what you said," I throw back.

"Miranda, I ..."

"Well, I have good news for you. Ta da! I'm now completely normal. I've learned to control my visions at night. I've learned to shut them out. I have a boyfriend, or at least a guy who likes to hang out with me and even likes to kiss me on the rare occasions when his little sister isn't getting in the way. I'm done taking care of dead people. I just want to live my life. Is that such a terrible thing to ask?"

"You've learned to shut them out?" Mom asks, like that's the most important thing in that sentence. She glossed right over my "first kiss" confession.

I shrug. "Yeah. I mean mostly."

"Mostly?"

I consider the connection I still have with the girl who won't leave. "Sometimes something gets through. But I can make them go away."

"How did you ..."

"Someone told me something I'd never thought of before. Someone told me I had a choice."

"So you've chosen not to use your gift?" Mom asks.

I give Mom a strange look. "I've always thought of it as more of a curse."

She smiles and pats my arm, like she's giving up a treasured part of my childhood that I've outgrown. "Like you said, you have a choice. But it seems to me, just suppressing your gift isn't the same as controlling it. It's not the same as using it the way you were meant to." She smooths my hair back and then kisses me on the forehead. "Since you're so into being a normal teenager these days, you'll love this. You're grounded for a week for lying to us."

Chapter Thirty-Four

It turns out I'm not just grounded, I'm in kind of a working imprisonment. I have to paint two of Dad's clients, a man and a woman, both who died of natural causes well into their seventies. I'm learning that it's much harder to paint someone from a picture instead of from up close and personal experience.

The time in my room gives me time to think about how Remy's lie about seeing Bianca die somehow changed into Bianca almost actually getting killed in the same kind of accident. Does this mean that Remy has some kind of power to decide who lives and who dies? That she can somehow draw a person's fate?

The other thing I keep thinking about is whether Mom and Remy are right. Is it wrong for me to shut things out and try to be normal? Is it wrong for me to wish to be as oblivious as the rest of the world when I might have the key to catching a killer? If the killer is even a person. It's starting to feel like something supernatural, like accidents are conjured up when Remy doesn't like someone.

I leave the unfinished painting on my easel and get out one of the big pieces of paper I used at the street fair. I spread it across my bed and try to draw out everything that's happened. I draw quick pictures of everyone who has died and add details about how they died; Kari, Ron, and the old woman who cleaned the church. What do they all have in common? Kari wouldn't listen to Remy's warning and she told

Adam I was a freak. Ron took my place as the drawing instructor and Remy didn't like him. Adam seemed oddly jealous of Ron. Bianca made fun of me. Actually, Bianca and Kari both made fun of me. They both went swimming with Adam. So do they have more to do with Adam or more to do with me? What about Remy? What if the accidents happen because Remy gets mad and then draws how she thinks they should die? But how does she or Adam have anything to do with the woman from the church? And what about her, the girl I've seen in visions and felt all around me? The one that Remy says can't move on?

I lie on the bed, staring at my crazy drawing. My head is swirling like it did when I had a concussion. What would I see if I let her back in? What would I see if I let Remy in?

"Hey, you sleeping?" Marshall knocks and opens my door at the same time.

I sit up, pushing the paper between my bed and the wall. "Working." I roll my eyes to the easel.

He smiles. "It's funny to watch you play the pouty teenager. I've never seen that side of you before."

"Oh yeah? So if I'm a pouty teenager isn't this the part where I ask you what you're doing in my room?"

He sits on the chair next to my bed. "I thought you'd like to know your boyfriend has mostly been cleared from the accident with the hammerhead. Well, in a 'don't leave town in case we have any further questions' kind of cleared."

"Really?" My heart leaps. I'm dying to text Adam, but my phone is part of the grounding.

"So they know what went wrong with the ride and why it broke like that?"

"Not exactly, but they're pretty sure the ride was set up wrong the night before. Something I missed in my safety inspection."

"You did the safety inspection?" I ask. "What do you know about rides?"

"Not much. Not enough I guess. I worked with a carnival for a while when I was a few years older than you, after I ran away from the last foster home for good. The carnival operators do their own safety inspections, but the city council asked the fire department to go in and do a backup check. I had the manuals and the safety checklist, but I didn't see the problem. I guess neither did Adam or anyone else. So it's just another freak accident."

"But no one died this time. Thanks to you."

"Yeah, I guess." He looks at me sideways. "Adam's not a bad kid. I feel bad that everyone here blames him for all this."

"Yeah. Even Mom doesn't want me around him now, and Mom likes everyone."

"Maybe I can help you there, let your mom know that I think he's okay." I must look surprised at his offer because Marshall adds, "I've gone over a couple of times, to see his aunt. She's great."

Something like jealousy creeps into my stomach. I didn't realize I felt so possessive toward Adam's family, especially his aunt, who I barely know. I push the feeling away. "How's Remy doing?"

"A lot calmer than she was the night of the street fair. What was she so upset about? I got that she lied, but ..." He trails off, waiting for me to supply an answer.

I consider what I'm going to say carefully. I trust Marshall, but I'm not sure how much I should tell him about Remy's visions or her drawings, especially since I'm not sure I understand them myself. It's not really my secret to tell, but I need someone else's opinion. I start slow. "She drew a picture of Bianca, remember?"

"The one I saw? I thought you drew that."

"No. It was her. It's not the first time."

"First time for what?"

I take a deep breath before I move on the crazy part. "First time she drew someone who looked like they were dead."

"Like the picture from your art class, the face in the water." He hesitates a minute. "The one that looked like your picture."

"Yeah."

"And she drew Bianca dead, because she was mad at her?" The last part ends in a question.

"Yeah, I guess so." I answer. "And it would just be a stupid drawing that an angry little girl drew, except, except—"

"Except there was an accident, and Bianca almost died."

"And it all could be just a coincidence, except it's happened before." A mix of fear and guilt settles into my stomach, like I've said too much.

"I think you should tell me everything you know." Marshall's voice is fading away, drowned out by a rushing in my ears, like a windstorm in my bedroom. Maybe my concussion hasn't completely healed yet. I focus on Marshall's face and struggle to understand what he's saying. "Tell me everything about Remy; what she's seen, what she's drawn, and how it relates to the accidents this summer." Fear and guilt twist together into a knot of insecurity in my stomach.

"I ... she ..." I'm trying to raise my voice above the noise in my brain, but my tongue feels heavy. "She's drawn all of them."

"Drawn all of them?"

The presence is heavy on my chest, in my throat and my ears. She doesn't want me to tell him anything about Remy. I concentrate on forcing her out of my head. My choice. My choice. I repeat it over and over.

"Miranda, are you okay?" Marshall's hand on my shoulder startles me and I jump.

I refocus on his face. It feels strange and familiar at the same time. It's just Marshall. "I'm fine. Remy has drawn them because she—"

The easel falls against my dresser, knocking the vase and the long-dead lilies Adam gave me to the floor. It shatters. The picture I was working on lands face up and red paint is streaked across the unfinished face of the man I was painting and over the corner of the canvas. Her anger and frustration isn't inside me this time, it's all around me. She's furious. Furious at me, but I don't know why.

Marshall bends over to pick up the painting. He stops for a second, holding it closer like he can see something. His face changes.

Dad pushes through the door. "What's going on in here?"

Marshall drags his eyes away from the ruined painting. "Wind caught the canvas and it fell, knocked over the vase and made a big mess."

"Miranda will have to clean it up. I need you to head to the office and get a copy of the death certificate for that girl from Morton and get it in the mail. It's already been filed." He glances at me. "I'd do it myself, but tonight is our anniversary and we have dinner plans."

"Right. Sure." Marshall leaves the broken vase and the painting and follows Dad out.

After they're gone I pick up the painting. In the corner where the red spilled I see what Marshall was staring at. He must have thought it was just the way the paint spattered, that his eyes were playing tricks on him. But I recognize the design smeared onto the canvas—two intersecting Ts, just like the one on my picture before. Just like the drawing from the camp.

Chapter Thirty-Five

"Why don't you just talk to me? What are you afraid of?" I say out loud, but the room is as quiet and emotionless as an empty grave.

I think back to the things she said to me before: Find out who I am. And what Remy keeps telling me. Names have power.

After all of this, I still don't have her name. Against my resolve I go to my computer. I type in Amberlea Dawn Beal, and her death date, July 31, 1996. I hit on her obituary. At the top is a picture of a beautiful, curly-haired girl—the one I saw in the casket, by the fire, and last, in the cabin at the old camp. I skim the text, picking out details I guessed, but wasn't sure of.

Amber was a counselor at the camp. More than that, she was the counselor, the one who died by falling into the ravine. I stare at her picture, trying to conjure up the feelings I had in the vision, the murderous hatred that she had for Amber. I get nothing. I do searches on the camp, but I don't get much information beyond what I already know of the accident. There isn't a list of the other counselors anywhere, but I'm almost sure the girl who can't move on was a counselor at the same camp at the same time as Amber.

Maybe the girls had a fight over the boy, the one I can never see clearly. Maybe she killed Amber and that's why she can't move on. But what does that have to do with me and with Remy? Or with the other people who've died recently?

I close my laptop. I'm being sucked in again. I can't do this. I get on my knees to clean up the broken glass. Because I'm so distracted I cut my finger. The blood bubbles up on the tip of my finger. The dream where I wore another girl's face comes back to me. I was consumed by guilt and shame, so much guilt and shame that I drew the knife across my own wrist.

My fault. I lied.

I go back to my laptop and try the word "suicide" associated with summer when Amber died, but suicides aren't reported the way accidents are.

Dead end. Dead end.

Dead. I'm a mortician's daughter. Not only that, but I'm the coroner's daughter and before my dad, my grandpa was the coroner for the entire area. At the mortuary, Dad has three big file cabinets full of death certificates. Some of them have to be from my grandpa's time. If the girl from my vision died in Morton, my grandpa probably signed her death certificate.

I suck on my cut finger and think about how I'm going to get into the place I've avoided for years. I have to go to the mortuary, but I can't do it anytime Dad might be there. Tonight is the perfect time, maybe the only time. My parents never go out. Their anniversary is the one exception.

Marshall at the firehouse tonight, so that just leaves me with Mark to deal with. At twelve, I figure he's old enough to spend a few hours on his own while I go to the mortuary. But I have to figure out how to get there. Despite my resolve to be a normal teenager I'm still without a driver's license. The mortuary is too far away from me to walk to and from within the span of time my parents will be

gone. The city bus doesn't run by my house, and I never learned to ride a bike. That leaves me with only one choice for transportation.

It's time to find out how well my first relationship holds up against the freak test.

Chapter Thirty-Six

I'm still without my phone. Mark has one, but it's already going to take some bribing to keep him from telling my parents I snuck out while they were gone. We have a landline, thanks to the funeral business, so I go into the little cubbyhole that serves as my mom's office on the days when she can't get to the mortuary to do her secretarial stuff.

He picks up on the third ring. "Miranda?" I wonder what he thought when Pine Grove Mortuary came up on his caller ID.

"Hey." I try to come off casual, flirty even. I'm sure I'm failing miserably, but Adam actually sounds happy to
hear my voice.

"Are you still grounded?" he asks.

"Yep."

"I figured that's why you haven't been answering my texts, or at least, I hoped that was why." An evil part of me likes the insecurity in his voice.

"Yeah, that's why I had to use this phone." I take a breath and dive in. "What are you doing tonight?"

"Babysitting. My aunt is working the night shift. Why? What are you doing?"

"My parents are out, it's their anniversary, and I was wondering if I could see you." I hold my breath, waiting
for his answer.

A smile comes through in his voice. "I think that could be arranged. I mean, Remy would have to come, but at least we can be together."

"I'd like that." And then, so it sounds almost like an afterthought, "But I also need to go by my dad's office.
I left something there and he won't get it for me." I should have come up with a better excuse, but I'm not ready to tell Adam the real reason for my nighttime escape.

"Your dad's office." He pauses for a long time. "At the mortuary?"

"Yeah, I'd really appreciate it if we could swing by there. You and Remy don't have to come in. I'd just slip in
and slip out. I have the key." As I say it I start rummaging through Mom's desk drawer, hoping her keys are where they usually are. I pull them out of the middle drawer.

"Yeah. Sure." He doesn't sound excited at the idea, but he didn't say no. "We'll be there in about ten."

I stand up to leave Mom's office, debating between just telling Mark I'm going to bed and then sneaking out and trying to come up with a way to bribe him not to tell. I get the answer as soon as I open the door.

"Why are you going to the mortuary?" Mark asks.

"I left something there." I say.

"You haven't been to the mortuary in years," Mark points out.

"I just need to get something there. And I need you to not tell Mom and Dad." I work to sound like a big sister. One that actually commands respect from her younger sibling.

He looks at me like I'm a new specimen he's never studied before—the normal, at least, almost normal teenage sister. "I might be able to do that, if ..."

"If?"

"If you give me the money I need to buy the newest version of the Planet Arcadia game. Mom said I have to earn it."

"How much is the game?"

"Sixty dollars."

"And how much have you saved?"

"Like two dollars."

"So you want me to give you fifty-eight dollars and then you won't tell Mom and Dad I left tonight?"

"That sounds about right," Mark says. "And you have to swear if I ever want to sneak out you'll cover for me."

I really don't have time to debate it with him or with myself, so I just say, "Sure."

Adam pulls into the driveway a few minutes after I pay Mark. By the time I get out the door Adam's on the steps, waiting for me. The first thing he does is kiss me, like it's a normal thing between us now. He steps back, holding both of my hands. "I'm glad you called me. The last few days, actually the last few months, have been kind of insane."

"I get that." I say.

He lets go of one hand and leads me down the stairs. "So, mortuary first?"

"If that's okay?" I'm studying his profile as we walk to see how far I'm pushing this. He looks nervous, but not quite to the running stage yet.

He pauses by the car door. "I don't think I've ever been inside a mortuary at night, actually, I'm not really sure I've ever been inside a mortuary. I mean, except after my mom died."

I squeeze his hand, wishing I had more comfort to give him. "I haven't either. I mean, I haven't been inside one at night ever, and I haven't been inside one in years."

"But your dad owns one."

"Yeah, well, I kind of got myself banned when I was a little kid. I didn't know how to keep my mouth shut." He opens the door without asking me to elaborate on that story. I'm glad. I'm not ready to get into all the reasons this town thinks I'm a freak.

"So what do you need to—"

"Hey, Remy." I intentionally don't give him time to finish his question.

"Hey, Rand," Remy says when I get into the car. "Come sit in the back with me, I need to show you something."

"No way," Adam says. "You're the tagalong. Tonight Miranda is mine."

Remy screws her face into a pout that makes me feel guilty, but not guilty enough to climb in the back seat with her.

The deserted mortuary looks creepy, even to me. Once it was almost my playground. I remember crawling under the pews and playing with the different settings on the organ when I was a little kid. There's only one light in the parking lot. I direct Adam to the back door that Dad uses to take the bodies inside.

"You can stay in the car. I'll just be a minute." I don't know how true that is, I only remember that Dad has file cabinets. I'm not sure if he keeps them locked or how he organizes them. If it's by date or area I have a chance. But if it's just by name, I probably won't be able to find the file I'm looking for.

"Are you sure? I could go with you," Adam says weakly. I know he doesn't want to go inside with me, but at least he's willing to make the offer.

"Nah, this place doesn't bother me." I'm already halfway out the door. Honestly, I'd love to have Adam come in with me, so I don't have to face the mortuary alone, but I'm not willing to press the freak thing that much.

I stand for a second, facing the heavy metal door in front of me. More than anything I want to turn around and go back to the safety of Adam's car, the comfort of his arms, and the normal life I've wanted for so long. A voice in my head pushes me forward, not another ghost, or my mom, or even Remy. This time it's all me. I know if I back out now more people will die and I'll never know if I could have stopped it.

I slip the cold metal key into the lock and pull the door open.

Chapter Thirty-Seven

The back door leads directly into the embalming room, a room I went in a few times when I was a kid, but it didn't bother me like it does now. I walk though without looking to either side, but I'm still aware of the steel table, the wall of instruments, and the white board on the wall with the diagram of a body. Dad uses it to take notes when he does an autopsy.

The office is down the hall. I purposely open my mind as I walk toward it, but I don't sense anyone else here. I guess a mortuary isn't a very pleasant place for anyone, living or dead. The keys I found in Mom's desk drawer open Dad's office. The three big metal filing cabinets against the wall look intimidating. I take a deep breath and move to the one that looks the oldest. I pull out the first few files and find receipts for funeral expenses. I check the next drawer. It's full of financial stuff, supplies purchased and things like that.

I find what I'm looking for in the next cabinet. My grandpa and then my dad kept impeccable records. This one is by area, by date and then by last name. As I reach Morton, 1996, the outside door opens. I freeze, my hand still poised over the file. It could be Marshall, just coming by to pull the death certificate Dad asked for. The worst-case scenario is Dad got a call and left dinner to come here. Okay, that's maybe not the worst-case scenario, but I'm still not eager to get caught.

"Miranda?" Adam's voice echoes down the hall. He, or Remy, or both must have gotten tired of waiting. I cringe as I realize they would have had to follow me through the embalming room door. It's the only door that's unlocked.

I dig through the drawers as fast as I can, hoping to find what I'm looking for before I have to explain to Adam why I'm searching my dad's files.

"Miranda?" he calls again.

"In my dad's office." I find the July, August, September files and start skimming death certificates.

"Remy has to use the bathroom." Adam is standing at the door. "Where is it?"

"Next to the chapel," I say without looking up. "I'll be there in a minute."

Natural causes. Too old. A guy. A car accident. A drowning. I stop on that one when I realize the drowning happened in the same lake near the camp. It was before Amberlea died, too late in the fall to have been during the camp, but it seems like it might be important.

Adam and Remy are in the foyer of the funeral home. They've turned all the lights on outside my dad's office. I hope that Dad and Mom don't happen to drive by the mortuary and wonder why the lights are all on.

Too young. Too old. Too old. Too ...

And then I'm looking right at her. The picture clipped to the file was taken before she dyed her hair black with the blue tips. It looks like the kind of picture you put on a student ID card. Her hair is mousy brown and she's hardly wearing any makeup. She isn't smiling. She's pale and plain, not really pretty, but her

eyes are a deep blue. I remember staring into those eyes. I remember seeing them reflected in the mirror. I read the whole report, purposely avoiding her name, the entire reason for my search.

Distinguishing physical characteristics: blue eyes, dyed black and blue hair, some grown out to brown. Tattoo on left shoulder. Injuries: Blunt force and multiple broken bones and internal injuries, consistent with a fall of approximately three stories. Spine severed at C-5 vertebrae. Death immediate upon impact. No water in the lungs. Despite the location of the body, drowning was not a factor in death. I skim down to coroner's determination of cause of death.

Suicide.

It hits me hard, even though I guessed that was how she died. I remember the feelings of guilt and helplessness when I was inside her mind. She thought killing herself was the only way to stop him.

I look back at the name, Tiffany Starr Farrell. One of the two Ts intertwined in the design on the bunk. I take a breath and say her name out loud. "Tiffany, Tiffany Starr Fa —"

Before I can finish an icy wind whips through my dad's office, scattering death certificates everywhere. I grip the paper in my hand to keep it from being sucked away. The lights around me dim and flicker. I can't move. I can't speak. My tongue feels too heavy.

I can feel her behind me, beside me. Her presence fills the room. She's furious. Terrified. Ashamed. She doesn't want me to know who she was. She doesn't want me to speak her name. She doesn't want to give up her secrets. She doesn't want to end her game.

I force my tongue to obey me, pushing her name out in a single breath. "Tiffany Starr Farrell!"

I turn, knowing she's behind me.

Her face is reflected in the dark glass of the office window. Her blackened lips twist into a malicious smile.

The lights go out.

Remy screams.

Chapter Thirty-Eight

"Remy!" Adam yells.

"Adam!" I yell back. "Adam, where are you?"

"Remy!"

Something crashes in the next room. I come out into the foyer, moving as quickly as I dare in the pitch dark. I kneel, feeling along the floor. "Adam?"

"I'm here." The little table that sits in the foyer is tipped over. Adam is tangled in the tablecloth and fake flowers that usually sit on top of it.

I reach for his hand. "Are you okay?"

He wraps his fingers in mine. "Yeah."

"Where's Remy?"

Adam stands, letting go of my hand and standing. He turns on the light on his phone. "She was heading to the bathroom."

I move to open the bathroom door, but I know she's not there. I turn around. The air pulsates with Tiffany's presence. I follow the sensation toward the door to the embalming room.

Adam follows me. "Where are you going?"

"Shh." I move toward the door and stop just outside. I know Remy and Tiffany are both in this room. I'm afraid to see what's inside. I don't want Adam to go inside either, but I can't leave Remy to whatever Tiffany wants from her.

I reach for the doorknob, expecting to have to force my way in, but it swings open as soon as I touch it. On the other side of the room is the steel enbalming table. Behind the table are rubber tubes and jars of fluid. Next to the table is the white board. Remy is standing at the board, drawing as if she's in a trance.

"Remy," I call to her.

Adam steps comes in behind me. He grips my shoulder, breathing hard in fear and exertion. He shines his light at the picture she's drawing in red marker. For a nine-year-old, Remy is a good artist, but there's no way she's drawing the face on her own. The style is different, more like what I saw in the cabin, urban graffiti. It's a man, surrounded by flames. After a few more strokes I recognize the face.

I breathe his name. "Marshall."

"Remy!" Adam grabs Remy's shoulders, but she doesn't respond. He tries to drag her away from the white board, but she resists him with superhuman force, and keeps drawing. He gets in her face. "Remy, listen to me."

"Tiffany, let her go!" I scream.

Remy stiffens and drops the marker. Then she turns around. "Find him."

Chapter Thirty-Nine

She slumps like a marionette with her strings cut. Adam grabs her before she hits the floor. The lights in the mortuary come back on.

I kneel beside Remy; her hands are shaking and covered with red marker, as if it was blood. "What did you see?"

She turns her head, her face innocent and confused. I try to feel for her vision, but it's gone.

Marshall's in danger. We have to find him.

Despite everything that's happened, it's the only thing that sticks in my mind. I run back into my dad's office. He keeps a police scanner there. I slip on the forgotten death certificates. They don't matter anymore. I flip on the scanner, going through the channels. The chatter begins to make sense. There's a fire, a big one. Marshall is probably already there. He may already be gone.

"Miranda!" Adam yells from the embalming room. "We need to get out of here. We need to get Remy back home or to a hospital or ..." He chokes like he's fighting back a sob.

I ignore him, waiting for the information I need. As soon as I hear the address, I scribble it down, not trusting my memory. Then I run back to Adam. "My uncle is in trouble. We have to find him."

"What? I can't go anywhere with Remy like this. She needs to leave. I need to get her—"

"We have to find him." Remy's voice is calm and flat, but it's definitely her. Tiffany is gone.

Adam looks from me to Remy and then back to me. His expression is a mix of fear, bewilderment, and frustration. Finally he says, "How are we going to find him?"

"There's a fire, a big one. I heard it on the police scanner. He's at the station tonight, so he has to be there. Please, Adam. Something is going to happen to him."

He stares from his sister to me and then back again, incredulous. Finally he speaks. "Okay, but if there is anything dangerous, anything at all, I'm taking Remy and leaving."

There's a change in his voice. Bringing him and especially Remy here was a mistake. I've put his sister in danger. That's not something he can forgive easily, or maybe at all. I barely had him and I've already lost him. That realization settles in the bottom of my stomach even as I'm pushing him out the door. Marshall's life is worth losing Adam over. Bianca's accident taught me that Remy's visions can be undone.

The Falcon's Nest is probably the most rundown apartment complex in town. By the time the GPS directions on Adam's phone leads us there, nearly the entire building is engulfed in flames. Adam drives behind the fire department barrier and parks. He doesn't turn the car off. I undo my seatbelt and push the door open. Before I can get out, he puts his hand on my shoulder. I turn around.

"Miranda I ... I don't think you should go near that building. Just stay. Stay with me." I look into his eyes, filled with fear and pain and the tenderness I know I'll miss.

"I have to go. I'm sorry." I slip out of his grasp and head across the parking lot. Even without looking back I know he's driving away. I know he won't stay.

A wave of heat from the flames envelopes me like a hellish embrace as soon as I cross the street. I keep walking. The whole scene is chaos and confusion. There are small groups of bystanders. Some are here to gawk, others watch in silence as what little they have crumbles into smoke and flame. I duck around the side of the barrier. No one stops me. Everyone is watching the fire and who might come out of it. No one cares who's heading toward it.

I step into the eerie red and gray shadows made by the bushes beside the building. I open my mind to see if I can hear anyone or anything. Waves of panic hit me. I cower behind a car. I can't do this. But then I think of Marshall, always teasing me, always patient, always on my side. I can't let him die. I stand up and walk closer.

"Marshall!" I yell with my voice and reach for him with my whole soul. The answering silence gives me hope. He's not dead yet.

The heat and the smoke grow heavier. Panic grips my heart. I'm surprised when I realize the feelings aren't mine. I don't think they're Tiffany's or Marshall's. It feels like someone else— someone who died in the fire or maybe someone who is dying, someone who needs help.

There's an outside door into the apartment complex that hangs on broken hinges. I'm not sure if it's always been broken like that or if the firefighters broke it down. The panic is coming from that part of the building. I pull my T-shirt up over my mouth and nose and step into the smoke-filled hallway. The air is as thick as night. I drop to my hands and knees to catch a breath. I follow the overwhelming emotions of whoever is still inside. I have to try to save them.

"Marshall!" I yell, but the effort makes me choke.

The door to my left is thrumming and swelling like it can't hold the fear contained behind it. I reach up and feel it. It's warm, but not hot. I reach for the knob, praying it's not locked. The door falls open when I push against it, like someone already broke the lock. I stay low to the ground and crawl inside. "Is anyone here?" I try, but my voice is drowned out in the roar of the fire. Above me, flames lick the ceiling like a hungry demon. I crawl over filthy, threadbare carpet, past a tipped-over chair and down another hall. The panic makes me hesitate more than the heat. Every inch brings me closer to being enveloped in sheer terror. I fight the urge to run, pushing my way into a bedroom at the back of the apartment.

He's on his hands and knees, bent over a figure wrapped in some kind of blanket. From the back, in full gear, it could be any of the firefighters, but I know it's him.

"Marshall." It comes out more of a croak than the scream I intend.

He turns. His face mask doesn't hide the shock and then horror in his eyes. His voice is amplified through his mask. "Miranda? What the hell are you doing?"

"We have to get out. The ceiling is going to come down." I don't know how I know that's what's going to happen, but as soon as I say it, I know it's true.

Marshall keeps staring at me, like he doesn't believe I'm real. I crawl closer. There's a woman wrapped in the blanket. She isn't moving, but I know the panic I feel is from her. "Is she …"

Wood splinters and crashes somewhere down the hall. Someone screams. I don't know if it's someone outside or if the voice is in my head and coming from the woman in front of me. Marshall crouches low, picking me up. "What about her?" I strain against the smoke.

"I can't save her!" Marshall yells.

"We have to try." I'm fighting to get to her. The flames crawl up the door frame. In a couple of seconds we'll all be trapped.

"She's already gone." Marshall throws me over his shoulder and runs through the door.

What's left of the woman leaves her body and gets sucked into the flames. Marshall carries me through the burning hall. Sparks land on my clothes and burn through to my skin. The smoke is so thick that I feel like I'm being suffocated. I press my face into Marshall's back. A piece of the ceiling falls on his shoulder. He yells and drops to his knees, still holding me. When I look in his eyes I see defeat. "Why did you come here?" he says.

"I had to save you."

"I can't … I can't let anything happen to you." He pulls off his face mask and fits it over my nose and mouth.

I take in a deep breath. Then I put my arm under Marshall's. "We can still … we can make it."

He nods and then leans on my shoulder. All hell is breaking loose around us. I can't see anything, but I reach out, feeling through the smoke and flame for something to guide us toward the door. I focus on the crowd I saw watching the fire. So many emotions, fear, despair, even excitement. I use the emotions as a beacon until my fingers scrape a door. I reach for the handle, but my head is swimming, full of smoke and clouded by other people's feelings.

"The door," I say and then slip into the smoky abyss.

Chapter Forty

"What do you think?" I toss my hair dramatically.

He comes up behind me, but instead of commenting on my hair he asks, "Who is she?"

It takes me a minute to figure out he's talking about the drawing I left on my bed. He's holding my sketch pad in front of him. "I'm actually not sure." I move beside him as he studies the face of the girl. She came to me in a dream last night, her arms and legs thrashing as she's fought to keep her head above water. But I can't tell him that. "Just a face that's been stuck in my head."

"Interesting." He leans closer, examining distinct gray eyes that fade into a half-finished nose. Irritation bubbles in my stomach. He always wants to talk about my drawing. I know I should be flattered, but he asks so many questions. Too many questions.

"Do you notice anything else?" I flip my hair again, this time it catches his attention.

"You dyed it, wow, it's ..." He takes a handful of pitch-black hair, tipped with blue, and lets it run between his fingers. "It's a big change."

"It's something I've wanted to try for a while, but I was never brave enough." I hate the insecurity in my voice.

He steps next to me and kisses my hair just above my jaw. He moves his hands from my shoulders to my waist and leans his lips against my ear. "I think it's incredibly sexy."

"Thank you." The insecurity fades and I bask in the glow of his approval.

He moves his hand under my hair and brushes my neck. "Have I ever told you how gorgeous you are?"

I shake my head. "Stop teasing."

"No teasing. I've watched you for a long time. There's something about you." His lips move down my neck. "The way you move." He kisses the fresh tattoo, still sore on my bare shoulder. "The way you talk." He kisses the corner of my mouth. "The wrinkle you get right here when you're concentrating on a drawing." He hands me the sketchpad. "Tell me what inspired the girl in the picture, another dream?"

I close my eyes, fighting a wave of annoyance. I want him to shut up and kiss me. For once the perfect line forms on my lips. I turn to face him. "You talk too—"

I see his face clearly for the first time.

"What's wrong?" Adam asks.

I force my eyes open, my heart racing as I sit up. It can't be Adam. It can't be him, but the image of his face is burned into my mind.

"Miranda, thank God."

It takes a second to get my bearings. I'm in a stark white room; something plastic is covering my mouth and nose. My eyes burn. Everything is hazy and too bright at the same time. I'm in a bed that's not mine.

"Where ... how?" The plastic mask makes it hard to speak. I pull it off. "Where am I?"

"In the hospital, baby," Mom says. "What do you remember?"

Swirls of dreams come back to me—the mortuary with Adam, a death certificate, a face in the window, Remy drawing, but it wasn't Remy. Fire. Lots of fire and smoke and someone, someone dying.

"Marshall!" I sit up so fast it makes my head swim.

"He's okay, baby. Thanks to you. He said he could have never found his way out without you," Mom says.

"What possessed you to run into a burning building?" Dad's voice is harsher than Mom's. I'm sure by now he's discovered the mess of paperwork all over his office. More than likely he's seen the drawing on the embalming room wall as well.

In a heartbeat I decide to leave off any mention of Remy and Adam. "I saw Marshall, dying in the flames. I couldn't let him die."

My parents exchange a glance. Seeing visions of dead people is one thing, but this vision almost ended with my death. Even Mom looks horrified by what I just said. I lie back on the pillow, beyond exhausted. My chest feels like it's been burned from the inside and there are pricks of pain whenever I move.

"Where is he now?" I ask.

"Upstairs, recovering from shoulder surgery. His collar bone was shattered by falling debris. You were lucky. You just got some bad smoke inhalation and a few burns on the way out. By all accounts you should be the one lying on the table in the mortuary instead of the woman who's there now, the one that Marshall was trying to save when you came in." Any bit of patience has left Dad's voice.

Mom rests her hand on his shoulder. "Doug, don't, not now. She's still so weak."

"No. Maybe now is the best time for this discussion. She has to stop this. She has to get help before she ends up dead." He turns to me. "You snuck out of the house, ransacked my office, drew on the board in the embalming room, and then ran into a burning building. Does this sound like the kind of thing a rational, sane teenage girl does?"

"You think I'm crazy," I spit back at him.

For a second he looks ashamed, but he shakes his head and continues. "I think you need some kind of help. I can't do anything else with you. I won't bury another child, Miranda, do you understand me? If I have to keep you locked up, if I have to put you in some kind of hospital, so be it, but I won't lose you." His voice breaks on the last few words and tears start flowing down his cheeks. He doesn't try to hide them or even wipe them away. He leans against the bed and grips the bars at the side hard. "I won't lose you."

I've never seen my dad like this. He's the always calm, always stoic mortician, so desensitized to death that it doesn't affect him. At least that's what I thought.

After a few seconds he steps back, muttering something about needing air. When he's gone, Mom stares straight ahead, gripping one of the pillows. It takes her a long time to speak. When she finally, does her voice cracks with emotion. "Did I ever tell you how excited Dad was when we found out I was pregnant? Or how excited he was when we found out we were having twins?" I shake my head. "I was scared to death, but your dad ... he couldn't wait to be a father."

She takes a shaky breath. "And then that horrible, beautiful night when you were both born. I was bleeding, unconscious. You were whisked away to the NICU before you could even cry. They didn't think either of us would make it through the night. Your dad was left with your sister; perfect, but blue and cold, his baby girl who would never cry. He held her for hours. When it was time for her funeral, he dressed her and prepared her for burial himself." She turns to face me, her eyes swollen with fallen and unfallen tears. "Dad's business is death, but that doesn't mean it doesn't get to him." Her eyes flash with protective indignation. "Why would you go into that building? Why would you put yourself in that kind of danger?"

"Marshall would have—"

"Marshall is a grown man and an experienced firefighter. It is not your job to keep him safe. And it is not your job to find out who or what might be killing people. You said you could shut it off, that you could make them go away. You told me you had a choice. Choose to be safe. I never thought I would say this, but choose to be normal. If nothing else, choose to be alive."

Chapter Forty-One

M om's words and Dad's breakdown haunt me long after Dad has gone back to the mortuary and Mom has gone to try to get some sleep. Any minute I expect a smiling doctor with a clipboard to come to my room to give me a psychiatric evaluation. I know I'm not crazy. If my visions were just some kind of psychosis, they wouldn't keep coming true. I need to talk to someone who will be on my side.

Adam?

His face in my dream comes back to me. What if I was wrong about him? What if it was him all along?

Don't love so much that you can't see what he is.

Could the warning from the woman at the church be about Adam? But how could he be tied to the murders that happened years ago? Unless the warning wasn't about someone coming back to kill again, but a similar situation; falling in love so hard that you're willing to hide a killer.

She was trying to protect him.

Is that the mistake she made? Is that why she thought it was her fault, because she knew what he had done, but she loved him too much to turn him in?

If Adam is a killer, could I turn him in?

I need to talk to someone, someone who will listen without thinking I'm a freak. Someone who likes Adam, but might be able to help me see clearly.

Marshall might be the only one who might be willing to listen now.

There's a little bag in the corner of the room that Mom brought in. It has some extra clothes, a toothbrush, and a few other things. I pull on a pair of sweats, a T-shirt, and shoes. Not wanting to panic them if they come back, I write my parents a note:

Went to see Marshall. Be back soon.

I sneak out of my room when there are no nurses close by. I step into the elevator. Mom said upstairs, so I try the next floor up. When I step off I head to the first nurse's station I see, trying to act like I'm a visitor.

"I'm looking for Marshall Wheeler." I'm hoping my voice doesn't sound too raspy or shaky.

"Are you a relative?" The nurse asks, barely looking at me.

"I'm his niece."

She consults her computer. "He's in B hall, room 303, but he might still be groggy from the anesthesia."

"Thanks." I'm grateful that she's too distracted to ask me anything else. I head toward Marshall's room, my strength fading with every step. I stop a few feet from his door and lean against the wall to rest. The door is open, just enough that I hear voices inside. I move a little closer, afraid that he's talking to my dad.

The man's voice that comes through isn't familiar. After a few seconds I realize he must be a police officer, or a detective, or maybe a fire investigator. "What condition was the woman in when you found her?"

It takes Marshall a minute to answer. "She was already dead."

"Smoke inhalation?" the other man asks.

"I'm not sure. I ... I actually don't think so," Marshall says. His voice is thready and weak. I've never heard him like this. Marshall is the strongest person I know.

"Yeah, that's what our investigator thinks too. We're waiting on the coroner's report. The body was badly burned, but not completely destroyed in the fire."

"I'm sorry I didn't get her out. I had to save my niece."

A pang of guilt rests in my stomach. Could he have saved the woman from the fire if I wasn't there?

"Like you said, most likely she was beyond saving." The man hesitates for a second. "Any idea why your niece was at the fire? Or in that particular room?"

I hold my breath, waiting for Marshall's answer.

"I think she was driving by and saw the fire. She came in because she was worried about me. Actually, I wouldn't have made it out without her."

"Driving around? Maybe with a friend? That new kid?"

"I don't know," Marshall answers.

"I don't have to tell you, the fire seems pretty suspicious, even without a dead girl in one of the apartments."

I hold my breath, realizing I tied Adam to another crime scene last night. But it couldn't have been him; he was with me at the mortuary. Unless he started the fire before he came to get me. How long had the fire been burning? My head hurts and my throat hurts. I just want the investigator to leave so I can talk to Marshall. I need his cool head to help me sort everything out.

Finally, the man says something about "going over things later." I step behind a linen cart and wait for him to pass before I go into Marshall's room. He's leaning back against the pillows with his eyes closed. A huge white bandage covers his shoulder.

"Hey," I say softly.

His eyes flutter open. "Miranda?"

"Yeah." I step closer.

"What are you doing out of bed?" he says.

I perch on a chair next to his bed. "I needed to talk to you. No one else will listen to me. Mom and Dad think I'm crazy."

"Maybe it has something to do with you running into a burning building," he says.

"That's your career and no one thinks you're crazy."

He sighs. "You saved my life. I'm grateful for that. But if anything had happened to you ..." He trails off, shaking his head.

"I already got it from Dad."

"Why in the world did you decide to go into that building, and then how did you find me?"

"The truth, even if it sounds completely insane?" I ask.

He looks into my eyes and I remember how Remy drew them last night. Even in the midst of flame he looked serene, peaceful even. "The truth."

I hang back, not sure if this is the right thing to do, but I can't keep this to myself any longer. "Remy drew your picture on the board in the mortuary. There were flames around your face. When she draws someone like that, it usually means they're going to die."

"It means they're ... going to ... die?"

"Yeah. I know it sounds crazy."

Marshall leans back like he's thinking hard. "Like the girl at the fair. Remy drew that? I thought it was you."

"No, it was Remy."

"The picture in Ron's car, was that Remy too?" I nod. "But you painted the picture of Kari."

"After I saw her in a dream, a dream that Remy shared with me."

"Remy shares her dreams with you?" Marshall looks even more confused. "How is that possible?"

"I don't know. The caretaker at the cemetery said I have a connection to death, because of my twin sister, that I have empathy for people who died, so they pour their memories into me." I shake my head, knowing it sounds crazy. "Sometimes, it works with people who are still alive, or people who are close to death or ... I don't know."

"So you don't see people before they die?"

"No. Before Remy came I only saw people who had already died, just before they crossed over. Remy sees them before they die, but she doesn't know how to save them. I think that's why she shared what happened to Kari with me. She thought I could help her." I look down at the floor. "But I couldn't."

Marshall breathes for a few minutes, like he's trying to understand. "Have you considered that maybe Remy doesn't actually see anything? What if she and Adam just decide that someone is supposed to die? She draws the picture and Adam makes it happen? Every one of the people who died did something that made Remy or Adam mad."

"Adam's not a killer," I say. But for the first time, I'm not sure. "He couldn't have killed the woman in the apartment or started the fire. He was with me at the mortuary."

"You were at the mortuary last night? Why?"

I take a deep breath. That's going to take a lot more explaining. "I think this has all happened before."

"Before?" Marshall asks.

"Years ago there were a bunch of girls who died from accidents in the same summer, but maybe they weren't accidents. There was a girl, one of the girls who died. I think she's trying to—"

The monitor next to Marshall's bed sounds an alarm. He leans forward, holding onto his shoulder and gasping for breath.

I've said too much. I spiked his heart rate with my crazy stories. Marshall falls back, pale as the pillow he's lying on. A thunder of feet sounds in the hallway. Two nurses then a doctor come running in. One is pushing a cart.

They swarm Marshall's bed so I can't see him anymore.

"Marshall!" I try to yell his name, but it comes out as more of a whisper.

One of the nurses sees me. "You can't be in here." She grabs my hand, pulling me away from him.

"No! I have to—" They roll him to one side as I fight to see if he's okay. Between the crowd of doctors and nurses I see a tattoo on Marshall's back, one I've never seen before. I recognize it immediately—intertwined Ts, a rose with a thorn, and a drop of blood.

Chapter Forty-Two

"He'll be fine," Dad says when he comes back into my room. His blood pressure bottomed out. They think there might have been a blood clot. They're running some tests." He slumps on a chair at the far corner of the room. "I suppose it's not going to do any good to ask you why you went up there."

"I just wanted to make sure he was okay," I say.

"Focus on being okay yourself," Mom says. "I nearly coded too when I walked in here and you were gone. At least you left us a note this time."

"At least," Dad grumbles.

I reach for the paper and pen I used for the note and draw as fast as I can.

A nurse comes in with a little paper cup. "Someone told me that one of my patients has been wandering around the hospital." Her voice is cheerful and grates on my nerves like bone on bone.

"It won't happen again." Dad's statement is more of a threat than a promise.

"I hope not." She hands me the little cup. "This will help you relax, so your lungs will heal." I tip back the pills into my mouth because everyone is watching me. "Well, that's an interesting design." The nurse leans toward the drawing I made. It's the closest approximation I can make of the drawing on the underside of the bunk in the cabin.

"Thanks." I fill in the shading and then hold it up so Dad can see. "Have you ever seen this before?"

Dad looks at me like I'm crazy, but he gets up, crosses the room, and studies the picture anyway. "It looks a lot like the tattoo Marshall has on his back."

We should get matching tattoos.

"When did he get that tattoo?" I ask.

Dad looks perplexed, like he doesn't know why I'm asking, or if he should answer. "When he was nineteen, I think. He had it when he came home after being away for the summer."

"Where was he that summer?" My voice sounds hollow and far away.

Dad sighs like he's humoring me. "Different summer work. I'm not sure if it was the summer he worked with a carnival or the summer he worked at some kind of youth camp."

I lie back on the pillow. My head spins, calculating the years. His nineteenth summer. It would have been the same summer that Amber and Tiffany died.

Marshall.

It can't be him. It has to be a coincidence. But too many pieces fit. The coroner's report said Tiffany had a tattoo on her left shoulder, just like Marshall's. Marshall was there the night Kari drowned. He went down into the ravine to rescue Ron. Ron, who Adam was sure was still alive after his fall. But Marshall saved Bianca.

He saved her after Remy said she lied.

And the woman in the building. The one who was so scared that her panic led me right to her. Marshall was bent over her when I found him.

We have to find him.

Remy, or Tiffany wanted me to find Marshall last night, not because he was in danger, but because someone else was in danger because of him. It's horrible and twisted and doesn't make any sense. I can't process it now. I'm so, so tired. My chest hurts. My head hurts. My mind is getting fuzzy. The pill. Something to help me relax ... right.

Rain pours down my face, but I can't feel it. I'm standing alone next to a smashed guardrail. Below me is Tanner's car, crushed against a tree. Through the cracked and rain-streaked windshield I see him moving. I try to leave, but whatever I took to help me relax makes it too hard to pull myself out of the vision.

Headlights come behind me, a familiar truck pulls over and parks at the side of the road. I hold my breath as Marshall steps out. He leaves the door open and leans against the guardrail, taking in the accident scene below him. He picks up his phone like he's contemplating something. Then he shoves it in his pocket and pulls his climbing gear out of the truck. He puts it on, secures his rope to the guardrail and then starts to climb down. He looks up once and I see the intensity in his eyes: a look of determination mixed with something like regret.

It hits me with a flood of icy horror. He's climbing down the cliff, not to save Tanner, but to kill him. I have to stop him. I slip and slide down the muddy ravine until I'm next to Marshall.

"Stop," I scream in his face. He keeps climbing down. "Stop!"

He can't hear me or see me. In frustration, I reach for him and dig my fingers into his shoulder. I expect the vision to evaporate, like it always does when I touch one of them, but I'm still here. Marshall isn't dead. This isn't his memory. He can't feel me, but I cling to him anyway, screaming myself hoarse. "How could you kill my friend? How could you kill any of them?"

He reaches the door to the car and then he does something I don't expect. He stops, his hand against the side of the car and reaches into his pocket. He pulls out a wrinkled piece of paper. The colors fade and run in the rain, but I know what it is.

My fault.

Right after the middle school dance, when I was hurt and angry at Tanner for calling me a freak, I painted a picture of him. I wanted to hurt him as much as he hurt me. In the picture his face is bloody, his eyes are closed. He looks dead. When my anger cooled, I shoved it in a far corner of my drawer and forgot about it.

Marshall must have found it.

Through the car window Tanner turns. His face lights up in relief when he sees Marshall. I can't watch anymore. I know what comes next.

Chapter Forty-Three

"He killed him. He killed him. He killed him." I'm sobbing into my pillow on the hospital bed. "It was my fault. All my fault."

"It's okay honey." The voice is unfamiliar. I look up to see a nurse standing over me. "You were having a bad dream."

"No. He killed them. He killed them all, Tanner, and Kari, and the woman in the church, and Ron, and the woman in the building last night. He's done it before and he'll do it again."

The nurse exchanges a look with a doctor who just walked in. The doctor sits down next to my bed. "Who killed them?"

My throat closes over. I can't say his name. I can't tell them what he's done.

The doctor waits, but I can't make myself tell her. Maybe I could tell Mom or Dad, but I can't tell a stranger what he did.

You have to tell them. You have to do what I couldn't do.

Her voice is faint, but I follow it to the corner of the room. She's standing in the dark, her face veiled in dark hair and shame. Now I understand why I couldn't ever see Marshall's face in the vision. The memories were hers to share and she couldn't give him up either.

My mind is still fuzzy from the drugs or the vision or both. I forget where I am, and that I'm with people I don't know. I stare at the figure in the corner that only I can see. "How could you protect him after everything he did?"

"Miranda, who are you talking to?" The doctor's eyes scan the corner of the room. "Can you tell me what you're seeing?"

I ignore the doctor as I strain to hear Tiffany's whispered confessions.

I didn't know what he was. I didn't know what he wanted from me. I thought he loved me.

The vision around the campfire suddenly makes sense. "You lied. You lied about Amber in the game because you were jealous of her. Then he killed her."

He thought what I saw gave him the right to kill them. That they were supposed to die anyway, so what he did wasn't wrong. He's been looking for someone like me ever since I took myself out of the equation.

"Remy." I sink my head into my hands. He knows that Remy sees people who are going to die, just like Tiffany did. He knows because I told him.

He'll use her. Now that he knows, he won't ever let her go.

Tiffany tried to keep me from telling him about Remy. First when she left the mark on the painting and then when she made Marshall's blood pressure bottom out. But I gave her secret away anyway. "How do I keep her safe?"

Find her. Find her before he does.

The doctor speaks. "Miranda, can you tell me who you're talking to? Can you tell me what you see?"

I look back to the corner, but Tiffany has faded into the shadows. I try to focus on the doctor's face, but she's the one that doesn't seem real. Her face is wavy and blurred by the fog in my head.

"I know these things seem real to you right now Miranda, but we're here to help. We'd like to move you to a different room for the rest of your recovery. Your parents have agreed, but we need you to sign some paperwork. We'll probably be able to get a court order to have you kept here, but it would be so much easier if you'd just agree."

He's going to find her.

"No!" I push the pen away.

He'll use her until there's nothing left. Until she only has one choice.

"I have to find Remy. I have to warn her."

"Miranda, please calm down," the doctor says. She motions to the nurse standing by the door.

"Where are my parents? I'm not signing anything without my parents here."

The nurse steps out and comes back with my mom and dad. Their faces are pinched with worry and shadows of betrayal darken their eyes.

"We're here," Mom says, leaning over the bed. "We're here, baby. We'll make sure you get the help you need. We're with you all the way."

"Mom, you have to listen to me. The visions are as real as they've ever been. You told me this was a gift. You told me I should use my gift to help people. I have to help Remy. I have to save her from—"

Marshall is standing in the doorway. I shrink to the corner of the bed. He doesn't seem to notice my reaction. "Hey. I just stopped by to see how you're doing."

"Marshall, how are you here?" Dad says.

"It was a false alarm. The machines somehow went haywire. I thought I saw ... I'm fine. How's Miranda?" He moves closer. I try to make myself smaller. All I can see is his face in the window of Tanner's car. All I can see is a murderer. I should tell everyone what he is, but the doctor is watching me. Everyone is watching me. They wouldn't believe me.

"We were just talking about that," the doctor says. "But it's a private discussion."

Marshall flashes my dad a look of genuine concern. "It's okay, Marshall. I'll tell you everything at home. I'm glad they're going to let you leave. Can I call someone to pick you up? I can't leave Miranda right now."

Marshall looks from Mom to Dad to the doctors to me. "No, I'm fine. Kasey's coming to pick me up."

I reach to stop him. "No. You can't. You have to—"

"Get well, Rand. I'll see you soon." Marshall touches my cheek and then smiles.

Murderer. Murderer. Murderer.

But I feel more than hatred and vitriol coming from the spirit inside my mind. It takes a second to recognize the other emotion—jealousy. Despite everything he did to her, Tiffany's lost soul still clings to Marshall.

Chapter Forty-Four

Observation.

I'm being watched for the next twenty-four hours. Closely. Luckily there isn't a bed "downstairs" in the psych ward yet, and ironically my regular doctor wants to continue his observation up here to make sure my singed lungs are okay. I'm being double observed, but at least for now it's in a regular hospital room. It still feels like a prison.

I'm desperate to get out of the hospital and get to Remy or at least warn Adam. Mom's phone is poking out of her purse about a foot from the edge of my bed. Mom and Dad are at the little bedside table discussing details with the doctor. I'm supposed to be part of this little council, but right now they're talking around and about me and not to me.

They might be too busy talking about me to notice what I'm doing. I lie on my side, casually, like I'm tired. All the while I'm inching my fingers down the side of my bed toward Mom's purse and my only link to the outside world.

"How long would you say these hallucinations have been going on?" the doctor asks.

I freeze, my fingers gripping the edge of the sheets. I consider a lie that would make me look less crazy, but I really don't have the brain power to come up with one. "My whole life." I say it like a prisoner holding her ground in an interrogation. "My dad can tell you about the little girl I saw when I was four."

My distraction works. Dad is left to explain something he's wanted to forget his whole life. The first time I told someone I'd seen a ghost. While he hems and haws the story of the little girl whose funeral I interrupted by telling her parents I'd played with her the night before, I finish my descent into Mom's purse. I squeeze her phone between my fingers and slide it up the side of the bed until I can slip it between the edge of the sheet and the mattress, tucking it in so it won't fall. No one notices. Now I just have to find a moment of my observation when no one is observing me to call Adam.

My parents talk to the doctor for what seems like hours. I answer questions whenever I'm asked, but don't volunteer any information. I think I'm truly going to go crazy when the doctor finally stands. "We can start moving her things to the psych floor tomorrow morning." She hands my mom a piece of paper. "This is a list of the 'can' and the 'cannot' haves for Miranda while she's under our care. You might want to go home and get her a couple of changes of clothing to take down with her."

"But I thought this was just a twenty-four-hour observation," Mom says.

The nurse gives the doctor a look that screams family in denial.

"I can get her things," Dad says. "Why don't you stay with Miranda?"

"I don't need her to stay." I need them all gone. "I mean, I want Mom to pick out my things. Am I allowed to bring my paints?"

"Not in the beginning. We have therapeutic art classes, but personal items need to be earned." Everything the doctor is saying reeks of "long-term imprisonment" instead of "observation." My parents don't seem to catch it, or they've already decided that having me committed is the best option.

I have to get a message to Adam, now. "I need to pee."

My parents look at the doctor as if to ask if that's okay. She waves me on. "Certainly. We need a urine sample anyway. This will save you having to do it later." The nurse produces a white bottle as if she's been waiting for this moment the whole time.

I slip Mom's phone into the bra I probably won't be allowed to wear downstairs. The doctor explains to my parents in a not-hushed-enough voice that the sample is to check for things like drug use or pregnancy. I take the bottle, mortified, and go into the bathroom.

As soon as the door is closed I start typing as fast as I can, hoping Adam can forgive me for what happened with Remy, hoping he doesn't completely hate me.

> Adam, this is Miranda. Do you have Remy with you?

I wait forever, sweating in the bathroom, imagining my parents and the doctor discussing me and wondering why I'm taking so long. I try again:

> Don't let her out of your sight. Don't leave her alone with Marshall.

He still doesn't answer.

> I can't explain now. Just please believe me. I might not be able to talk to you again for a while. I'm sorry for all the crazy things I put you through. I'm sorry for putting you and Remy in danger. I hope …

But I'm not sure what I hope as far as Adam is concerned anymore.

I finish with:

I hope you'll give me the chance to explain all of
this.

I hit send and stare at the phone forever, waiting for an
answer or for three dots or anything to indicate that he got
my message.

Nothing comes.

Mom knocks at the door. "Are you okay in there?"

"Sorry. It's hard to pee on demand." I'm surprised at the
crack in my voice. I reach up and brush away stupid tears I
didn't know were sliding down my cheeks. How did I get
myself into this mess? Why did I ever leave my room? Why did
I make a connection with Adam and with Remy? It's my fault
Marshall found her. Now my parents, even Mom, think I'm
crazy. Maybe they're right. More tears come. I let myself slip
into a puddle of self-pity. It feels like I've lost everything, and
tomorrow morning I'll lose the freedom I never wanted.

"Baby, are you okay?" Mom says. I can tell she's leaning
against the door. I let the silence sit between us. "Miranda?"

I want to scream at her that I'm not okay. I want to ask her
why she suddenly can't accept who I am and what I see. I just
want to go home and curl up in my room with my paintings
and my benign nighttime visitors and my stupid online
homework. Maybe if I promise to never leave the house again
they won't make me stay in this place.

"Everyone else is gone. You can come out."

I can't decide if Mom is lying to get me to leave the
bathroom. I take a couple of deep breaths, slip the phone
behind the garbage can, and then slowly open the door.

"I'm so sorry, baby." Mom folds me in her arms, but I stiffen.
Dad, the doctor, and the nurse have all cleared out, but I'm not
sure I can trust Mom. I feel like they're listening, just outside
the door, probably a sign that I'm paranoid.

I pull away from her. "Why are you doing this? You're the
one person who's never treated me like a freak."

"Dad." She shakes her head. "No, this is from both of us. We
were terrified when they told us that you had run into a
burning building. Whatever the ghosts, or the spirits, or the

voices in your head are telling you, it's gotten out of hand. Maybe it's time we controlled them with … other means."

"You mean you want to pump me full of drugs until everything I am is gone."

"I just want you to be safe," Mom says.

"Perfect. Lock me in a hospital. That should do the trick. But wait, I thought I was supposed to pretend to be a normal teenager?"

"Miranda, I—"

"What if locking me in a hospital means other people are in danger? What then?"

"Why do you think being in the hospital will put other people in danger?" Mom says the words slowly like she has to consider each one carefully.

I breathe out. Anything I tell her now without proof will just make me sound crazier.

She breaks in before I can think of what to say. "I know you think you see things, or hear things … even I thought … but the truth is … I …"

"The truth is you've never believed me. Or you believed me when it was a cute, convenient fairy tale, but now that it's more than that, now that I can actually use my gift to help someone else, to save someone else, then it's all in my head."

She lowers her head like she's ashamed. "I'm sorry, baby. I only want you to be safe."

I pick up the list of acceptable items from the bedside table. "You'd better go, then. You need to go through all of my things and decide which of my things I can still be trusted with. Pro tip, real underwear and shoelaces are 'out' for crazy people."

Chapter Forty-Five

I'm standing on a metal bridge. It's night, but the moon is bright and reflects off the dark water below, so far below me. The wind blows my hair into my face—black with tips of blue. I brush it away, hard, as if my stupid hair was the cause of all of this. When I had it colored I thought I was being brave, like a new hairstyle and a tattoo would make me stronger. Turns out it was just another cover for my weakness. I step closer to the edge. I know what I have to do, but I'm not ready yet.

I'm waiting. I need to know that he cares, cares enough to understand what the picture I left on his bed meant. That he cares enough to come find me. I have to know if I meant anything to him. If I'm being honest, I want him to be here to witness what he's done to me. I want him to feel pain and regret. I want him to be sorry for what he's done, the way he's never been sorry for anything.

Headlights chase away the shadows around me. His truck announces itself with a rattle of metal as it crosses onto the bridge. Despite where I'm standing and what I'm planning, I smile. From the deck below, I must look like a ghost.

Ironic.

He stops just below me. I wait for him to climb up the bridge, hating the flutter in my stomach that comes even now that I know exactly what he is.

"Tiff!" He calls up to me. "Baby, what are you doing?"

I don't turn around. "I won't let you use me anymore. I won't let you use me as an excuse to kill."

His feet clang against the metal girders as he climbs up to me. "They were all supposed to die. You saw it. I was just—"

"No!" Red hot anger flares, and I turn on him. "Don't try to justify what you are to me. Do not try to pretend you're anything more than a cold-blooded killer!"

He doesn't even flinch. He reaches his hand toward me. "Let me help you down. It's cold out here. Let's go somewhere warm and talk about all of this."

I shake my head, pushing against the control he's always held over me. "Not this time. It's over."

His calm expression melts into near-panic, like he just realized I'm serious. He inches closer to me, still reaching out to stop me. "Don't do this. I'll never find anyone else like you."

"That's what I'm counting on." I release my grip on the metal ropes and step backward, my eyes locked on his.

My own scream wakes me up. I'm back in the hospital bed, the sheets and my hair dripping with sweat as if my plunge into the river were real.

"Tiffany?" I whisper into the dark.

A blue light shines through the sheets. I reach for my mom's phone, holding it up to read the text that just came through. The two words Adam typed fill me with more terror than the vision I woke up from.

She's gone.

I text back:

How? When? Where?

I don't know. I fell asleep on the couch and when I went in to check on her, her bed was empty.

Call the police. Tell them

But what proof do we have that Marshall is anything more
than what everyone thinks he is?
I erase the text and start over.

I'm coming to help you find her.

Aren't you still in the hospital?

I'll find a way out.

I climb out of the bed and go to the bathroom. Quietly, yet
frantically, I pull on my regular clothes. Getting out might be
hard tonight, but if I wait any longer it will be impossible. I
should have left sooner, as soon as it got dark.

No.

The one-word text stops me. My shirt hangs half over my
shoulder.
He adds:

You've done enough.

I sink onto the toilet in the bathroom. His words sting as if
he had slapped me. He blames me for all of this. I'm frozen
with indecision. The police can find Remy. Running out in the
middle of the night is a sure way to ensure my parents will
keep me locked up until I'm thirty.
She needs you.

It's not Tiffany, just an echo of the words she used on me before. Except those words were. They need you. But Adam obviously doesn't need me.

I stand up. This was never about Adam. This was never about anyone but Remy, Tiffany, and me. We all share a gift, or a curse. Tiffany is dead. No one is going to be able to help Remy but me.

Chapter Forty-Six

I slip my mom's phone into my pocket, make my bed up to look like I'm still in it, and then sneak into the hallway. The hall isn't dark, but it is quiet. A couple of nurses are at the desk between the elevator and the sign for the stairway. I'm going to have to get past those nurses to go either way. I duck behind a linen cart. It's tall enough that I might be able to hide behind it, push my way past the nurse's station and toward the stairs.

The linen cart has one squeaky wheel. I push it a few steps, squeak, squeak, squeak—then I stop. This is going to take forever. I need a distraction. "Tiffany, Tiffany," I whisper. No answer, not even the feeling of her being near. Names may have power, but I guess that doesn't mean I can call her on demand. I remember the distraction she used in Marshall's room. Some kind of ventilator is plugged into the wall to charge. There's a red switch on the side of it that says, "alarm."

I park the cart next to the wall and crouch behind the machine. I visualize my escape route in my mind, considering how fast I can get past the nurse's station and down the hall to the stairs. I take a deep breath and reach for the switch.

As soon as I touch it, the machine screeches to life. If I was trying to sneak out and be inconspicuous, I choose the wrong way to do it. It takes me a second to react and remember my plan. The nurses hurry toward me. I flatten against the wall, preparing to run. They run past me. The alarm isn't from the machine next to me after all. The sound comes from a room a few doors down the hall.

As soon as the nurses pass, I walk, not too fast, but fast enough, toward the stairs. Another nurse steps out of a room as I walk by. "Can I help you? Where are you supposed to be?" I break into a run for the elevator, but at the last second slip through the doors marked "stairs."

I run down one, two and a half flights of stairs. My own footsteps are so loud that I can't tell if anyone is following me. I pause, panting for breath and check behind me. I'm face to face with a man in a uniform.

"Where do you think you're going?"

I try to come up with an excuse, but I can only stand with my mouth half-open, gaping at him.

His eyes soften in recognition. "Katherine, is that you?"

I stare at him. His face breaks into a wide grin. "It is you. I knew you'd come. I knew you'd forgive me."

I study his uniform. He's not a cop or a security guard. His jacket looks more like an old pilot's uniform. Like something from the Vietnam war. There was a man in the hall in a wheelchair earlier today. He was wearing a hat that said "Vietnam Vet" on it. The man in front of me is the reason for the alarm. He must have died. He thinks I'm Katherine, whoever she was.

"That girl didn't mean anything to me. It was war. That's not an excuse, I know, but things were different, more stressful." He hangs his head. "What I did was inexcusable. I deserved for you to leave me, but ..." His eyes raise, hopeful. "If we could just go back to the beginning. Like we just met."

"Like nothing before ever happened?" I find myself falling into the role he needs.

"That's not fair either. Is it?"

"No. It's not."

Above me, I hear the clattering of footsteps.

The man doesn't notice them. "Kat, I just need you to know, I never stopped loving you." A real security guard rounds the corner above me. I don't have time to think. I run straight into the ghost.

"Katherine!" The man dissipates like a puff of smoke as I pass through him.

On the bottom floor, I burst through the door. Two women in scrubs are sitting on the sidewalk, talking and smoking. They barely spare me a glance, like they're used to crazy things happening in the hospital at night.

There's a little garden with a path in it to the side of the building. I run until I'm sure no one is following me. I stop to catch my breath. My lungs are burning and ragged. I take my mom's phone out. As mad as I am at my parents I can't let them worry. I compose a text to my dad:

> I'm okay and I'll come home as soon as I can, but first there's someone I have to help.

After a few heartbeats I add:

> I love you.

I don't want to have any regrets in case this goes badly.

Chapter Forty-Seven

It's still dark when I reach the house. The lights are all off and Adam's car and his aunt's car are both gone. I go to the front door and rattle the handle. The door is locked. I walk around the house until I see a half-opened window in the back. I push out the screen with a loud screech. I hold my breath, waiting for someone to come check the noise. No one does. I climb through the window and into a bedroom. The room is dark.

"Adam?" I call softly. "Remy? Kasey?"

No one answers. There's a bed and a little desk, piled with drawings: Remy's drawings. I pick them up, afraid to see what she's drawn. Even in the dim moonlight the faces are familiar. She must have drawn all of them more than once. She has pictures of Kari, the old woman, Ron, and another woman I don't recognize. I assume it's the woman who died in the fire. The pictures are interspersed with more innocuous ones: an apple tree, a rainbow, a gray kitten. I'm almost to the bottom of a pile when I find a drawing that makes me gasp. The face peeking out from the car window is crude and cartoony, but there's no mistaking the vanity plates—T-MAN.

I whisper his name out loud. "Tanner."

He died months before they came here. How could she know? Even with everything I've seen, I can't wrap my head around this one. The room suddenly feels warmer. There's a familiar scent in the air—like the school locker room, faintly covered by sandalwood cologne. Eyes bore into the back of my neck.

"Rand."

I spin around at the sound of my name. Even though his voice is as familiar as his scent, I'm still shocked when I see his face. "Tanner?" He nods. "But you're ..."

"Dead, apparently." He says the words like he wants me to correct him, but he knows it's the truth. "That's what you said, isn't it?"

"Yeah."

He's quiet for a long time, like he's taking it all in. "Then why am I still here?"

I step toward him and then stop, not wanting him to leave. "I don't know. I think it has something to do with the way you died."

"I wasn't supposed to die." His voice is thick with regret.

"I know."

He looks so downtrodden and defeated that I wish I could wrap my arms around him. I want to say something that would help, but how do you take back a death that wasn't supposed to happen?

"What do you remember?" I ask.

He shakes his head. "Not a lot, the last few days ..." He trails off, waiting for me to help him.

"Months," I supply.

"Months." He repeats it like he can't believe it's been so long. "The last few months have been like walking through a dream. I saw my mom, I saw Brie, but none of them saw me. Only you. Why can you still see me?"

"I don't know. I've always been able to see people who aren't all the way gone yet. Remember, that's what makes me a freak."

He cringes at the word. "Look, Rand, I'm sorry for—"

I don't have time for his apologies. "Tanner, I need your help. I need to find a little girl before something bad happens to her. Can you help me find her?"

"I don't know. I'm not even sure how I ended up here." He looks around him. "Or even where I am. Usually I can only go places where I've been before."

"I think I called you here. I said your name and then you were here."

"Then why don't you call her name?" Tanner says it like it's the easiest thing in the world.

"She's not dead. I'm not sure how—"

The front door rattles and I step back into the gap between the desk and Remy's bed. Tanner fades into the shadows by the window until all that's left of him is a dark formless shape. The bedroom door is open, but I don't have time to close it. Adam steps into the kitchen. He sets his keys and phone on the counter. He opens the fridge and then closes it again. He slumps into a chair and rests his head in his hands. His hair is disheveled and his eyes are rimmed in red.

His phone rings. He pushes the button for the speakerphone, and stares down at it.

"Adam?" His aunt's voice is shaky.

"She's not back home. I'm going to go check the woods and the park."

The voice on the other end gains strength. "Stay put in case she comes back. I can check those places with Marshall."

"Why is he even part of this?" Adam snaps into the phone. "Miranda said we can't trus—"

"You know Miranda isn't … isn't well."

"I don't believe that. It's been two hours. Have you called the police yet?"

There's a long pause on the other end of the phone. "You know why I can't do that."

"Then let me help. If anyone should be out looking, it should be me. I'm her brother and—"

"Stay there!" the voice on the other end commands. "I don't want to have two missing kids."

Adam hangs up his phone and slams his hand down so hard on the cabinet that it makes me jump. For a second he seems to see me as he stares through the door into Remy's room. He shakes his head, goes back to the fridge, and gets himself a soda. He sits back down, pulls a piece of paper from his pocket, and lays it on the counter in front of him. "Meri, where are you? What did you see? Tell me how I can stop it. Tell me how I can find you."

"Meri?" I say the name out loud and stand up so he can see me. "Who is Meri?"

Adam jumps and spins around. "Miranda! How did you ... why are you ...?" He looks down at the bracelet still on my wrist. "You ran away from the hospital."

"Yes. I did." I move closer to him. He stuffs the paper he was looking at into his pocket. "Who is Meri?"

"I told you not to come." He won't look me in the eye.

"I didn't come for you. I came for Remy. We need to find her before he, before he ..." But how can I explain to Adam what Marshall wants from Remy?

He crosses the room to me, blocking me in Remy's room. "Before he what? You said that Marshall took her. Why? And how are you so sure it was him? My aunt said he was home in bed recovering from his surgery when she called him. He got up and went to help her search. She said you were ... that you see things that aren't real. But you knew my sister was in danger. And you ... you know more than you should. About a lot of things."

I take a deep breath and glance toward the corner where Tanner was. He's gone, not that he would have been able to back up my story. I guess if I'm going to be put away for being crazy, I might as well make it good. "What do you know about the pictures Remy draws?" I indicate the pile on the desk. "What do you know about the people she draws?"

He hesitates, like he's considering whether to trust me. He slides his hand into his pocket and for a second I think he's going to take out the paper he put there. Instead he folds his hands on the counter in front of him. "When she was like five or six, we had this neighbor, Mrs. Harris, who was really old, probably over eighty. Remy used to go play on the swing Mrs. Harris had in the backyard while I did jobs around the house. Mrs. Harris paid me pretty well and she always gave Remy cookies. She was really nice to both of us.

"One morning Remy came into the kitchen and started drawing with her crayons. She drew a picture of an old lady, lying down, next to a blue mug that was missing the handle. There was something brown spilled all around her. When I asked Remy who it was, she said it was Mrs. Harris, and that she was going to go see her husband. I really didn't think very much about it. Mrs. Harris had been fine when I'd raked her leaves that afternoon.

"She'd asked me to come back and help her carry some boxes downstairs the next morning, but when I went to her door the next day, no one answered. I went around to the back. Through the porch window, I saw Mrs. Harris lying on the floor. By her hand was a blue coffee mug with the handle broken off. Her coffee had spilled all around her. My aunt said Mrs. Harris died of a heart attack. I didn't dare tell her about Remy's drawing. I thought it was just a crazy coincidence."

He leans against the counter, fear and exhaustion stamped into his face. "But it happened again and again. Sometimes it was just a cat, like Puffers, and sometimes it was a stranger, someone we didn't know about until we saw their picture on the news. Sometimes she just drew people and I never knew if they had died or not. Remy's drawings got better and it was harder to pretend that the people she drew were just a coincidence, even for my aunt. Then last year, Remy drew a picture while she was at school. It was a picture of a police officer, one who was shot and killed during a traffic stop the next day. There was no mistaking who he was. She had written his name on the badge. His daughter was in her class."

I close my eyes against the pain in his voice.

"The cop had been targeted for the hit and they couldn't find the person who shot him. Somehow the picture got out and someone decided that me or my aunt knew something about what happened to him. There was no connection and no proof, but people were weird around all of us after that. Then my dad showed up. We hadn't seen him for years, but he said he wanted us back. That he was going to fight for custody. I think he heard what Remy could do and figured he could make some money off her visions. My aunt freaked and moved us here." He pauses for a breath. "But none of that explains why Marshall wants my sister."

"Actually. It does." I say. "Remy sees how people die. She's exactly what he's been looking for."

"So you believe me? You believe that Remy sees people before they die?"

I almost laugh at the look on his face, like he's shocked that someone actually listened to his story without telling him he was crazy. "Of course I believe you. I've seen what she's seen. I see them too."

His eyes get wide. "You see people who are about to die?"

"Not until recently. It used to be just people who were already dead. People on their way out. They share their memories with me." I brace myself for Adam to tell me everyone is right, that I am crazy, or at least for that "freak" look to pass over his face.

His expression looks more studious than skeptical, like he's trying to put the pieces together. "But you don't see them before they die, not like Remy does."

"I didn't until ... until she shared her visions with me."

"Shared ... her visions with you?"

"I can't explain it. But she can show me the things she sees. The night Kari died was the first time I'd seen someone die." I look back at Adam. "That all sounds pretty crazy right? Kind of explains why my parents want to lock me up in a psych ward."

He's shaking his head. "If I hadn't seen the proof, if I hadn't lived with Remy and seen what she could do all this time ... but I didn't understand it. I didn't know she saw the people die, I just thought she saw faces and then she drew them."

"I can't imagine what it's like for her to see those things. To see how someone is going to die and not be able to do anything to stop it. Or actually, I can imagine, because she's shown me."

Adam puts his hand over his pocket again, like he's protecting whatever he put there. "So how does your uncle fit into all of this? You said she's exactly what he's been looking for. How do you know that?"

It takes another deep breath for me to delve into the next layer of insanity. "This has happened before. All these deaths: Kari, Ron, even the woman in the fire, they look like accidents, but they aren't. About twenty years ago, the same thing happened. There was a girl then too, someone like Remy, who could see who was going to die and how. She was Marshall's girlfriend. He found out what she could do and he used her to figure out who he should kill. She said what she saw gave him permission to kill them, because they were meant to die anyway."

"Permission to kill them?"

"I think in some twisted way it relieved his conscience, like if those people were supposed to die anyway, then he's not doing anything wrong by killing them."

"And you think he's the one who killed Kari, and Ron and ..."

"And maybe a lot of other people."

"If we know Marshall is the killer, why don't we just go to the police?"

"And tell them what? We have no proof Marshall did anything, now or then."

"What about the other girl? Where is she now? If we could talk to her she's all the proof we need to get to Marshall. She can tell the police what he did before."

I shake my head. "She's gone. She said she couldn't let him use her like that anymore, so she killed herself."

"Wait, this happened twenty years ago, and she just barely killed herself?"

"She killed herself when she was seventeen."

"But you just said she told you ..."

I breathe out, hoping he stays with me for at least one more crazy revelation. "Not everyone who dies moves on right away."

"The girl who can't leave," Adam says. He lets out a long slow breath as another layer settles onto his shoulders.

"Yeah. She's been hanging around me, and apparently around Remy for a while now, hoping we could stop him. Her name is ... was Tiffany. Marshall has been looking for someone like her ever since she died. That's why ..." I trail off, understanding for the first time why Marshall always favored me, why he spent so much time with me, why he was so interested in what I saw, how I felt, what I painted. Betrayal cuts through my chest like a knife, so painful that I actually double over.

"Are you okay?" Adam puts his hand on my back. I turn and see the concern in his eyes. I remember what it felt like to kiss him and feel like he cared, before I chose Marshall, the killer, over him. "Maybe you need to rest. You just got out of the hospital."

"I'm fine." I stand up straight and pull away. Connections for either of us are a bad idea right now.

I see something like hurt flash in his eyes, but he steps back. "So why does Marshall want Remy?"

"He figured out it wasn't me who drew all those pictures. He knows it was her. He knows she sees people who are going to die." I can't bring myself to tell Adam I was the one that gave away Remy's secret.

"So how do we find him? How do we keep him from killing the next person Remy draws?"

"That part I'm not sure of. The good thing for Remy is he's not going to hurt her. He needs her to tell him who's supposed to die."

Adam stays silent for a long time. He reaches into his pocket, touching the paper he put there. "What if she's already drawn the person who's supposed to die next?"

"Then we need to find that person. Bianca proved that someone can be saved even after Remy predicts their death."

"Marshall saved Bianca," Adam points out.

"Because he heard Remy say she lied about Bianca dying. But it doesn't matter. If we can figure out who's next and then find that person, we might be able to save them. "

"Finding her isn't going to be hard." Adam pulls the paper out of his pocket. He spreads it out on the table. I lean close, then jump back. It's a picture of me. My hair is dripping wet. I'm in the center of dark water. My mouth is open in a scream, just like Kari. Adam meets my eyes. "It's keeping you safe that I'm worried about."

Chapter Forty-Eight

The room is dark and smells like pine trees, sweaty socks, and dank musty wood. A little girl in a white nightgown is curled up on the floor, hugging her knees and crying. I know it's Remy, but I can't get to her. It's like I'm trapped on the other side of a wall of glass. She can't see me or hear me. I can't help her.

I try to smash the barrier between us, beating at it with my fists. "Remy!"

I open my eyes. Adam is standing over me. It takes me a minute to remember how I ended up sitting on the floor in his room. It was his idea to try to contact Remy. I almost did, but there's something about the space between us that I can't cross.

"Did you find her?" he says.

Before I can answer, the outside door opens. Voices come from the next room. "We'll find her." Marshall says to Adam's aunt. His voice is liquid sympathy coated with honey. Even though I know he's lying I can't pick out the deception.

"I promised my sister I'd keep her safe. And now I've let him get to her." Kasey's voice is thick with tears. I imagine Marshall wrapping his arms around her and pulling against his chest. I imagine him stroking her hair. The mental image makes me sick, sick and jealous. I look around the room. Tiffany is here somewhere. Her jealousy and rage is almost palpable, even if I can't see her.

"You let who get to her?" Marshall asks.

"The kids' dad. I know he's the one who took her. We ran from Canada to get away from him. We left everything—my job, our house, the kids' school." Kasey's voice wavers. "I made the kids change their names."

Something clicks in my mind. Names have power.

She starts sobbing. "But it didn't do any good. He still found us."

"You need to pull yourself together," Marshall says. "I think it's time you went to the police and told them everything about Remy's dad. It's more important that we find her now. You can sort out the legalities of who should have custody of the kids later."

"You're right," Kasey says. "Of course you're right. I was stupid to think we'd be safe here."

I turn to Adam. He's listening as intently as I am. His hands are balled into fists. I put my hand on his arm, trying to loosen the tension with my touch.

Marshall's voice is muffled, as if he has his face buried in her neck. "Don't be so hard on yourself. You call the police. I'll go out again. We won't stop until we find her. I promise." I hold my breath until the door opens and closes and I hear Marshall's truck start. Probably going wherever he's keeping her.

An idea comes to me. "Tanner, Tanner can you follow Marshall?"

Adam looks at me like I am crazy. "Who's Tanner?"

But I'm listening to the voice he can't hear.

"I'm not sure." Tanner says. "I've never tried to follow anyone."

"Try. Please. Go after her. Tell Remy we're coming. She'll be able to see you. She'll be able to talk to you."

"I'll try." His answer is a fading whisper.

"Thank you." I say, but he's already gone.

"Miranda, who are you—" Adam starts.

"What's your sister's real name?"

"Her real name?"

"Your aunt said she made you change your names. What was Remy's name before you came here?"

"Meri, Amerie." He says the name with a little bit of a French accent I hadn't noticed from him before. "Is that important?"

"Very." I close my eyes, trying to recapture the vision—wood floors, musty smell, Remy crouched in the corner.

"Amerie, Amerie." The vision comes back in sharper focus. A cabin, a wood floor, Drawings on the bottom of the bunk bed. Remy turns her head. "Rand?"

I smile. "We're coming to find you."

Her face twists in panic. "No, Rand, you can't come here."

My mind fills with images of gray waves, a faded red canoe. I'm inside it, in the middle of the lake. Something bumps against the boat. I move to the far side as the boat tips. There's something deep in the lake, something dark, just like when Kari died. The boat tips and I'm plunged into the icy water. Something grabs my feet, pulling me down. I thrash against the pull.

My scream shatters the vision into a million pieces.

"What the hell?" The bedroom door bursts open. It's Adam's aunt, standing at the door. "Adam, what is she doing here?"

I'm gasping for breath. My whole body is as cold as if I really had been in the water. I can't stop shaking. Adam wraps his arms around me. "She came to help, help us find Meri."

"No, no, no. She can't be here now. Why would you bring her here?" Kasey is talking about me like I'm not here. "She's not okay." The adrenaline from the vision mixes with rage and boils inside of me. I start to shake with anger instead of cold. I clench my fists until my nails dig into my palms.

"She's supposed to be in the hospital. Marshall told me what's been going on with her." The sound of his name on her lips makes a sick green jealousy churn in my stomach. "It's not safe for her to be here. She needs to go back. We have enough issues with Meri disappearing. We don't need your crazy girlfriend to—"

I stand. A wisp of smoke streaks across the floor. Kasey throws up her hands to defend herself, but it's too late. Her scream is cut off as she's knocked to the floor. She lies still.

I'm not sure if Adam saw the streak of black and blue that flew across the room before Kasey was knocked to the ground. He might even think it was me, but I know exactly who and what attacked Kasey.

Chapter Forty-Nine

"Tiffany!" I scream at her.

For a second her face appears in the mirror, distorted and grinning. "You're welcome." Her image dissipates, but I still hear her voice. "Now go find the little girl. Before he finds you."

Adam bends over his aunt.

"Is she okay?" I ask.

He looks like he's afraid of me, but he nods. "I think so. Who ... what?"

"Tiffany. The girl who can't leave. She has a temper, and ... and apparently she still has a thing for Marshall."

Adam looks at me like the world is shifting out from under his feet. I know how he feels. I'm way more used to this paranormal stuff than he is and it still feels insane to me.

"Are you okay?" Adam says. Kasey moans. "Help me lift her on the bed."

"What was that?" Kasey asks once we have her settled on Adam's bed.

Adam and I exchange a glance, simultaneously deciding that "vengeful ghost" may be the correct answer, but it's the wrong one to give her right now.

"You fell and hit your head," Adam says instead.

"It was you!" She sits up, her face inches from mine. "You did all of this. You're crazy. You're dangerous, just like Marshall said."

"Lie back, calm down," Adam says. He tries to pry Kasey's fingers from my shirt.

"Oh," she moans, her head slumps to the side, and her eyes roll back.

I shake her shoulder. "Kasey, stay with us!" She moans again. She yells at me again. This time her words don't make sense.

I turn to Adam. "Your aunt has a concussion. We need to get her to a hospital."

"I need to find my sister." The intensity in Adam's eyes is scary. "Did you see her? Do you know where she is?"

I don't want to tell him what I saw. I'm still shaking. "I think she's at the camp. In the cabin with the writing on the bottom bunk." I look back at the thrashing woman on the bed. "We need to get Kasey to the hospital."

"Call an ambulance and then stay with her. I'm going to get my sister."

"I don't think you should go alone. I'll—" But the image of my death is etched in my mind.

"No. You stay here. I'll go after Remy. If Marshall has seen what she drew ..." He trails off, but I know what he's thinking.

I can't tell him what Remy showed me. I fight back the panicked feeling that I'm drowning. "We shouldn't split up. We can call the ambulance, and then we can both go."

"Look, if your theory is true, Marshall won't hurt me because I'm not meant to die. You stay here. Watch over Kasey. Try to contact Remy or your other friend or ... whatever it is you do. I'm going to go after my sister."

"I don't think it's a good idea for you to go alone."

"And I don't think it's a good idea for you to be going anywhere as long as Marshall's out there." I open my mouth to protest, but he stops me. "You know I'm right."

The coward in me gets the best of me. I nod. "Okay. Promise you'll be safe."

He leans over me, cupping my face with his hand. I expect him to kiss me, but he just runs his finger over my cheekbone, looking at me as if he still can't wrap his head around what I am and what I see.

I lean into his hand. "What's your real name?"

He shakes his head. "Adam is better."

"Please tell me. It might be important."

He rolls his eyes, but then he leans down next to my ear. "Andre."

A shiver goes up my spine, as if he just told me something intimate. "Andre." I repeat. "I like it."

He kisses my cheek. "Stay safe, Rand."

"You too, Dre."

Then he's gone.

Chapter Fifty

I look down at the woman on the bed. She's finished yelling horrible but incoherent things to me, and she's slipped into unconsciousness again. "Why don't you act like that around Marshall?" I say to the empty room, even though I know Tiffany has made herself scarce. "Why don't you go after him?"

"Who are you talking to now?" The voice behind me makes my blood run cold.

I turn around to see my uncle, smiling at me. It takes me a second to remember that he doesn't have any idea that our relationship has changed. He doesn't know that I know what he is. He walks over and leans over Adam's bed. "What happened to her?"

"She fell and hit her head. I was going to call for an ambulance."

"But you don't have a phone," Marshall finishes. I realize he's right. I left my mom's phone in the garden by the hospital so they couldn't track me.

"Can you call?" It takes me a few breaths to calm my heartbeat and force my voice to be normal. I can't let him suspect how terrified I am of him.

"No need. I'll check her out." He pulls a flashlight out of his pocket and shines it in Kasey's eye. "Couldn't stay put in the hospital, huh, Miranda?"

"You know I don't belong there."

"Your parents are going insane with worry." He moves his light to Kasey's other eye. "See what I did there? 'Going insane.'" Something in his voice makes me nervous, like he knows more than he's letting on.

"You aren't going to make me go back, are you?"

He laughs. "Why would I do that? Why would I let them lock up My-Rand-a?" It's the nickname he had for me when I was a little kid. "Naw. I have other plans for you."

"Plans?" My voice squeaks.

"You didn't answer my question, My-Rand-a. Who were you talking to when I came in?"

"Kasey," I lie. "I was trying to keep her awake. In case she has a concussion."

"She does," Marshall says. "What exactly did you hit her with?"

"It wasn't me. I didn't do anything to her."

"Your boyfriend, then. What did he do to her?"

"Adam didn't touch her either."

"You're sure." He moves his hand down the side of Kasey's head. "This lump definitely feels like someone hit her with something, and hit her hard." He doesn't turn around, but the tone in his voice changes. "The other thing I'd like to know is, how do you know exactly where Remy is?"

"How I know … what?"

"I heard you and Adam talking through the open window. When I saw his car was still here, I thought you might be with him. Your mom called me, frantic, about an hour ago. I decided to drive away and then double back to see if I could find you." He stands, putting the light back in his pocket. "So how do you know where Remy is?"

I decide it's better to tell the truth than to try to lie to him. "I saw her in a vision. It looked like she was in the cabin Adam and I stayed in, back at the old camp."

He turns around. "You saw a vision of Remy?" He smiles. "That's a bit ironic, don't you think?"

"Why would that be ironic?" I take a step back.

"Because little Remy drew a vision she had about you." He reaches into his pocket. For a strangled heartbeat, I think he's pulling out some kind of weapon. It's just a piece of paper, a drawing nearly identical to the one Adam just showed me. "What do you think about this picture?"

I take the picture with trembling hands. "She's getting better at drawing people."

"I'd say your class has helped her out a lot. It's certainly been educational for me."

I'm eyeing the door, trying to decide what it would take for me to get from this side of the room to the door on the other side. Marshall is twice my size. He'd have me in a second. I'm waiting for the vengeful ghost to come back and attack Marshall, but Tiffany doesn't appear. Tanner is gone and so is Adam. I'm alone with a man who thinks I'm supposed to die.

Kasey groans again. "We have to find her."

Marshall turns back to her, leans over her, and strokes her hair out of her face. "I'll take care of everything. Don't worry about Remy anymore." He adjusts her pillow and for a second I think he's going to put it over her face and smother her. Instead he kisses her forehead. He stands and looks at me, then pulls his phone out of his pocket.

"9-1-1, what is your emergency?"

"This is Marshall Wheeler. I'm at 422 Ravenwood Lane with Kasey Vincent. She appears to have a concussion. She was struck with a heavy object by her nephew, Adam. Please send an ambulance immediately. Tell the police to be on the lookout for a gray Honda, license number K0319P. The nephew fled the scene. He should be considered armed and dangerous."

"Copy that. We're sending aid units to the scene immediately."

"Thanks." Marshall closes the phone. "That should take care of Kasey and your boyfriend. Now the only thing that's left is to decide what to do with you."

I realize too late that I should have screamed or made some kind of noise while he was on the phone with dispatch. My mind races. I make a move like I'm going for the door. Marshall goes to intercept me. I scramble the other direction, through Remy's open window. I crash through the screen, curling into a ball and rolling on the ground to break my fall. I stand and start running.

"Tiffany!" I scream into the wind. "Tiffany help me!"

The front door slams open. Marshall is chasing me. He covers the distance faster than I imagined he could. I'm almost to his truck when he catches me around the waist. He picks me up.

"Shh, shh, Miranda." He holds me against his chest, gently, almost lovingly, but firm enough that I can't move. He leans down, whispering in my hair. "I won't hurt you here. This isn't the right place. This isn't where you're supposed to die." He squeezes tighter, cutting off the air to my lungs. I fight against him until the world goes gray. In the fog I see her face again. Tiffany's expression is full of regret, but she doesn't move to stop him.

Chapter Fifty-One

The smell of damp pine trees, mold, and dust permeate the air around me. A hard wood plank creaks as I roll over. I'm covered by a heavy, scratchy wool blanket. Someone is quietly sobbing in the corner. I open my eyes. Directly above me is the drawing Tiffany left of the interlocking Ts, the heart and the bloody rose. This isn't one of my visions or even a dream.

I sit up slowly, expecting to be tied, but other than the sharp pain in my head that comes with any movement. I'm free to move around as much as I want. I don't see Marshall. The windows that used to be covered only with curtains are boarded up from the inside. I'm sure there's a new lock on the door. Pale light seeps through cracks in the cabin walls and between the floorboards. It must be sometime after dawn. There's an old folding table in the middle of the room with a box of cereal and a couple of oranges on it.

"Remy? I mean ... Ameri?" I call out.

She sniffles. "You can still call me Remy if you want."

I move slowly out of the bed, keeping the blanket wrapped around my shoulders, and move to sit by her.

"I'm sorry!" She leans over and I wrap my arms around her. "I didn't know it was him. I didn't mean for him to see what I drew." Her sobs get louder, shaking against my body.

"It's okay, it's okay." I stroke her hair. "Adam knows where we are. He'll find us."

"Are you sure about that?" Tanner is leaning against the wall, the way I saw him lean against his locker at school a hundred times.

"You found her," I say, remembering I'd told him to follow Marshall.

He shrugs. "I've been here before. My dad used to take us hiking along the trail to the lake. I followed Marshall, like you asked, but when I heard what you said to Adam, I just thought about this place and boom, I was here. This being dead thing has a few advantages." I don't tell him that it might have been better if he'd stayed with Marshall when he doubled back. "Of course, I can't do the things she can do."

"Tiffany?" I look around the room and then close my eyes and try to feel for her presence.

"She's not here. She won't or can't come inside this cabin. I'm not sure which. I saw what she did to that woman though. I wonder how long it took her to figure that out. I can't touch anyone who's alive." He flexes his hand in front of him, like he's trying to understand why he's not solid.

"What woman? What did Tiffany do?" Remy asks.

I hesitate. "She got a little upset. I think she's jealous of your aunt. But she's okay." I hope. Since neither Remy nor I have seen her, I'm going to assume Kasey is going to recover.

"If your boyfriend knows where you are, why hasn't he shown up yet?" There's an odd jealousy hanging around the room, even without Tiffany here.

"I don't know. Do you think you could find Adam?" I ask.

"I doubt it. Marshall was one thing. I knew him. I'd even been in his truck before. Unless Adam is somewhere I've been before."

"But you can try," I say. "Please."

"If I find him, then what? I can't talk to him. You two are the only ones who can hear me."

"Are you sure?" I ask.

He gets quiet for a minute. "I think other people, people I knew, like my mom and my little sister, can tell when I'm with them, but they can't hear me."

"But you could tell us if you find him," Remy says. "Then we'd at least know he's okay."

Tanner looks at me and lets out something like a breathless sigh. "I'll try. But call me back if anything happens; if Marshall comes back or Tiffany. Maybe she can show me how to do what she does, so I could help if … if …"

"Thanks, Tanner." I swallow. "It's good to talk to you again. I really … I really missed you."

"You too, Rand." He raises his hand in a goodbye and then fades into shadow.

Once he's gone, I look around the room. Besides the box of cereal and the oranges, Marshall has left a bag of jerky, a box of crackers, some cookies, and a pile of art supplies on one of the other bunks. I'm not sure how long he plans on keeping either of us here, but I'm betting he's planning on keeping Remy longer than me.

"I can't fight it," Remy confesses, leaning closer to my shoulder. "When I see people die. I have to draw them. I have to. I tried not to draw you, but it was too hard."

I spread the blanket across both of our laps. "I understand that need. Have you tried shutting down your mind? Have you tried not letting them in? The minister at the cemetery told me there's always a choice. You just have to practice. It was hard for me at first too." Even as I coach her I understand the advice is probably too late for me, but it might help the next person she sees. What would Marshall do if she just refused to tell him who was supposed to die next? Would he kill her?

Then there's the question of whether the people she sees would die anyway. Marshall thinks so. He thinks he's just acting as fate's executioner. If that's true, then am I meant to die anyway? The vision comes back to me, the boat, the icy water, the dark shape and then losing my breath as I'm plunged underneath.

I stand up. I can't spend any more time thinking. It's time to act. Even if I can't save myself I have to save Remy. I walk around the room, examining the boards covering each window. The wood is new and screwed on tight. The lock on the door is solid. I get down on the floor and peer between the cracks. The floor of the cabin is elevated on concrete blocks so there's about ten inches between the floorboards and the ground. The floorboards have big gaps between them and some of them have splintered or cracked and don't look very sturdy. If I pried them up, at least Remy could crawl out. I put my fingers through the largest gaps and pull. The board gives a tiny bit. I tug harder and the board breaks in half, splintering and cutting into my hand. I sit back, cradling my bleeding palm. The hole left behind is barely the length of my foot.

"It's no use. We're stuck here." I turn to face Remy. She looks stricken and terrified. "It will be okay. Whatever he does to me, he won't hurt you. As soon as you have the chance I want you to get away."

Remy stands up. Her cheeks are wet with tears, but her expression hardens. "We can't give up. There's always a choice. I won't let him kill you." She moves the lamp off the little folding table and then shoves the table over.

I wrap my arms around her. "It's okay."

She pushes me away. "No. It's not okay." She starts wrestling with one of the table legs. "Are you going to help or what?"

I realize what she's trying to do. The metal legs might be strong enough to use as a lever to pry up the broken floorboards. I help her pull until the leg finally breaks off. We start close to the edge of the cabin, so we don't have as far to crawl. The first few boards splinter when we try to pry them up, leaving a jagged hole that's too small. I start looking for boards that look sturdier—strong enough to come out in a bigger chunk, but still weak at the nail points.

It's slow, painful work. The first leg snaps after just a few boards. We break off the next table leg, and then the next. It seems like hours have passed before there's a space big enough for Remy to crawl through.

I push her toward it. "Go. I'll keep making the hole bigger and follow as soon as I can."

She shakes her head and sets her mouth in a stubborn line. "Not until we can both go."

I know better than to argue. "Okay, but we need to hurry." I work the next board loose. Then I hear the roar of a familiar engine, Marshall's truck. "Remy go!" She shakes her head, stamping her foot to try and break off the last bit.

The engine dies and a truck door slams. I push her toward the opening in the floor. "You have to go."

"No!" Remy looks toward the ceiling. "Help her! If you let her die, it's your fault."

For a second the room is silent. I'm not sure who Remy is talking to. Then, as if it were a gust of emotional wind, a wave of anger and frustration overtakes me. I clench my fists. The floor creaks and buckles under my feet, like some massive creature is pushing it from underneath. The last few boards in our path give way and splinter into a thousand pieces. I throw myself in front of Remy to protect her.

When the cracking stops, Remy grabs my hand. She drags me toward the hole and then climbs in, pulling me after her. I scrape up my back on the splintered boards as I duck into the space under the cabin. The door opens behind us.

The space under the cabin is dusty and full of spider webs and rat droppings. We sprawl on our bellies and crawl as fast as we can until we reach the edge of the cabin. Even then we stay low, army crawling away from the cabin.

"Remy! Miranda!" Marshall's voice echoes behind us.

Remy and I stand at the same time and run. We head away from the cabin, down the embankment and past the fire pit. Only when we reach the lake do I realize we've left ourselves only one path of escape. The faded red canoe is tied to the dock. The oars are inside, waiting for us.

We both stop dead, staring at the canoe. Marshall walks toward the dock, casually, as if he was planning a row on the lake. This was his plan all along. I'm here, playing things out exactly the way Remy saw them. He's just waiting for the events to unfold he knows are supposed to happen.

Chapter Fifty-Two

I turn to face him. "You don't have to do this, Marshall."

"I don't want to, Miranda, but I don't have a choice." His voice is gentle, and there's a note of genuine regret mingled with an undercurrent of excitement. His face has the same look of grim determination I saw in Tanner's memory.

"There's always a choice." I'm trying to keep my voice calm and even.

"But you're supposed to die." Marshall's voice is gentle and low, like he's explaining a basic fact to a six-year-old. "You know that as well as I do."

"What if I'm not supposed to die? What if none of them were supposed to die? What if you aren't the one who gets to decide that?"

"I didn't decide it." He nods toward Remy. "She saw the visions. I'm just the one who has to carry it out."

"But why you? You've been my uncle, my friend, my protector for my whole life. Why do you have to kill me now? Just because of some crazy dream? That's not who you are."

He laughs, but it's a deep, evil, cold laugh. His face changes into something I don't recognize. "Actually, that's exactly who I am. I'm just very good at hiding it. I've always wanted to kill. Ever since I was really young there has been this pent-up urge inside me that I can't control. The idea of having power over someone like that, to take the light out of their eyes. It's like some kind of drug. I know it isn't right to feel that way. I don't have the right to choose who lives and who dies. But if someone is supposed to die … if they've already been chosen. Then it's not wrong, is it?"

"Yes!" I scream at him.

He continues walking forward like he didn't hear me. "As soon as I met Tiffany, as soon as I knew what she could do, I knew I had the answer. She could tell me who was going to die and how. I didn't have to kill without reason. I could just help someone meet the fate that they would have met anyway. But she lied to me. She made me kill someone who wasn't supposed to die. She couldn't deal with that guilt, so she killed herself."

"No. Tiffany killed herself so you'd stop making her tell you who was supposed to die. She couldn't play dark prophet to your grim reaper anymore. She told me she killed herself because she knew what you were doing was murder, and she couldn't be a part of that anymore."

His calm expression twists in anger. "How would you know why Tiffany did what she did? You didn't know her. She died before you were born."

"I didn't say I talked to her when she was alive. She's the one who warned me about you. She's the one who showed me who you were and told me to stop you."

He stops coming closer. A shadow of doubt and something like fear crosses his face. "You're lying. When people die they're gone. They can't come back."

I laugh. Not because it's funny, but because it's ironic. After all those years of trying to figure out what I can do, after all that he's seen, Marshall still doesn't believe there's something after this life. "I've seen her. She's shown me what you did to all of them. She's shown me what you did to her."

His lips curl in anger. "No. Tiffany wouldn't have done that. She understood me like no one ever did. She loved me."

"She knew what you were doing was wrong. She knew it enough that she was willing to die before she let you hurt anyone else. She knew it enough to come back to me so I could stop you."

"No! Tiffany understood me. Tiffany loved me."

"No. To her you were nothing but a cold-blooded killer." Something else occurs to me. "A cold-blooded killer who is going to have to answer for the blood on his hands. It doesn't matter if it's in this life, or in the next."

As if to punctuate my point, dark clouds cover the sun. The wind picks up and the lake gets choppy. Tiffany is in the storm around us: anger, regret, and jealousy mixed together with a terrifying obsession. Marshall feels it too. I can see it on his face. He cowers, covering his head with his arms.

I dare to move a little closer, yelling above the wind. "It doesn't have to be like this. You can choose to stop right now. Enough people have died. It's time to end this."

For a long time Marshall stays on his knees, almost as if he's praying for forgiveness. I think it's over, that he's changed his mind. He stands up. "You're right. This is wrong. But I have to kill once more, or I'll never be free."

He rushes toward me. I step back and trip, landing in a sacrificial heap at his feet. He goes past me and grabs Remy. "If I don't know who's next to die, then I won't be tempted to kill again."

I'm so shocked by his sudden change that I don't move. Marshall carries Remy toward the boat. She kicks against him, her little body crashing into him as uselessly as the foamy waves beating against the dock. The wind howls. The boat creaks and strains against the rope that tethers it in place. Marshall drags it in, steadying it with one hand. He drops Remy to the bottom of the boat like a fresh caught fish, unties the rope, and steps inside.

I run after him and jump into the boat. It rocks violently and I'm sure we're all going in the water. "You can't do this!" I grab his arm. "Let her go."

He turns to face me, his face contorting into a malicious grin. "Miranda, when did you become so noble? What happened to the little girl who was afraid of everything?" Suddenly I understand that I've played right into his hands. He throws both oars out of the boat. He picks up Remy and jumps overboard. He pushes the canoe so it drifts away from the dock toward the center of the lake. Then he swims back to shore with Remy, carefully keeping her head above water even as she fights him.

The canoe drifts farther out into the lake, the wind pushing it toward the middle. I can't do anything to stop it or change its course. Marshall disappears over the embankment, carrying Remy back to the cabin. I stare into the gray water, not sure whether it's better to stay in the boat, waiting for him, or take my chances swimming to shore. I can barely swim, thanks to a few harrowing swim lessons insisted on by my dad. Water was one of my first and most unreasonable fears. Turns out I had a pretty good reason to be afraid.

"Tiffany!" I yell into the wind. She doesn't answer. "Tanner!" But he doesn't appear either.

Marshall appears back on the shore. He's in full scuba gear, a Pine Grove Search and Rescue patch sewn to his wetsuit. I remember the dark shape in the water behind Kari, not quite human. It was Marshall then, just as it's Marshall now.

He spends a lot of time at the dock preparing, adjusting his goggles and turning on the air hose. Finally he dives into the lake. His dark figure skims on the surface and then disappears into the murky water. I look around, frantic. I cling to the sides of the boat as his masked face breaks through the water a few hundred yards off the shore. He dips back under the waves. The next time I see him, he's just a few feet from me. Something bumps underneath the boat. His fingers grip the edge. I scream and pound my hands against the dark gloves and the masked face. His voice is calm. "I'm sorry Miranda."

"You don't have to do this!" I scream at him.

"I do."

The canoe flips. I'm in the water, bobbing on the waves, frantic to get back to the boat. He lets me get almost to the overturned hull before his hand encircles my ankles. I kick at him, but his grip is as tight as a pair of shackles. I gasp in a breath and he pulls me down, down, down. I fight to get to the surface, but he's too strong for me.

"Go limp, go limp, go limp." The voice playing over and over in my head sounds like mine, but it's not me. I force my body to relax, even as my lungs are screaming for air.

He brings his face to mine, his eyes shining with anticipation behind the mask. I want to tear his mask off and dig my nails into the corners of his eyes. But I know I'll never beat him that way. I stare back at him and allow my eyes to roll back as my body goes limp. He pulls me against him in a morbid embrace. "I'm sorry My-Rand-a."

He releases me. My body is so heavy that I couldn't move if I wanted to, so heavy that I feel myself sinking. The blackness of the water fills my head. I don't have to pretend to be limp anymore.

Chapter Fifty-Three

I'm the little girl in a pink party dress from the days before I was a freak. I'm back in the kitchen at home, when it was painted yellow instead of white. There's a big blue cake with three candles burning on top.

"Make a wish, Miranda," Dad says.

"Make a wish, Meredith," Mom whispers and touches the bulge of her stomach that will become Mark.

I look at the seat next to me. Another little girl who looks just like me leans in to blow out the candles as I do. She turns to me and smiles. "What did you wish for?"

The kitchen dissolves. I'm on the grade school playground, alone, listening to the shouts and laughter all around me. No one wants to play with the freak. One boy comes up behind me. "Hey, ghost girl!" He pushes me into a mud puddle. Everyone on the playground laughs. I look down at my new purple jeans, covered in mud.

The little girl with my face reaches her hand out to help me up. "Who cares about them? We have each other."

Scene after scene passes through my mind: the hardest times of my life, the best times. She gets older as I get older. My twin sister, but instead of being dead, she's with me through all of it, part of everything I do.

Finally, I'm standing in a familiar hallway. Light and music and the stench of perfume and body odor float through the doors to the gym. I look down at the blue dress Mom took me shopping for. I hold up my hand and my nails sparkle with the polish she painted them with this morning. Without looking, I know my hair is done up in ringlets. My lips are sticky with pink lip gloss, my lashes are heavy with never-before-worn mascara.

The girl beside me is in a white dress that catches the light the same way my nails do. Her hair is down and straight. She reaches over and squeezes my hand. "It will be okay."

But I know where I am. I know it won't be okay. "I don't want to be here. I remember what happens here."

"Give him a chance," Meredith says.

Tanner is standing just beyond the open door to the gym, exactly where he was when I was thirteen. His silhouette is easy to pick out against the darkened dance lights. Tall for his age, already filling out the way most boys wouldn't for several years. He was the hottest boy at the eighth-grade dance, already a football star. My friend. At least I thought he was.

I turn away. "I did. Three years ago. I won't go through this again."

The girl beside me smiles with encouragement. "This time isn't for you. It's for him."

I stare into my sister's gray eyes. It's like looking into a mirror, except she wears a perpetual expression of peace. I'm suddenly angry at her. "Why are you here? Why show me what my life would have been like if you'd been part of it? Is this my biggest regret, not having my twin sister to go through life with?"

Meredith smiles and shakes her head. "I'm not showing you what your life would have been like if I'd lived. I'm showing you your life as it is, and as it was, and as it will be."

"But you weren't there, not for any of our birthdays or when James pushed me down, or any of that other stuff. And definitely not here. I was alone. I've always been alone."

She shakes her head again and her peaceful expression turns to regret. "You of all people should understand that there are those who walk with us that we can't see. You were never alone. You will never be alone."

I stare back at her, trying to understand. Tanner said that the people who he knew were able to sense he was there. I understand now that I've felt that too. "Maybe I did know, sometimes. But I didn't see you and you didn't talk to me. You aren't like the others."

"That's because I've moved on and they haven't."

"Does this mean I'm dead? But not moved on, not yet?"

"That's up to you. Remember, there's always a choice. Dead or alive, we have to live with our choices. But sometimes we're given the chance to make a better choice." She nods toward Tanner. "I think he deserves that much."

I walk toward the gym door, exactly as I did before—my legs shaking, my palms wet, and my mouth dry. This was Tanner, my cul-de-sac buddy, my best friend. But he'd stopped talking to me at school. He hadn't come over to watch TV or to tell me how football was going for weeks. We were getting ready to go to high school. This was my chance to figure out where I stood with him. My only chance to feel like I was still somebody to him, and maybe that would make me somebody with everyone else.

He's standing with a group of the popular kids, his friends. It took all my courage then and it takes all my courage now just to say, "Hey, Tanner."

He turns. It feels like the whole room goes silent. His friends stop talking. One of the girls giggles behind her hand. One of the boys says something I can't hear, but they all laugh. Tanner stares at me. Just by saying his name I've broken some middle school code of social conduct that I didn't know existed.

I turn away, not wanting to see the smirk on his face and hear the words, "What do you want, freak?"

I'm prepared to run for the bathroom and slide onto the floor to cry off my first ever coat of mascara, just like I did that night. Then I hear footsteps behind me. When he speaks, he only says my name. "Rand?" I turn around, still waiting for him to say the word, freak. Instead he asks, "Do you want to dance?"

I can't move. He laces his fingers through mine and leads me to the dance floor. His friends all stare, but he doesn't even look at them. He puts one hand on my waist and then holds my other one. I must be dead. His touch doesn't make the vision dissolve into scattering lights. We step side to side in an awkward middle school interpretation of dancing.

He looks at me, almost shyly. "You look really good."

I stare up into his soft brown eyes. "Thanks, you do too."

We sway in silence for a few more beats. I don't think he remembers anything about his accident or asking me to help him or being dead. It's a perfect moment. I lean into him, enjoying this new, better memory. He holds me against him, his chin barely resting on the top of my head. If this is what heaven is, I don't want to leave.

Finally he speaks. "This is how that night should have gone. This is how I wanted it to go. But Mia laughed and Brian said something stupid that everyone else thought was funny. I was in this stupid place where I was worried about being cool and ..." He steps away and hangs his head. "I'm sorry, Rand. I should have never said those things to you. I should have asked you to dance. I should have talked to you in the halls. I should have been your friend. I wanted to do all that and more. But I was too stupid and too afraid to understand what I had and what I could have had."

"Hey." I put my hand under his chin so he has to look me in the eye. "It doesn't matter anymore."

He looks back at me, his face painted with regret. "I found him. He's going to save you. At first I didn't want him to. I thought if I didn't bring him back, if he didn't save you, you could come with me. You'd forgive me and we could be together. But that's not the way it's supposed to be." He brushes back a curl that's stuck to my cheek with a tear I didn't know I'd let slide past my lashes. "Don't cry, Rand. He's going to be so much better for you than I could have been. I just ... I had to leave you with a better memory of me."

He leans in and our lips touch. For a beatless heartbeat pure energy flows between us. I can feel everything he feels. I can see everything he wished he'd been for me. I can see everything he's lost. I feel it when his regret fades into peace. For a shimmery moment I can see where he's going.

The vision explodes in sparks of pain and dark and cold. Someone else's lips are pressed against mine. I choke and my body convulses. Water gurgles up from my throat and I vomit. My chest explodes in a fit of coughing.

Adam's face comes into focus. I take in a wheezing breath. He lays his head on my chest, listening as my shallow breathing grows deeper. He raises his head. Our eyes meet and he starts sobbing.

I pull him against me. "It's okay. It's okay."

Chapter Fifty-Four

Adam carries me back into the cabin. He sets me on the wooden plank of the bunk and wraps the wool blanket around me. I'm too much in a daze to move anything but my eyes. Remy and Marshall are gone. He left everything behind except for Remy's drawing supplies.

I take in a ragged breath. "Where is Remy?"

"He took her. I couldn't go after her and let you drown." His voice shakes. He stands and moves toward the door. "I'm going to go start my car. As soon as it's warm I'll come back for you."

"Where are we going?" My voice still sounds far away, underwater, or back with Tanner—not quite real.

"I'm taking you to the hospital," Adam says. "I would have called for an ambulance, but my phone was in my pocket when I went in after you."

I'm still shaking, barely comprehending that I'm back in the world of the living. Something under the pried-up floorboards catches my eye. It's a rolled-up piece of paper. I'm drawn toward it with an almost uncontrollable force. I stand up and walk across the floor. Adam stops at the doorway. "Miranda, what are you doing?"

I kneel down in front of the jagged edge of the hole and retrieve the paper. I sit back, unroll the canvas, and look at the face in front of me. It's a much younger version of Marshall. His face is full of terror and his mouth is frozen in a silent scream.

Everyone has to live with their choices.

I recognize the voice in my head as much as I recognize the face in the picture.

"Unless you get the chance to make a better choice," I whisper back.

"Miranda, what are you ..." Adam stares at the picture in front of me.

"She wasn't the one who was supposed to die." I look up at him. "I know what I need to do."

"We have to go back to town and go to the police. We have to tell them everything and let them figure it out."

"They won't believe us. They think I'm crazy and they think you're a murderer. Marshall told them you attacked your aunt. Besides, by the time we sort things out he might have taken Remy far away from here."

"We're just kids. We can't stop him."

I turn to face him with a determination I hope he understands. "Adam, what if we're the only ones who can stop him?"

He looks at me like everyone is right about me being crazy.

I put my hand on his arm. "Trust me. I know what we have to do to save your sister. We just need to give her a chance to make a better choice."

"Wait, what? What choice did Remy make? How can you—"

"Not Remy. Tiffany. Look, I don't have time to explain or argue about this. We need to find some kind of costume shop or thrift store."

"A thrift store? You really are crazy."

I take in a shaky breath. "Maybe, but I need to get some things if we're going to save Remy."

Whether Adam thinks I'm crazy or not, at some point he gives up arguing and drives me into town. There's a little thrift store in what passes for downtown Morton. He has the heater cranked up as high as it will go, so by the time we get there I'm not completely soaking wet, but I'm also not particularly dry. It takes me just a few minutes to find a pair of black jeans, a vintage T-shirt advertising a long-ago concert for some heavy metal band, and a dark jacket. A stroke of luck leads to a long ratty black wig. It won't fool Marshall close up, but by the time he gets close enough to recognize me it will be too late.

I hope.

This would be a lot easier if I thought I could trust Tiffany. Even though I think I've finally figured out what she wants, she's still unpredictable when it comes to Marshall. My plan hinges on Marshall's ability to see his dead girlfriend. If it can't be Tiffany, it has to be me.

I change out of my wet clothes in the dressing room and wear my new outfit to the checkout counter. Luckily Adam left his wallet in the car when he dove in after me. After the thrift store, we make one more stop at a drugstore for some cheap eyeliner and mascara.

"You look ..." He stares at me for what feels like a long time. "Really, really different."

"That's what I'm counting on." I lean back on the seat. "I need you to be quiet."

"What are you ..."

I reach my finger to his lips. "Trust me." I close my eyes. "Amerie, Amerie." I reach for her emotions: for her fear, her pain, and especially the guilt I know is consuming her. She thinks I'm dead, but I can't let her know I'm still alive, not yet.

She's in the back seat of his pickup. The art supplies from the cabin are scattered on the seat beside her. She's leaning against the window, tears sliding down her cheeks. Marshall is rattled, driving too fast. I'm not sure if he has a prick of conscience from killing me, or if what I said about Tiffany unnerved him. I'm actually hoping it's the latter. The more he has her on his mind, the easier it will be to convince him she's back.

"Amerie."

I feel the connection surge across the miles between us. I conjure the scene in my head. My brush with death makes it easier to communicate with Remy. I'm able to share my thoughts with her, the way she shared them with me. More than that, I'm able to take a vision I've seen before and manipulate it, as if I were controlling a dream. As soon as the vision forms in her mind, Remy reaches for a pencil and a piece of paper, scattered among the objects on the seat beside her. I purposely make the image of the person indistinct, so she'll draw it that way. The location I make crystal clear.

Marshall's eyes light up when he sees her drawing. She sees him watching and stops, throwing the paper away from her.

"Draw!" he demands.

"No!" she yells back at him.

I'm proud of her for denying the urge inside her, but I need her to draw what she sees. I try to send her more urgency. "You need to show him this. It's important."

She shakes her head as if to clear it. "Rand?"

"Yes." I have to risk her giving me away. Marshall is watching in the rearview mirror, his eyes hungry and dark. "Draw what you see. It will be okay."

She takes the pencil and draws with shaky hands. Marshall pulls over. She barely finishes when he snatches the drawing from her. "Who is it?"

"I don't know. Just that she's waiting on the ... the bridge."

He nods and puts the paper on the seat behind him. He grips the steering wheel with an expression I recognize. He turns down the road that leads to the bridge where Tiffany died.

As soon as I'm sure they're going to the bridge, I look at Adam. "I'm not sure where they are, but we have to get there first."

"Where?"

"The bridge."

"What bridge?"

It hits me that I've only seen the bridge in a vision. I don't know where it is, but it can't be too far. Tiffany died in this town. I take a gamble, lean out the window of Adam's car and ask the first person who walks by. It's an older woman who gives me a strange look. Fortunately, when I ask, "How do we get to the old iron bridge?" she seems to know exactly what I'm talking about.

"Are you sure about this?" Adam asks after I get directions.

"Honestly, no. But I think it's our best chance of saving Remy."

"You have a plan?"

"Actually, yeah. I gave Remy something to draw, but we don't have very much time." I close my eyes, reaching for Tiffany. Even though it doesn't feel like she's near, I address her. "Tiffany, I figured out what you want. This is your chance to make a different choice." No answer comes. I'm going to have to do this by myself. I catch Adam looking at me. He takes my hand and squeezes it. His look of stupid, desperate trust makes me realize that he believes I can do this. That thought both comforts and terrifies me.

Chapter Fifty-Five

We make it to the bridge before Marshall gets there. I roll up the picture and tuck it into my jacket. Then I stand, staring at the top of the bridge, trying to figure out how I'm going to climb to the upper deck where Tiffany was. My body hurts everywhere. My chest burns. My limbs feel like noodles.

When I hesitate too long, Adam moves next to me. "What's going on?"

I point to the deck above us. "I need to get up there. That's where she jumped from. That's where he'll expect her to be."

He measures the distance with his eyes. "That's insane. As weak as you are, you'll never be able to climb that far."

"Thanks," I shoot back at him sarcastically. "Maybe you could help me?"

"Before I help you to almost certain death, you know, after I risked everything to save your life, can you explain to me why you're doing this?"

"Marshall's girlfriend, the one who could see people who died, killed herself here. She did it so she didn't have to show him who was meant to die, but she wasn't the one who should have died that night. I'm giving her the chance to make a different choice."

"So your whole plan hinges on the vindictive ghost who attacked my aunt doing what you want her to do?"

"No, this all hinges on me doing what I know she wanted me to do all along. But if she can't do it, then I'll have to." I swallow hard, realizing the choice I'm about to make. Tiffany wasn't strong enough to stop Marshall that night. She loved him too much to kill him. She sacrificed herself instead of him. But he was the one who was meant to die, not her. Despite everything Marshall has done, I don't know if I have the strength to do what she couldn't.

I don't know if I can kill him.

"Okay. I'll help you. Just be careful." Adam boosts me up on the edge of the bridge and then stays behind me, helping me climb. When we reach the top, I stand, clinging to a braided metal rope. "Now you climb down. Wait for Marshall to come. He'll probably leave Remy in his pickup. Be ready to get her out. Break a window if you have to, whatever it takes. Don't worry about what happens to me."

He shakes his head. "I'm not leaving you."

"You can't be here. None of this will work if he sees you."

He hesitates, looking around the bridge as if to find a hiding place. There isn't one. "I can't leave you alone for him to find you."

"Just get Remy someplace safe." I reach for his hand. "I'll be okay. One way or another." For the first time in my life, I really believe it. I still don't have any desire to die, but after what I saw when Tanner crossed over, I know if I do, it will be okay.

He hesitates for a second, like he's trying to come up with a better choice. Then he pulls me against him. He whispers in my ear. "Whatever you do, don't die. I think I'm in love with you."

Brave behind the dark eyeliner and black wig, I pull away and kiss him gently on the lips, buying myself a few seconds to think about what he said. I finally whisper back. "I think I might be in love with you too."

He climbs back down the girder. Footsteps echoing across the bridge mark his retreat. The wind whistles through the rails of the bridge. It's cold and I'm already shaking. Far below me, the moon reflects in the dark water. I grip the iron rope tighter, hoping I have the strength to hold on until Marshall comes.

You're braver than I was.

Her whisper on the wind is all the reassurance I needed. I'm not alone.

Chapter Fifty-Six

The wind blows the black hair of the wig into my face. I brush it away, wondering if this whole thing is a bad idea. Where is the line between bravery and insanity and how long ago did I cross it? Headlights illuminate my back. His truck announces itself with a rattle of metal as it rolls onto the wooden tracks of the bridge. From the deck below, I must look like a ghost.

I'm counting on it.

He stops just below me. "Tiffany?" His voice is hoarse and breathless.

I don't turn around. I don't have the voice to answer him, so I stay silent.

His feet clang against the metal girders, climbing up to me. I grip the metal rope and try to keep from shaking.

"Tiffany, is that you?"

I straighten my back and reach for the paper tucked inside the jacket. I turn slowly. "It was never meant to be her that night."

I unroll the paper in front of him.

He doesn't even flinch. "Miranda!" His arm snakes around my waist before I realize what's happening. I reach for the metal rope and let go of the picture. It floats away, drifting toward the river like a wounded bird.

"Why would you lie to me? Why would you make Remy lie?" He doesn't seem surprised that I'm alive. He keeps one arm around my waist and pulls out another picture. Where the image I fed Remy was purposefully indistinct, the one she drew is clear. The person standing on the edge of the bridge is him. The image behind him is shadowy and inhuman, but the dark hair flecked with blue is unmistakable.

My hold on the metal rope is so tight that the fibers are digging into my hands. "It's not a lie. You were the one who was supposed to die that night, not her. Tiffany drew you. She sacrificed herself to give you the chance to make a better choice, but instead—"

He tightens his grip on my waist, choking off my words. "This is better, so much easier to explain to your parents. You were distraught, driven crazy by the voices in your head and you tried to kill yourself. You climbed to the top of the bridge and were about to jump when I saved you."

He lets me go. I stumble back, still clinging to the metal rope. "Saved me?"

"You cheated death and won, Rand. Who am I to take that away?" He shakes his head at me. "Of course you're still going to have to spend time in that hospital. You may even be there the rest of your life, especially after they find your boyfriend's body on the side of the road all bled out. From there it won't be much of a leap to determine that you were the one who killed all of them. With a little creative investigative work, I might even be able to pin Tanner's death on you."

Adam is lying on the ground, a red stain blooming across his shirt. He's struggling to breathe. I sense Remy's panic as she pushes the vision into my brain. She's locked in the truck, pounding on the window to try to get to him. I can't tell if this is something that's happening now, has already happened, or is going to happen soon.

"Tiffany!" I shriek into the wind. "This is your chance! Your choice!"

The wind answers back with a howl. Marshall laughs. "She's long gone, long ..."

He trails off and I follow his gaze to the bridge support above me. Graffiti takes shape against the rusted metal, a face, drawn by an invisible hand. The image is the same style as Tiffany's other drawings. The face is Marshall's.

"No!" he screams.

Meant to die, meant to die, meant to die.

Her voice is in the shriek of the wind, reverberating through my head, ringing against my ears. Marshall curls up in a ball, covering his ears, but he can't escape the sound. The air swells around us. The bridge vibrates with the words.

Meant to die, meant to die.

The bridge is going to collapse underneath us or Marshall and I are going to be swept into the river from the force of the howling wind and the screeching of her cries.

Everything goes silent.

I open my eyes. Tentatively he uncovers his ears. He uncurls himself from the ball of fear he's molded into. He stands up, dazed, like he's in a dream. His eyes grow wide.

I turn around to see what he's staring at. Tiffany hangs in the air in front of us, her arms outstretched.

Marshall looks astonished for a long moment. Then he nods like he understands something unsaid between them. He rests his eyes on mine. He digs something out of his pocket. He stretches out his hand and gives me his keys and cell phone. "You'll need to stop the bleeding as soon as possible. There's a medical kit in my truck. I wouldn't have stabbed him if he hadn't surprised me with the knife. I don't kill people who aren't meant to die."

I take both from him, stunned. "Come with me. You can save him and—"

"Then what? I can't stop it, Miranda. If you take Remy I'll find someone else. It's not something I can control. I've tried. Just, if possible, let them think they were all accidents. Don't tell my brother what I really was."

Tears are streaming down my face. I thought I was prepared to let him go, maybe even prepared to kill him, but I was wrong. "You can stop it. You always have a choice."

He looks out at the dark figure in front of him, what's left of Tiffany with her hair flowing in the wind, and her face serene as she waits. "I do. And this is it. After all, who am I to keep her waiting?"

He steps into her arms. I swear she holds him for a few seconds before he falls.

Chapter Fifty-Seven

The line of police cars and fire engines stretch for miles down the road to the old church. The speakers all talked about Marshall's bravery, about his selflessness, about how he overcame the trials of his youth to become a hero.

It's a funeral of lies, but I can't say anything to stop it. Marshall even got credit for rescuing me from an "unknown assailant" who he pursued across the bridge before ultimately falling to his death. There's nothing that Remy, or Adam, or I can say that would change anything that's happened. If we tried to explain it we'd all end up in mental institutions.

"You okay?" Dad says after the service is over and people are standing around the cemetery in small groups, talking about the tragedy.

"Yeah, I just need to take a walk."

"Can I come with?" Adam looks so tenderly protective that for a minute I almost say yes. But I can't take him with me, not this time.

I shake my head. "I need to be alone." I reach out and squeeze his hand. "But thanks." I feel his eyes on my back as I walk away. I'm not sure we'll ever reconcile his inherent extroverted need to be part of everything with my need to be alone, but we're working through that.

I move away from the crowd. Marshall is buried in the newer part of the cemetery, next to his mother. Only after he was gone did I realize she was the woman who cleaned the church, the other woman who kept his secret and died because of it. Ironically, they're both buried just a few plots over from Kari.

I'm not sure it's better that her parents believe her death was an accident, but again, it's not something I can change. I walk toward the back of the cemetery, past Amber's conspicuous red headstone, and stop at the nearly unmarked grave.

The flat gray headstone is overgrown with weeds and nearly hidden by ivy. I bend down and clear the vines away. Tiffany Starr Farrell, no inscription beyond her name and the dates, a lonely and forgotten marker. I don't feel Tiffany with me anymore. I don't know if she moved on with Marshall or if she's still lingering somewhere.

In an odd way, I miss her.

Adam says Remy sleeps peacefully now. Her latest passion is drawing mythical creatures—dragons and unicorns and fairies. I don't know if she'll be haunted with visions of people dying ever again. I hope not.

They still come to me, wanting to relive and repair the choices they made in life. Most of them pass peacefully, but not always.

He's pulling weeds under a tree, like any normal groundskeeper would, but I recognize him for what he used to be and what he is now. I stand in front of him and unfold the painting I made after my visitor disappeared last night.

He looks up, a handful of weeds still gripped in his palm. His expression is peaceful, but expectant.

"I need a name."

THE END

To read more books like this or to subscribe to Jennifer Shaw Wolf's newsletter, visit jennifershawwolf.com.

I'd Love to Hear From You

One of my favorite parts of being an author is connecting with readers. If you'd like to send me a message, read more books like this, and recieve advance news and promotions, including my free short story, "The Extra," please visit my website at jennifershawwolf.com to subscribe to my newsletter.

THE EXTRA
A starving student gets much more than a free meal when she signs up to be an extra on a B-list horror movie.

Enjoy this book?

Leave a Review.

Please take a few minutes to leave a quick review. Reviews are the best way for me to earn attention for my books and to show retailers that this is a book worth supporting.

Thanks in advance!

Also by Jennifer Shaw Wolf

Dead Girls Don't Lie

In an unanswered text, Jaycie chooses her new boyfriend
Sklyer, over her best friend Rachel. But when that text turns
out to be Rachel's last, Jaycie must rise above a small town's
prejudice and find out what really happened to Rachel before
her killer strikes again.

Breaking Beautiful

Allie doesn't remember anything about the night her
boyfriend Trip died, and what she does remember about him,
she doesn't want anyone to know. When the investigation
into Trip's accident turns to Allie's best-friend-turned-
boyfriend, Blake, she has to decide whether she has the
strength to remember everything and the courage to finally
break free.

For Kristy. Thanks for being so much braver than I am and for always showing me the way.

Acknowledgements

I began Meant to Die just before I sold the manuscript that would become Breaking Beautiful In the excitement of acquiring an agent, selling my first book, and then my second on proposal, the manuscript that would become this book was set aside. It was paranormal and I was now a contemporary YA mystery novelist. It sat for years, although I would pull it out now and then, dust it off (metaphorically because it was on my computer hard drive) and write a bit more.

One day on the drive back from girl's camp, my young friend Grace H. introduced me to the quarter game. In it she posed the question, "Who will be the first to die?" (In case you're wondering, the answer was me.) I knew that had to go in my story. Still, there were elements I couldn't get right. In the midst of a retreat, during a late-night intensive plot hammering-out session, and over too much chocolate, I came up with the ending. Even with all of that, it wasn't until the dark days of Covid when all the elements finally came together and I had the courage to finish this book.

Since this is my first indie published book, you might think I'd have fewer people to thank, but no book is born in a vacuum, so here goes. Many thanks to my darling agent Sara Megibow, who gave me the encouragement to keep going, the freedom to do what I wanted, and then the courage to let go.

Immense gratitude goes out to Val, Sarah, Jolinda, Grace, Rachel, Medea, Angela, Gail, and Peter (the Rainy Day Writers) for the late night encouragement and on-the-fly plot fixes. To Dakota for being willing to beta read. To Grace H. (now G, my, how the time flies) for inspiring me with thoughts of my own untimely demise. To my husband, David, for believing in me even when I stopped believing in myself. To my kids, David (and now Shylah too), Sabrina, Zach, and Daniel for standing by me even when it meant the house was falling down around us and we were eating boxed macaroni and cheese for dinner again. To Val, Joan, Blessy, Michele, Annie, and another Sarah for being there with first comments and suggestions when this story was barely a twinkle in my eye. (I really miss our awesome critique group.) To Lynda for her editing prowess and Sarah (H this time) for her amazing cover design. To Amy Solo and our high school Write Club for continually inspiring me with their writing, their passion, and their total acceptance of each other and anyone who's brave enough to join our ranks. To all the readers who have inspired me to write and keep writing. To Tiffany and Miranda for sharing their names and the inexpressable joy of dreams coming true. To Elana and Lyndzee and all the presenters at Storymaker's 2020 who gave me the tools and encouragement I needed to do this on my own. To my older sister, Kristy, and my sister-in-law, Angela, for being braver than I am and staring this journey way before I found the courage to.

An inexpressable gratitude goes to my parents (Dale and Linda) who taught me that I can be anything I want to be and to my Savior who continually teaches me that I can be more than I think I can be, and that there is so much more to look forward to beyond this life.

About the Author

Jennifer Shaw Wolf lives in the lush green (rainy) forests of Western Washington with her husband, a very spoiled dog, and the one of her four children who hasn't yet deserted her for adulthood. She spends her days working at a high school library among two of her favorite things—books and teenagers. She's one of the few people in the world who would be absolutely thrilled to get locked into her workplace over the weekend. (As long as there were snacks.) She writes happy, fluffy books for teenagers with rainbows, unicorns and titles like, Dead Girls Don't Lie, Breaking Beautiful, and Meant to Die. She loves horses, skiing, and making readers second-guess everything they thought they knew about the characters she writes.

Made in United States
Orlando, FL
28 August 2022

21682776R00150